Brethren of the Black Spot

ISBN: 978-1-63950-131-1   [Paperback Edition]
         978-1-63950-132-8   [eBook Edition]

Printed and bound in The United States of America.

Writers Apex

Gateway Towards Success

8063 MADISON AVE #1252
Indianapolis, IN 46227
+13176596889
www.writersapex.com

Brethren
OF THE
Black Spot

Dennis Davis

This book is pure fiction, but the Navy Seals are not fiction. They are the greatest military branch of services that are continually serving America.

This book is dedicated to their service, loyalty, teamwork, and, most of all, to their ability to take names and break things.

In the pirate vocabulary of the 1600s, the word Black Spot meant "Mark of Death."

CHAPTER 1

On a Tuesday morning in June 2005 in the family area of the White House, George W. Bush and Laura Bush are having breakfast. A hardy breakfast of eggs (sunny side up) Jimmy Dean Sausage and hash brown potatoes with green chilies and onions with lots of coffee. "Keep the coffee coming," says George, "I have another important, stressful day, meetings, meetings will the meetings ever end?" Laura says, "Yes they will as soon as you're not the President any longer." "Believe it or not Laura I am looking forward to that day." says George. "Oh by the way did you hear Rush Limbaugh and Sean Hannity yesterday?" asks Laura, "No I didn't get a chance," says George. Laura says, "Well I was deeply moved by their support of the International meeting you put together, with Vice President Dick Cheney, Secretary of State Condoleezza Rice, Senator Orrin Hatch going to the peace meeting in Kingston Jamaica. With world renowned representatives from Great Britain, France, Germany, Iraq, and Saudi Arabia to find a solution for peace in the Middle East. I don't believe that any of our national TV stations or national newspapers has given any coverage or support to this very important meeting," explains Laura.

George says, "I've given up expecting any support from the leftist media even if it is their right to do it. The national press like NBC, CBS, ABC, and CNN are just water carriers for the Democrats, they have lost all credibility and integrity serving the Democrats as they do. It doesn't matter what I say or do they will never support me or my policies because they can't handle the truth. Thank God for Rush and Sean and the truth news media of FOX news and all the other right wing talk shows in America the truth does get out sooner or later. What I am thinking of doing is inviting Rush and Sean to the White House for a thank you diner this week." Laura says, "That is a grand idea those two men have always been fantastic supporters of you and your policies and your fathers administration from day one. They ask for nothing except to be able to do the job they were born to do and that's telling the truth and supporting our great country." "You're right Laura and I would enjoy their company just the four of us. I'll personally call them both today and extend the invite myself; I can only hope that Friday night is open for them both." Laura says, "I agree just the four of us not having twenty other people in the room at the same time, these are the type of get togethers I really enjoy the most with people we both respect, admire and like a lot."

At 11:00 A.M. the President has just finished with the morning briefings with the CIA in the oval office looked at his watch and thought I had better give Rush and Sean a call to invite them to dinner on Friday evening. George calls his secretary into the Oval office and asks her, "Please call Rush Limbaugh and get him on the phone so I can talk with him, then please call Sean Hannity for me as well." "Yes Mr. President right away," responds his secretary. The private phone rings in Rush's office Rush answers, "This is Rush how may I help you." The President's secretary says, "The president George W. Bush would like to talk with you please hold." "Rush my good friend how the heck are you?" Rush answers, "I'm doing just fine what do I owe the honor of this call to?" "Well Rush Laura and I were talking this morning and we both agreed that we would like the honor of your company at the White House this Friday for dinner, can you make it?" "Absolutely I can make it what an honor, thank you," says Rush. Laura and I were discussing your support for the International Peace meeting taking place in Kingston, Jamaica this week and this is our way of saying thanks to you and Sean." says George. Rush says, "It is my pleasure and my duty to support what will bring peace and stability to the Middle East." "Thank you Rush, you have been a good friend to me and to my father over the years," answers the

President. "I am also going to call Sean Hannity and invite him as well, cocktails at 6:00 P.M. dinner at 7:30 P.M. so be here at 5:00 so you can freshen up. A car will meet you at the airport to bring you to the White House at 4:00 P.M. on Friday, how does that work with your schedule Rush?" "That will work out just fine I'm really looking forward to having dinner with you and Laura." answers Rush.

The phone is ringing on Sean Hannity's private cell phone and the secretary says, "Will you please hold for President Bush?" "Well I sure will." answers a surprised Sean. George Bush gets on the phone and says, "Is this the real Sean Hannity or is it Memorex a recording." Sean laughs and says, "It's really me Mr. President what do I owe the honor of this phone call?" "Sean Hannity you are a great American." Sean answers, "No you're a great American Mr. President." As both men have a good laugh at the friendly banter that just took place. Mr. Bush says, "The reason for my call is Laura and I were talking this morning about your support that you gave to the International Peace summit tasking place this week in Kingston, Jamaica. We would like to thank you personally by coming to the White House for dinner with Laura and me this Friday and your undying support of me and my administration over the years." Sean says, "Mr. President when I believe in something I support it and peace in the Middle East is easy to support." says Sean. "The liberal media in this country does not support peace they support chaos, turmoil, and unrest anything not to support you and your admiration." George responds, "Because what they want is power to them and their agenda, screw the world." "You're right Mr. President I believe I will steal that line and use it on my radio show tomorrow," Says Sean. "Well Sean can you make it to dinner on Friday with Laura, myself and Rush Limbaugh can you make it?" Sean answers, "Oh my God what an honor of course I'll be there," answers a flabbergasted Sean Hannity. " George continues, "Cocktails at 6:00 P.M. dinner at 7:30 be here at 5:00 to freshen up and a car will pick you up at the airport at 4:00 P.M. along with Rush Limbaugh does that meet with your schedule?" Sean answers, "That will work out perfectly I look forward to seeing you and Laura for dinner on Friday."

Both Sean and Rush arrive at the airport at the same time a limousine is waiting to bring them both to the White House. They greet each other with a friendly hand shake and a big bear hug with friendly smiles on their faces. They see a sign held up by the limo driver with their first names and they proceed to get in for their ride to the White House. Both men begin the walk toward the front door of the White House shoulder to shoulder. Sean says, "Can you believe it you and I doing what we love to do two radio jockeys being invited to dinner at the White House by the president of the United States himself. I believe that God has been good to us and has given his blessing for what we do, that is loving America to the best of our abilities." Rush responds, "I agree just like I say on my radio show, a talent from God." As both men smile and reach the front door a secret service agent opens the door and welcomes them to the White House. "Welcome Mr. Limbaugh and Mr. Hannity it is my pleasure to meet you I have been a fan of both of you guys for some time now. I want to thank you for what you do every day to get the truth out," says the secret service agent. "The secretary is waiting to escort you gentleman to your rooms." The secretary is standing just inside the door. "Welcome, welcome gentleman," says the secretary. "I have been such a fan of both of you guys forever this is a real pleasure to finally meet both of you I will escort you to your rooms. Rush you have been given Lincoln's bedroom since you liked it so much the last time you were here. Sean your room is just as nice just across the hall now you are to relax get refreshed I will return at 4:50 P.M. to meet with George and Laura Bush for cocktails."

As both men settle down to rest for a little bit, Rush is so full of energy he knocks on Sean's door. "Sean it's me Rush got a minute?" "Yea sure come on in the doors unlocked," answers Sean. "Whats up." Rush answers, "I am so honored to be here I just wanted to talk for a few minutes, I couldn't lie down and rest if I wanted to. I'm rested and ready to get this show on the road." "I know how you feel I feel the very same way anxious as hell just being here to break bread with the President and his lovely wife Laura this evening I'm stoked." says Sean. Thirty minutes passes on the clock the two men end their conversation showing great respect for each other. Rush returns to his room takes a shower and changes into a very nice suit and Sean does the same. At precisely 4:50 P.M. a gentle knock is heard at their doors. Gentleman will you please follow me," says the secretary. As both Rush and Sean enter the living room George and Laura are standing in the center of the living room. With big smiles and hands extended to welcome them to their home the living quarters of the White House. The living room is quite large with couches and comfortable chairs and family pictures on the wall it is rather homey and comfortable. The room is absolutely elegant and very well decorated to show the flair and warmth of the President. "Welcome to our home," says Laura. Then George with his Texas hospitality shakes hands and gives them both a friendly pat on the back. "Sit down make yourselves comfortable remember the White House belongs to all Americans," says George with a friendly smile. Rush and Sean take a seat on the most comfortable white couch they have ever had the pleasure to sit on. "May I get you gentleman a drink what's your pleasure?" asks the President. Rush speaks up, "I'll have a single malt scotch if you please with a twist of lemon on ice if you please." "I would like a glass of wine, Merlot if you please," says Sean. Laura speaks up, "I would also like a glass of wine Merlot if you please." The President says, "Coming right up I will fix myself a Pepsi with a lot of ice."

The President presents Laura and his guests with their drinks and then takes a seat beside his lovely wife. George then continues with the conversation, "I am so glad that you were able to make our little dinner party tonight. If I could I would have invited all the conservative talk show hosts that support my administration along with the people at Fox news perhaps that will happen on another day. Next week on your radio shows please make my apologies and tell them how much I appreciate their support." Sean speaks up, "We understand the old media news referred to as the drive by media that is losing its support daily has gone over to the dark side. I do not understand how the major newspapers and the TV stations NBC, CBS, ABC can support the anti-American rhetoric on the left never reporting the truth." Well Sean says Rush, "The congress is doing its best to pass an anti-free speech bill called the Fairness Act." "Let me say one thing about that bill," says George. "As long as I am President that anti-so called free speech bill will nerve pass my desk." "We thank you for your support to keep free speech alive and well in America," says Rush and Sean. Sean Hannity looks at Laura and says, "I just want to say from the bottom of my heart that you are without a doubt the most beautiful First Lady this great country of ours has ever had." Rush looks at Laura and George and says, "Ditto." Laura smiles and everyone has a good hardy laugh.

"One thing that I am sure about the democrats is. If you really want to make them mad and see their faces turn red and watch spittle come from their mouths and see their horns emerge from their foreheads is just tell the truth about them and their agenda," says Sean. "That I agree with," says Rush. "They can't handle the truth and one more note is if they ever told the truth about themselves and their policies and agenda they know is that no democrat would ever be elected again." The President and First Lady are nodding their heads in agreement and smiling at what was just said. The President chimes in and says, "Now that is so true what you just said." Laura smiles and adds a comment, "Gentleman I also agree with everything you just said, "Perhaps we should discuss something else other than democrats they are such a depressing subject." George rises from his seat and asks, "While I'm up can I refresh your drinks?" Sean says, "Just one more Merlot would be fine." "OK one more single malt scotch that will be my last." Says Rush. Laura says, "Honey I will have another Merlot please." The cocktail party is just what George and Laura envisioned it would be relaxed and informal having a good time with good friends. Sean speaks up, "I would like to add one more one last comment, and the liberal democrats do not care about American people they only care about power, control and money." "Now that is the Gods honest truth," adds George. Rush chimes in, "I have one last question why do the leftist democrats hate so damn much? They hate organized Christian religion, they hate babies in the womb, and they hate free speech, freedom of assembly it appears that hate is in their DNA when it exposes the truth about them. They hate the free market and capitalism and our strong military and so much more." "I don't know," answers George. "Neither do I," adds Sean. "But I will predict this; their hatred for America will be their down fall because America is the greatest country ever created by God." "God bless America," says George. For the next thirty minutes they talk about other subjects having a good time.

The head of the White House staff enters the room and announces that dinner now being served and to please follow him to the dining room. The table is set with fine china and silverware Rush and Sean are impressed knowing that they will be having a great dinner with great friends. First the salad is served a tossed salad with tomatoes and other fixings with five different salad dressings are on the table for you to choose from with plenty of blue cheese crumbles. Then the main course is served a prime rib dinner with the cuts to everyone likes, along with a baked potato and all of the trimmings and creamed spinach a perfect dinner to be enjoyed by everyone. President Bush starts the dinner conversation with, "Have you guys ever eaten Ostrich?" Both Sean and Rush nod their heads in a negative movement. "Well when I am no longer President and I am back on my ranch in Crawford, Texas I intend to raise them and sell their meat and other parts the meat is so different and tasty." The desert is served it is Baked Alaska one of Laura's favorites. Then the President asks, "Would you like an after dinner liquor?" Before anyone can answer a commotion is heard outside of the dining room door loud voices are talking then a persistent loud knock on the door occurs. Then Karl Rove enters the room, "Sorry for my intrusion but an emergency has occurred that needs the Presidents undivided attention." Karl Rove looks as though he has seen a ghost. "George says, "Go ahead tell me what is going on that has you so concerned?" Karl Rove hesitates and George says, "Go ahead spit it out man we are among friends I trust them with what you are about to say and will keep it to themselves," Karl Rove says, "The peace summit in Kingston Jamaica has just been invaded by the radical Muslim Jihadists connected with Usama Ben Laden. They have kidnapped Secretary of State Condoleezza Rice and Vice President Dick Cheney and Senator Orrin Hatch along with the primary ambassadors from the four main Middle East Countries at the conference. A total of six people were kidnapped it happened at the Pegasus Hotel where the reception and ball was being held." George speaks up, "Rush and Sean I trust what you just heard will never leave this room. I would never in a million years trust a democrat with this info they would have it published with in ten minutes even if I asked them not to say anything. "We know what you mean you can trust us not to say anything," says both Rush and Sean. "Gentleman I'm going to have to excuse myself you're in good hands with Laura she will enjoy your company. I fear this situation is going to be an all-nighter, let's go Karl call the Joints Chiefs of Staff and have them in the planning and war room with in the hour." Karl responds, "Yes Mr. president the call is being made as we speak."

The peace summit that is taking place in Kingston, Jamaica this week has a real important agenda on the table for world peace in the Middle East. The agenda developed by President Bush and his cabinet and his advisers is going to discuss the evil development of nuclear weapons by Iran and a plan to stop and end their nuclear development in its tracks. Also to stop the interference of Iran and Russia in Iraq and Afghanistan sending weapons and personal to the fight. Iran and Russia are a real enemy to peace in the Middle East and they must be held accountable and stopped. The peace summit is scheduled to begin on this coming Monday morning June 2nd at 9:00 A.M. All the parties were scheduled to arrive by Thursday to be able to attend the reception and ball tonight. The Pegasus Hotel was chosen because of its grandeur and easy access walking distances to so many International offices, Embassies and historical landmarks. Also to cultural venues and fine dining restaurants it is a four star hotel the best hotel in Jamaica.

The security to protect the guests attending the peace summit began over a month ago. Every country attending has had a hand in developing security for the summit; no one wants anything to go wrong and no trouble to occur, especially considering the attendees and the reason for the peace summit. The enemies of peace would like nothing better than to disrupt the peace summit and create chaos, showing the world powers to be weak and unable to protect their own people. So in the evil minds of the Muslim Jihadists that would prove that Allah is great and they are all powerful in their own twisted evil way.

The moment that the peace summit was announced at the United Nations and the world the Muslim Jihadists and al-Qaeda started to plan for its failure. The word went out for volunteers the best of the best to disrupt this peace conference and bring honor to Allah. Approximately 40 dedicated Muslim, Jihadists were chosen and they are now meeting in Tehran, Iran the leading terrorist's capital of the world. They are planning on capturing at least a dozen of the world's leaders attending this summit and demanding a ransom to get them back alive. Creating total chaos at the peace summit and derailing it showing the weakness of this peace folly. The ransom will be twenty million dollars and those who are foolish enough to try to stop them they will be killed. The plan is approved by the Mullahs of Iran. Now let the exact planning begin, time is short for such a grand plan. Mohammad Abdullah was chosen to be the leader; he alone is credited with killing ten American Army Soldiers in Iraq by his own hand and responsible for the deaths of another hundred American Soldiers on the battle field by planting land mines and directing battles. Abdullah calls together the volunteers for the first meeting and speaks in a loud and commanding voice. "We are the soldiers of Allah and we are going on a very important mission to capture the dogs of the west that want to destroy us and bring them to justice, our kind of justice after we get the ransom the hostages will all lose their heads. We are demanding twenty million dollars for their safe return to buy more weapons to kill more infidels and unbelievers. I will chose only 25 men to join me in our quest to go to Kingston, Jamaica you will be the fiercest and most dedicated to the cause and be willing to die if necessary. Remember when you die you will be rewarded in heaven as told by Allah himself of 72 virgin women to please you for eternity."

"Today I will begin the process of choosing who will join me in Kingston, Jamaica." The names are presented of the Muslim terrorists those who have the shown most glory on the battle field this takes place over twenty four hours to find the best of the best. The 25 have been chosen, now the real planning begins that will take place in one month from today they will strike. Passports are being made to provide safe passage in Tehran so no suspicion falls on them as some will register at the Pegasus Hotel and others will register in hotels nearby. The embassies of Iran and Syria provide the cover as they are now registered dignitaries on a peace mission. The planning continues with the help of local Jamaican terrorists that are Muslims to find the perfect place to take the hostages. The place that is chosen is a camp twenty miles up the Rio-Cobra River large enough to hold and hide their captives with four large buildings on the large property. The camp is not that well known in Jamaica only a few elite and wealthy people know if this place used as a get-a-way and a fishing camp. "This camp is perfect," cries out Abdullah. "Allah is with us and wants us to succeed to provide such a perfect place in all Jamaica, our planning is coming together." The first action that will take place is on a Friday night in the ballroom when all the dignitaries will meet for the first time at a large cocktail party in the ball room of the Pegasus Hotel. We will enter the ball room from different doors and demand everyone to stand by as we pick out who we want to take with us. If any guards are foolish enough to try to stop us kill them. The travel plans are made and reservations at the hotels are confirmed they arrive two weeks before the start of the peace summit.

Five of the men go to the camp where the hostages will be taken to scope it out and get it prepared. Fifteen Muslim Jihadists check into the Pegasus Hotel and six other Muslims check into hotels nearby. For whatever reason no one connected with the peace summit were concerned with these 26 Muslims arranging in Jamaica. Mainly because of the official diplomatic papers they presented at the airport and at the hotels. Mohammad Abdullah is working on his kidnap plan 24/7 since they arrived, walking through the Pegasus Hotel becoming familiar with every square inch of the large grand hotel, and finalizing the getaway plans along with five of his jihadists. Now that the plan is set and the Muslims know that they do not want to bring any unnecessary attention to themselves. So they either stay in their rooms or go sightseeing to blend in with the regular tourists. Muslim terrorists are very adept at fitting in and not being noticed as they did for their terrorists attack in New York City and the Pentagon on 9/11. No one should ever underestimate the evil planning of jihadists Muslims set on bring death to others.

Vice President Dick Cheney, Secretary of State Condoleezza Rice and Senator Orrin Hatch have just arrived in Kingston, Jamaica aboard the vice presidents plane without any fanfare on Thursday about 9:30 A.M. They do not want any publicity to over shadow the peace summit that is going to take place. The rest of the attending dignitaries will be arriving sometime today aboard their private jets and a few will be on regular airlines. A limousine whisks them to the five star Pegasus Hotel where they will be staying and three cars filled with security and secret service personal are close behind. There is no press taking pictures or trying to interview anyone the press has been told they are not welcome to cover this event. The American press has its own agenda that is to report untruths, lies and distortions to embarrass and bring about chaos for the Bush administration. As President Bush has said many times to his cabinet that the American press does not have America's best interest at heart any longer. Dick Cheney turns to Condoleezza and Orin and says, "I believe the three of us have the qualifications and the ability to make this peace summit a success. I am very proud of you and your abilities Condoleezza the President chose well when he chose you as Secretary of State." "Thank you for your confidence in me Dick, I look forward to contributing to this peace summit to bring about peace to the Middle East." Dick Cheney looks over at Orrin Hatch and says, "And you my good friend I am glad you're on this mission as well." Orrin in his very relaxed way says, "Thank you my friend I'm very pleased to be here as well." Dick Cheney says, "When we arrive at the hotel after we check in we should meet by the pool for a relaxing lunch at 11:00 A.M." "I like that idea that is a great way to start the day," speaks up Condoleezza. Orrin says, "I like that idea as well I will be in my bathing suit and take a refreshing swim." The rest of the dignitaries attending the peace summit begin arriving at the airport on this very sunny day such beautiful weather the temperature is around 94 degrees the sky is blue without a white cloud in the sky. The limousines and cars are all lined up to take everyone to the Pegasus Hotel. A calm seems to have settled over the dignitaries a feeling of something good is going to take place and that peace is possible in our time. Since everyone is arriving early the majority of them are taking this opportunity to go shopping and some sightseeing around Kingston.

The grand Pegasus Hotel is located in the heart of Kingston where the shopping in interesting and unique shops takes place. The people of Kingston, Jamaica are open and very friendly to the tourists. This site was chosen because of the natural beauty and relaxing feeling and it is so different from the standard places to meet in the world. All the people attending the meeting feel that here on this beautiful island of Jamaica they are safe and secure.

Dick Cheney, Condoleezza Rice and Orrin Hatch are sitting by the pool with their bathing suits on. Orrin is swimming laps and Condoleezza just jumped in the pool doing a perfect swan dive from the spring diving board. Dick prefers to sit and watch feeling the cool breeze surrounding him. The security is present but also out of sight blending in with the people around the pool area. Dick speaks up, "I think that I'm going to order the Jamaican jerk chicken with their special rice and fresh vegetables." Condoleezza yells out from the pool make that two that sounds so good." Orrin speaks up, "Dick make that three jerk chicken lunches and also order three Jamaican beers that helps the spicy jerk chicken go down."

Friday has now arrived the evening festivities are taking place in the main ball room at 8:00 P.M. A grand room it is very colorful with a lot of fantastic pictures on the walls all painted by local artists. This is supposed to be an informal cocktail party meet and greet with all the dignitaries getting to meet and introduce themselves around. The formal dinner party is to be held the next night on Saturday with an elegant dinner hosted by the government of Jamaica. Even though this cocktail party is informal everyone shows up dressed to the nines. The first people to arrive are the representatives from Saudi Arabia dressed in their traditional white robes. Then the representatives arrive from Egypt and Iraq they walk through the door in dark suits with a classy Italian cut. The English and the French are wearing dark blue sport coats with white pants, as though they planned to dress alike. Then Vice President Cheney and Condoleezza and Orrin Hatch arrive they are dressed in perfectly tailored dark suits with solid red and blue ties, Condoleezza is wearing an off the shoulder cream color long elegant dress she is dazzling. The informal cocktail party is in full bloom as there are about fifty dignitaries present all having a great time. Interesting Jamaican wine is being served both red and white along with Jamaican rum drinks with local fruit juices in tall glasses. The Hoes D' Oeuvres are perfectly prepared large shrimp and Beluga caviar on crackers and bread along with hot jerk chicken wings and different cuts of cheese. Also Blue Mountain Jamaican Coffee is brought around by waiters in red jackets and black pants serving the Hoes D' Oeuvres on silver trays. All the talking is informal yet crisp, shaking hands and telling stories just enjoying the evening together. Most of all the security is feeling secure that no problems were apparent and everyone is safe and sound as the cocktail party starts to wind down.

Then in the very next moment all hell breaks loose as 20 jihadists, terrorists Muslim men come bursting into the ballroom uninvited. Four men came swinging through the open windows from above screaming and yelling in Arabic. Then eleven men rushed into the room from the entrance doors and six came from the kitchen area. Everyone in the room was totally surprised and terrified at what is taking place. The Muslim Terrorists began firing their AK47's and Uzi weapons at anyone suspected to be security killing seven men without question. Chaos fills the room and fear is everywhere not knowing what to expect next. Then the leader of the Muslim Terrorists Mohammad Abdullah begins screaming, "We are holly warriors of Al-Qaeda and we are doing the bidding of our most holy profit Allah. Everyone in this room is our enemy and we bring justice our kind of justice to you all for the deaths you have caused in Iraq and Afghanistan killing our brothers. You men from Saudi Arabia are the worst kind of traitors to Allah you who bargain with the infidels to kill us. You twist the Koran the teachings from Mohammad to meet your own needs to sell oil to these infidels in the world. Then the Muslim Terrorists fire their weapons into the group of men from Saudi Arabia killing most of the representatives along with the ambassadors from Iraq and Egypt. We show no mercy to you infidels we have come for certain people in this room to take with us to our camp as hostages to bargain with your governments for large sums of money that is written on this piece of paper. Your lives may be spared if your governments give in to our demands in our time limits. The very moment that this so called peace meeting was decided on and the Saudi Government we intercepted a phone call that was made to our al-Qaeda headquarters to warn us of what is going on in Tehran, Iran. There are no secrets kept from us we have faithful agents in place everywhere. Security in the Muslim world those who stand against us is like a block of Swiss cheese full of holes. You people of the western powers had better understand this lesson."

Mohammad Abdullah continues speaking in an angry voice, "You Vice President of America, you Secretary Ms. Rice and Senator Orrin Hatch move to this side of the room and hurry. The ambassadors from England, France and Saudi Arabia join them now time is running out and we must go. I will leave our ransom demand note right here on the floor with our instructions we will contact you." The Muslim Jihadist Terrorists move from the ball room down the hall with their guns pointed at their captives the rest of the security gives them free passage so the captives would not be harmed. Four black SUV's with their motors running are waiting for them just outside the front door of the Pegasus Hotel they all get in and then drive away with their six hostages. The convoy reaches its destination about 3 hours later the hostages are told to get out and their hands are duck taped behind their backs and a heavy black hood is placed over their heads. Then they are helped into the three boats that will transport them to the camp deep up the Rio-Cobra River where they believe they will be safe from anyone finding them. The camp was well prepared with a lot of provisions, rum and weapons it will take over two hours by boat to reach their camp site. The terrorists now total 29 men 4 are Jamaica Terrorists with most coming from Iran and Saudi Arabia, Iraq and Afghanistan. Very little conversation is spoken in the boats by anyone quiet is what they wanted.

The letter that was left behind was picked up and read the letter was a real eye opener. **We are the Holly Warriors of Allah and we are seeking revenge for the atrocities of Infidels. We have captured some of the enemies of war against the Muslim World. We demand a ransom of $20,000,000 be wired to our bank in Tehran, Iran in 5 days from today**

and all Muslim prisoners in the world to be released. Or we will begin cutting off body parts of the prisoners and sending them to the Pegasus Hotel. This letter will change everything about how this situation will be handled especially the time frame these Muslim Terrorists are the worst of the worst this letter must be forwarded to Washington D.C. and the three other countries of the captured men. The secret service views the room of death and chaos that was a room full of happy people just twenty minutes ago. There are 9 people murdered and 6 people wounded that are on their way to the hospital the floor and walls are sprayed with blood what a terrible site to see. A call was made to the White House within minutes of this horrible event.

The boats are moving silently up the river only the sound of the 25 horse motors can be heard. The boats moving silently along high clefts and canyons a beautiful country to see even in the middle of the night. The leader of the terrorists is taking in all the terrain studying the landscape. Mohammed says, "I want lookouts placed here along the river with communications to warn us if anyone is coming up the river, they will be placed here three miles from our camp." The boats arrive at the camp and the captives are roughly pulled from the boats and marched to the main building that will be their prison or their grave depending if the world follows our demands. The six hostages are pushed to the floor and each is kicked and told to sit back to back in a circle in the center of the room and make no noise. If you do make noise you will be beat with a wire whip that will hurt and cut you. Mohammed sees a watch on Vice President Dick Cheney's wrist and he wants it and roughly takes it from him.

Back in the White House President Bush has entered the war room and has taken his place at the table as the Joint Chiefs of Staff the military leaders enter with a somber look on their faces along with the CIA and NCISS. President Bush knows the importance of moving quickly and decisively with all the might that the American Military can muster. President Bush calls the meeting to order the time is around 11:00 P.M. and informs every one of the death and destruction that just took place in the ball room of the Pegasus Hotel in Kingston, Jamaica. The Vice

President, the Secretary of State and a Senator have been taken hostage along with three other dignitaries. Nine people murdered and six taken in serious condition to the hospital and he passes around the room a copy of the letter left by the terrorists. President Bush speaks, "Gentleman we are faced with a terrible situation that began with 9/11 we must handle it differently. I am going to tell you what I want to happen but not tell you how to make it happen. I want all the hostages returned safe and sound and all the Muslim Terrorists killed we will not be capturing any of them and sending them to our country club camp in Gitmo, Cuba. The whole military operation will be supported leave nothing to guessing. We have less than 4 days to do this before body parts start showing up at the Pegasus Hotel. We will never negotiate with Muslim terrorists they are zealots and evil devils in human form. Now the ball is in your court how do you military men see our next move?" The Secretary of the Navy speaks up, "This is a clandestine operation I suggest that we develop a plan using our Navy Seals."

"Damn I like this plan already the idea of our Navy Seals getting involved," says President Bush. "They are trained for this type of mission not that the other branches of the military aren't well trained I mean no offence." "No offence taken Mr. President," adds the Joint Chief of Staff. "This operation will involve other branches as well even though the Navy will be front and center." "OK how will the Navy Seals be deployed, what exactly are the tactics and logistics?" asks the President. "Let's look at the whole picture and what we know at this moment," says the head of the CIA Operations. "We know that 20 men stormed the ball room at the Pegasus Hotel and that Mohammad Abdullah one of the worlds most wanted terrorists is their leader. And that there was a driver in each of the four SUV's that makes at least 26 that we know of perhaps more," adds the CIA director. "We also know that they drove towards the ocean and got on board four small boats, that means they are headed towards a river perhaps the Rio-Cobra River since it is the closest and the biggest river at this point on the map. The Vice-President, was wearing a special watch that provide GPS signals to our satalights we will soon learn the exact place where they were taken." The Air Force Commander suggests,

"We need to send our spy planes over Jamaica as soon as possible with our special electronics on board. That way we will be able to pinpoint their exact location and how many terrorists there are." The President says, "Make that happen now no delay that information is critical to a successful operation. Let's call this mission Operation Phoenix for the bird that rose from the flames." "Operation Phoenix is a perfect name Mr. President," says the CIA director. "Now for the specifics of Operation Phoenix what will be our next step?" asks President Bush. "The next step will be how many Navy Seal teams will go each team consists of 6 men will be deployed. Now we must plan on how we get them on site and then evacuate the hostages once all the Muslim jihadists are killed. This Operation Phoenix must move very quickly and in a stealth mode not letting them know we are coming if they have time to figure out that we are coming the hostages will be killed. "This is what I was born to do," says the Four Star General of the Army. "That is plan an operation like this one."

The President stands and says, "Gentleman if you will please excuse me I will leave you to your planning I want a complete plan of operation on my desk at 0700 in my office with all the plans in place. I am sure that your plans will be kick-ass plans I have all the trust in the world in your abilities to get Operation Phoenix running successfully, let's get our loved ones back safely. "Good night Mr. President we will see you in your office at 0700 with our plans ready for your approval," says the Navy Admiral. "Now let's decide how many Navy Seal teams are needed on this mission," says the Four Star General. "We know that there are at least 24 terrorists perhaps as many as 30 we will plan on 30 but we will know exactly within the hour how many terrorists there are." says the Navy Admiral. "I would recommend two teams of 6 Navy Seals be sent up river and 10 Navy Seals invade the camp by air. I believe that will be enough as I see it one Navy Seal can kick the ass of 20 to 50 Muslim Terrorists or more any day of the week." The Navy Seals can be dropped by a plane and they can parachute in right on target." "I think you're right about the number of Navy Seals needed but let's think more about getting men on the ground and getting the hostages safely out." says the Army Four

Star General. During this time the Commandant of the Marine Corps. hasn't spoken up. The Commandant of the Marines Corps. speaks up, "So far so good, I have an idea about getting the 10 Navy Seals on the ground and providing safe transportation for the hostages. I suggest that we employ a V-22 Osprey to deliver the 10 Navy Seals and that will also solve the problem of getting the hostages to safety quickly if medical attention is needed." The room breaks out with cheers and high fives with congratulations at this great idea by the Marine Commandant. "Just one more thing I think is important; we should also employ at least one AH-1Z Viper Helicopter for added fire power and cover to go along for the ride. The V-22 Osprey can carry the load and is about 75% quieter than most helicopters. We can plan the timing of the V-22 Osprey landing with the timing efforts by the Navy Seals from the boats when they are in position." Gentleman this is a plan of operation that the President expects from us now for the exact Navy Seals who are they and where will they come from?" says the Four Star General. The Navy Admiral Robert McCann speaks up, "First I want to say we have a perfect base of operations on Jamaica already to advance this mission from. It is about 90 miles from Kingston on the Northern side of the Island facing the water. This is a secret base that the Navy is now using and developing for our next generation of amphibious landing craft and Navy Seal boats with the help of the manufacturer Apex Boats of Costa Rica. I suggest that two of the teams come from the navy base at North Island, San Diego and the 10 additional Navy Seals come from our naval base in Norfolk, Virginia. I will place a call the two base commanders at both bases within the hour. The Navy Admiral makes the call to Captain Taylor the base commander in North Island, San Diego Calif. "Captain Taylor this is Admiral Robert McCann of the Joint Chiefs I have an emergency request that you make ready two Navy Seal teams both of Seal Team 6 to be shipped out at 0400 to a secret base in Jamaica. What the emergency is our peace summit that was to be held in Kingston, Jamaica was just attacked by radical, evil, bastard Muslims and they took Vice President Dick Cheney, Secretary of State Condoleezza Rice, Senator Orrin Hatch and three more world peace ambassadors to a secluded encampment on the Rio-Cobra River in upper Jamaica the terrorists are going to kill them if we don't save them in a matter of hours. I need you to choose wisely the best of the best Navy Seals but choose quickly we will talk within the hour."

Captain Taylor new immediately who he would send on this mission he would choose Seal Team 6, 007 and 008 both seal teams have seen military action in Iraq and Afghanistan. Both teams have returned to base four months ago ready for a reassignment between the two teams there are two Medals of Honors recipients four Navy Crosses. Their military jackets speak volumes about their dedication and bravery they are the best of the best. The twelve men are woken up and told to report to Captain Taylor's office on the double. As they are now in Captain Taylor's office sitting in chairs and leaning against the wall Captain Taylor speaks, "A troubling situation has occurred in Kingston, Jamaica tonight what was to be a peace summit on the Middle East. The fucking Muslim jihadists of Al-Qaeda kidnapped the Vice President and the Secretary of State along with Senator Orrin Hatch along with 3 additional world dignitaries attending the meeting. We need you guys to get them out and safe and kill the bastard jihadists that kidnapped them are you interested?" A loud war cry could be heard emanating from the captains office. "Damn right were interested let's get it on," yell the men in the room. "Good now be ready to leave at 0330 a jet plane will take you to a secret naval base in Jamaica. There you will get your final briefings on what to do and what your enemy looks like and how many of them needs killing.

Next Admiral Robert McCann calls Captain Kook the commander of the naval base in Norfolk, Virginia. "Good early morning Captain Kook this is Admiral Robert McCann of the Joint Chiefs we have a situation that need your personal attention. I am presently in the war room of the White House with a ton of military brass around me I need you to choose to Navy Seals for a special mission called Operation Phoenix as soon as possible and have them mobilized by 0400 can you do that?" "Eye, eye sir I certainly can do," says Captain Kook. A V-22 Osprey will be on your base at 0430 hours to take the 10 Navy Seals attached to Seal Team 6 to our secret naval base in Jamaica. What has taken place is a peace summit was scheduled to take place in Kingston, Jamaica on Monday at a cocktail meet and greet party tonight a number of fucken evil, Muslim, Jihadists, terrorists attacked and killed a number of those attending and kidnapped Vice President Cheney, Secretary of State Ms. Rice and Senator Orrin Hatch along with 3 additional summit meeting personal. We only have a few days left before the terrorists begin sending body parts of those they captured to the Pegasus Hotel as they said they would in their ransom letter. They also are demanding a lot of money but that will not happen. So Captain Kook chose well and choose quickly we have no time to waste we will talk later." Captain Kook has 10 Navy Seals rousted up from their sleep the ones he knows so well. These are the ones that have performed in Iraq and Afghanistan and have earned medals for their service and who have been back in the states for about six months. As the men muster into the base commanders office in the early morning they are all wondering what the hell is going on.

Captain Kook speaks up, "You guys are wondering why I called you to be here America needs your service again to save the lives of Vice President Cheney, Secretary of State Ms. Rice and Senator Orrin Hatch and three other important men who were kidnapped by Muslim Terrorists this evening as they were attending a peace conference in Kingston, Jamaica. They were taken to an encampment in Jamaica it will be your mission to save them and to kill all of the Muslims you see are you guys interested? ""You bet your sweet ass were interested," screams out a number of Navy Seals. "Good then get your asses out of my office a V-22 Osprey will be on the tarmac at 0430 to take you to a secret naval base in Jamaica now get ready and God Speed." says Captain Kook. The Marine Commandant speaks up, "The V-22 Osprey will be on the tarmac at the Navy base in Norfolk at 0430 to pick up the 10 Navy Seals along with all the weapons that the 22 Navy Seals will possibly need on Operation Phoenix. And the AH-1Z Viper attack helicopter will be sent directly to the secret naval base of operations in Jamaica they are presently in Gitmo, Cuba on a training mission. Admiral Robert McCann speaks up, "I can report to the President that 22 Navy Seals from Navy Seal Team 6 will arrive on our secret base in Jamaica by 0930."

In the meantime a report came in regarding the fly over of Jamaica from our unmanned spy plane that was deployed from a naval ship in the Caribbean that was on a military exercise. The unmanned spy plane was able to pick up the coordinates from the GPS watch worn by one of the American hostages. The spy plane was able to photograph and map the terrorist's encampment with its inferred camera and identify 26 Muslim Terrorists on the ground. Also we know that there are four buildings and the hostages are in the largest building used as a large meeting hall. As the plane was making one of its many passes the inferred camera picked up the heat signature of three men sitting in trees about three miles from the camp along the Rio-Cobra River most likely as look outs. The spy plane flew at 15,000 feet not making a sound so no one on the ground heard or saw anything flying around. The Muslim terrorists are congratulating themselves that they pulled off a grand Jihadist military operation and no one knows where they are. The evil, but very stupid Muslims feel real proud of themselves and their planning everything worked as they planned it out. The Muslim Jihadists are the most evil, violent and most hell bent on creating death and destruction to advance their evil religion ever seen in the modern world. Only the Nazi's and the Communists in Russia and China were as evil and violent and have created more chaos. But the Muslim terrorists are cowards as they use innocent women and children to carry bombs on their bodies and blow themselves up to create death and destruction in the market place.

The time is rapidly reaching 0700 when the military men are to present their plan to President Bush in his office on Operation Phoenix. The Joints Chiefs of the military are winding down their plans it appears that they have done all they can do for now. President Bust left the war room early to get some sleep but he did not sleep very well he tossed and turned for most of the night. At 0700 the President is at his desk in the Oval Office looking forward to the report on Operation Phoenix. The secretary notifies Mr. Bush that the Joint Chiefs are in the outer room. "Please show them in," was the Presidents response. All the men walk into the Oval Office and each is greeted by President Bush with a hand shake and asked to take a seat. President Bush speaks up, "I am anxious to hear your planning report on Operation Phoenix how did it go." Admiral Robert McCann speaks up first, "Mr. President I believe we have done well in our planning last night. As we speak there are 22 Navy Seals from Seal Team 6 on their way to our secret naval base in Jamaica ready for action they will be there by 0900. The boats that will carry the two teams of 6 up river are ready to go." The Marine Commandant speaks up, "There is a V-22 Osprey helicopter carrying 10 of the Navy Seals that will land at the base in Jamaica by 0900 along with all the weapons the Seals will need. And an AH-1Z Viper attack helicopter will be on the base by noon." The President speaks up, "Hell I didn't know we had a secret naval base in Jamaica but what the hell good work." We also have flown an unmanned spy plane over Jamaica and we know exactly where the Muslim encampment base of operations is because of the special watch Vice-President Chaney has on his wrist. We have also determined how many terrorists are on the ground and how many buildings are there and where the hostages are being kept." President Bush is very pleased with the plans so far and says, "I love it when a plan comes together, you men did well thank you all. Impressive very impressive your pre planning is excellent now for the execution of Operation Phoenix. Remember take no hostages alive they must all die not one of those bastards will be going to the country club prison in Gitmo, Cuba. It is important that this operation goes off without a hitch and rescues all the hostages. The prestige of the American military operations is on the line for the whole world to see. The newspapers and the TV stations like NBC and the rest who are in the back pocket of the leftist's anti-American democrats would like nothing more than for us to fail and the Muslim Terrorists to succeed. Success is on our side as God is on our side as well with that we cannot fail. I want a briefing every three hours or when something unexpected happens."

Only a special few in Jamaica are even aware of a military buildup taking place at a secret naval base in the northern part of Jamaica facing the sea. This is necessary to keep such a secret operation a success time is not on America's side. The two special jet inflatable craft that will carry the two Navy Seals teams designed by Apex Corp of Costa Rica are being prepared. And a ship the USS Kilgore is standing by that will carry them to their starting off point six miles off the southern coast is being made ready. Everyone is due to arrive within the hour. The two Navy Seal teams attached to the naval station on Coronado Island in San Diego are sitting on a jet plane excited to get the show on the road. Seal Team 008 is commanded by Lt. John Schneider better known as "Big Bad John" he is 6'2" a body of muscle and bone. It is said he has one fist of iron the other of steel of one doesn't get you the other one will. Lt. John is a gentle giant of a man to his Navy Seal team buddies and a good man to have on your side. He will never order you to do something that he would not do, or has not done before he is a real leader of men. Lt. John Schneider's second in command is Ensign Jeff Ohnmeiss also a dedicated and trusted navy man he is an expert with all the weapons at hand. Jeff Ohnmeiss is the perfect second in command if anything needs to get done you can count on Jeff to get err' done.

The other men on Seal Team Six are all handed picked and dedicated to team work and also very bad asses. The members of Seal Team 007 also Seal Team Six members are ready for action. Lt. Darren James is a man of action with the ability to lead men into battle and survive. He stands 6' tall all harden muscle at 210 lbs. His second in command is Ensign Jacob Blum a man deserving of his position he is also a weapons expert and a good leader of men. Ensign Jacob Blum has a wicked since of humor playing practical jokes and always has a new joke to tell. He has the ability to make the men laugh and relax even is the toughest situations. Then you have First Class Mitchell Davies the oldest on the team at 32 a real warrior he is also the navigator and electronics operator. He is also a history buff on the Pirates of the Caribbean he has been a student of the pirates of the Caribbean for many years it is a passion of his. Another important member of the team is Bobby Harold a hot head someone that needs to be looked after but a very necessary part of the team for his fighting ability at hand to hand combat. Bobby Harold once took on seven men at once who were harassing a pretty lady sitting by herself in a bar; he took them all outside and beat the crap out of them they never returned. Bobby Harold fears no man and has over 18 kills to his name in Iraq and Afghanistan of Muslim Jihadists in a number of fire fights. Then one man that everyone likes is Hunter, no one knows his last name no one cares they just call him Hunter. Hunter operates the boat as well as any piece of equipment that needs driven or fixed. He is the man that keeps the equipment going and a damn good man with an assault weapon. Then last but not least is Christopher Kirk he also has about 14 kills to his name in combat. Christopher was wounded in a fire fight in Iraq shot in the left arm but he managed to pull five men to safety and destroy a machine gun nest alone before he passed out. He received the Medal of Honor for his bravery but he never talks about it.

All the men on the Navy Seal teams are the best of the best our military has to offer. These brave men are dedicated to service, to country, and their team's men, in moments of need they answer the call of duty, and who would sacrifice their own life's to save a buddies life to take care of business. The jet is about to touch down at the secret naval base in Jamaica. Back at the Muslim Terrorists encampment Mohammed Abdullah walks into the building were the hostages are sitting in a circle with their hoods still over their heads for the last 12 hours. Mohammed says, "Take off their hoods so they can eat the soup of the day prepared especially for them and untie their hands. You're not planning on trying to escape or giving us any trouble I am sure that would be very bad for you all." The soup tastes like watered down pig slop not very tasty without any spice at all. Mohammed yells, "Eat your soup you infidel pigs you're going to need your strength. That's a good bunch of swine now stand and face the wall as my man Allie whacks each of you twenty times with a whip of justice until blood runs from your bodies on to the floor. I don't give a damn if one of you is a woman you will all receive the justice of Allah." Before the beating begin Vice President Cheney pleads with Mohammed to give him 40 whacks and not to give Condoleezza Rice any whacks. Mohammed thinks this is stupid and tells Allie to hit the old man 40 times as well as Condoleezza Rice 20 times as a lesson not to speak. As the beatings continue moans of pain can be heard from everyone but no one is crying for the beating to stop. Mohammed leaves the building with a smile on his face enjoying what was just done to the hostages. All the Muslim terrorists outside the building are screaming, "Praise be to Allah we are beating the people of the Great Satan."

Vice President Cheney tries the best he can to comfort the hostages telling them in a whisper, "I know President Bush at this moment he is working on a plan to set us free and to bring American justice to these evil bastard Muslims. He is not like democrat President Jimmy Carter who would rather hide under his bed not wanting to work on a plan of action. Or democrat Bill Clinton who would send an FBI team to Jamaica to investigate, without wanting to get into any real action to save us. Then Bill Clinton would call Monica Lewinski to the Oval Office for some stress relief." Then Vice President thinks to himself, those two democrat ex-presidents were phatic and were bad for America but that is what you get with a democrat in the White House. The hostages seem to get a little solace in what Dick Cheney has just said, even though they are tied up sitting in a circle with men pointing Uzi's and AK47's at their heads. The Muslims have a desire to beat or even kill them without blinking an eye oblivious to the pain they are causing they are having such a good time. Dick Cheney smiles to himself knowing that soon American soldiers will soon set them free and bring righteous justice to these fucken terrorists because that is the Republican way.

Mohammad Abdullah is sitting at a table in the building he has chosen to be his headquarters and his sleeping quarters during these hostage negotiations that could last 4 more days from today. Depending on how weak the Western Governments are at meeting his demands. Mohammad believes that it would take until Monday for the governments to even think or talk with each other long enough to come to some kind of agreement. Then it will take two additional days to solidify a workable agreement to settle with the demands. By Wednesday a transfer of Muslim prisoners should be released and by Thursday the money will be in our bank. What Muslim terrorists do not realize is that a Republican President is a different bread of cat then a democrat to negotiate with. Democrat Presidents would rather negotiate then take any action and rely on the FBI to take the heat not them. So the American people think they are doing the right thing and never take the direct heat for doing nothing at all, too afraid to do what is right. The liberal left news media that supports liberal democrat Presidents knows that bullshit investigations take place as a cover up for doing nothing at all. Republican Presidents are different they take the right action to solve problems and do not concern themselves with the leftist news media and what they will report. Mohammed talks with his terrorist's leadership and his second in command, Ayyub, Ismail, Magyar, and Adren and says, "Allah is blessing our movement and we are his chosen warriors, he knows the weak scared governments of the West and the phatic government of Saudi Arabia will do our bidding. That means we will all be home in our own land blessed by our people by the end of the week as the heroes we are." All the terrorists in the room yell out, "Allah is great blessings be to Allah." Mohammad speaks up, "We will go back to the room with the hostages in a few hours and give them more of Allah's justice upon their bodies."

Everyone in the Oval Office is smiling two of the men that are Joint Chiefs that are part of the planning of Operation Phoenix are ordered to go to the secret naval base in Jamaica to be the primary planners of Operation Phoenix. The two men are Admiral Robert McCann and the commander of the Marines Major General John George. Everyone that arrives at the base in Jamaica was instructed to be wearing street clothes, civvies no military uniforms at this time, just to reduce any appearance of any military buildup. The V-22 Osprey has already landed with the 10 Navy Seals they are shown to their quarters not very lavish just a place to rest their heads. The two Joint Chiefs of the military have arrived to start the next phase of Operation Phoenix. The AH-1Z Viper attack helicopter has arrived. The 12 Navy Seals from San Diego are set to arrive at any moment they are very late because their airplane had some trouble and had to land at the New Orleans airport for repairs. Their plane is met by a beautiful Jamaican lady a military person with a couple of cars to bring them to their sleeping quarters. She takes one look at Lt. Darren James as he walks down the plane ramp with the other 11 Navy Seals. The beautiful Jamaican lady's reaction is one of astonishment and also some panic it is as though she has just seen a ghost. Darren was somewhat concerned with the ladies strange reaction but let's it pass he had more important things to be concerned with at the moment. The seals are taken to their sleeping quarters then told to report to the operation center ASAP. The two men that will be in charge of Operation Phoenix are already hard at work in the war room. Large maps of Jamaica and the area where the encampment is located are being placed on the wall. All of the pictures taken by the unmanned spy plane are spread about in an organized fashion on the tables.

Four of the terrorists and Mohammad decide to go to the building holding the hostages to bring about more pain, harm and justice to all of them again because that's what brings them pleasure. On their way across the lawn Mohammed says to Ismail, "Bring the 7 pound rock you found by the bank of the river today I have a good idea." The Muslim terrorists enter the building and view the hostages still bleeding from their last beating and showing pain on their faces. Mohammed walks around the hostages still sitting on the floor and pointing a 6 foot bamboo stick at their heads. Then he says, "We Muslims find you infidels to be weak and phatic, when you dipped a few of the Muslim prisoners heads in water in the prison in Gitmo, Cuba your leftists on the democrat side went nuts and called that torture we really got a big laugh at that, hell you don't know what torture is but we do. Now Mohammad stops right in front of Dick Cheney resting his bamboo stick on his head. Then he says nothing and raises the bamboo stick up and slams it down on top of Dick Cheney's head causing excruciating pain. Then he moves in front of Condoleezza Rice and smiles at what he is about to do. He raises the bamboo stick up and slams it down on Condoleezza's right shoulder; Condoleezza winches in terrible pain but does not make a sound. Mohammad now moves in front of Senator Orrin Hatch and tells him to stand up then without warring jams the end of the bamboo stick into his stomach causing Orrin to bend over in terrible pain.

Then he moves in front of the dignitary from Saudi Arabia, Oman Fillah ll a son of King Oman Fillah and glares at him on the floor. Mohammad screams at Oman Fillah ll to stand and he slowly does. Mohammad Abdullah speaks in a very agitated voice, "You are a traitor to the true Muslims and so is your father you bed down with the infidels you trade with them your father accepts weapons from them to kill us and provides military basses for the Americans. My hatred for you and your kind knows no bounds I will punish you as Allah commands me to do. Today you will receive the most pain grab his arms and force him to the floor face up." Ayyub and Magyar do as they are instructed and stand on his arms, Ismail drops that 7 pound rock on his right hand breaking bones in his fingers. Mohammad says, "Now drop the rock three more times." Again the rock is dropped and more bones break and his hand begin to swell like a balloon causing excruciating pain. Oman begins to cry in pain and all the Muslim Terrorists smile and laugh at the pain they have just caused. Mohammad speaks, "I will not bring pain to the Englishman or to the Frenchman today but when I return you will feel my wrath I have something special in mind for you. All the terrorists go back to the main house and sit down on a rug to hear the wisdom from Mohammad written in the Koran. The tea is served and joy fills the room at what they have just done to the hostages. Mohammad speaks, "You are all aware of the so called torture that the American military in Iraq is accused of by the leftists, liberal senators and congressman and the news media in America. All they did was put woman's underwear on their heads and marched them around and poured water on their faces called water boarding. What they did is laughable American's do not know what torture is but we do. Their so called torture is phatic and ridicules the torture stopped because the leftist, liberal democrats are supporting our cause. They think we are their friends when we win the war with America and take over we will kill all the liberals first by cutting off their heads." Abdulla holds out his left wrist with the watch he stole from Vice-President Chaney and says, "Look at this fine watch I have it will bring us good luck."

The planning of Operation Phoenix in under way in Jamaica all of the Navy seals are in the room anxious to learn the particulars of the mission. John George the Major General of the Marines speaks first. "Men these are our plans the unmanned spy plane that flew over their encampment the other night confirmed that there is a football field at the camp big enough of support the landing of our V-22 Osprey with the 10 Navy Seals on board. The landing will be coordinated with the Navy Seals landing by boat then all hell will break loose. Our AH-1Z Viper attack helicopter will be flying above the camp firing its weapons of destruction at those bastards, the securing and safety of the hostages is your first priority when that is done bringing them quickly to the V-22 Osprey. Then you men make sure no evil Muslim lives that they are all killed then set hell fire to the camp burning it to the ground. Then the 12 Navy Seals that came by boat get in your boats and get the hell out of there. Today is Saturday 1700 hours we want to commence the fire fight on Sunday at 2200 hours. We have a lot to do to get ready especially with the boats that will take the Navy Seals up river to the camp now I will turn that part of the planning over to Admiral McCann."

Admiral McCann stands and speaks, "Men the boats that you will be driving the inflatable boats up river let me tell you some exciting news about them. The boats are unique in a lot of ways these specially new developed boats are built by Apex from Costa Rica, along with our help in the design. We have been working on the newest design, building the ultimate inflatable attack boat especially for the Navy Seals for two years now. The engines are water jet two of them with more power than ever before and they make very little noise partially silent. The boats can now travel in very shallow water and the engines have been developed to run on a variety of fuels not just gasoline but any fuel that will burn that makes them more versatile in hostile territories. The top speed can reach 65 knots with the boat fully loaded and can carry ten men and all their equipment. The boat is the color blue, black and sea green a perfect camouflage color making it almost invisible on the water. The normal interior beam of a Zodiac is 6' the beam of this new boat is 10' at the beam. The length is 33' giving it an exceptional stable ride in the worst of bad seas. The payload is 7,880 lbs. with a very deep hard V, fiberglass bottom we are very excited about this boat and what it will mean to our Navy Seals. This boat has been named the "Pegasus" history lore tells us the "Pegasus" was a flying horse now it is a flying boat. A couple of other things we have mounted on the bow a M1-34 Gatling gun that fires

3000 RPM, the cartridge size is 7.6 a devastating bullet when it hits its target. It is easy to learn to fire it and it has no recoil. This new boat was always intended to have this gun at the bow making it the most feared and devastating landing craft ever for the Navy Seals. Oh yes there is one more thing there are two lights high up on the back transom each providing 1,000,000 candle power each with all the latest electronics GPS and communication in the console and a loud speaker as well. The 10 Navy Seals that will be aboard the V-22 Osprey are envious as hell hoping some day they will get into these boats. The seal teams will be transported about seven miles from the southern shore by our transport ship the USS Kildare where you will depart from. This will end our meeting for today tomorrow we will have two additional meetings commencing at 0900. Now Seal Teams 007 and 008 muster to the docks in two hours for sea trials to get used to the boats but everyone your get your dinner first.

As the men are leaving the war room the beautiful Jamaican lady that met the 12 Navy Seals at their airplane was waiting outside the door. "Excuse me," she says to Lt. Darren James. "May I have a word with you please?" "Sure you can" says Lt. James, as the rest of his buddies gather around in a curious manner. As it turns out her name is Margo and she is the secretary to the base commander and has an extensive knowledge of the history about Jamaica and the Caribbean. Margo is a very beautiful lady and will always get a man's attention. "I know that I was rude when I first saw you and I want to apologize," says Margo. "No offence taken, "answers Darren. "But I am curious as to why I startled you so?" "OK I will show you if you will please follow me and your buddies can come along as well. There is a room with pictures and other information about Jamaica it is a small museum that we are very proud of." As the men and Margo enter the room what they see astonishes them. "There on that wall is your picture Lt. James no denying it," says Margo. That picture was painted in 1699 that is a picture of the most important Governor in our history sitting beside his wife the first lady of Jamaica. He brought civilized law to our island when it was overrun by pirates who ruled our island at the time of the biggest earth quake in our history in 1692. Ensign Jacob Blum speaks up, "Damn that is you Darren the same exact scar on your left cheek and your eyes the same as well and in the tattoo on your right forearm is your tattoo of the Navy Seal Trident no mistaking it. Who is the beautiful lady sitting beside him?" Margo answers, "She is the daughter of the Governor before she married the man in the picture and his name was Darren as well." "Well crap on a cracker," says Bobby Harold. "I've never seen anything like this before in my life and to tell you the truth it scares the hell out of me it is spooky." Lt. James is stunned and mesmerized at the same time to be looking at a picture of himself from 1699 and doesn't understand. Margo says, "Now do you understand my surprise when I first saw you getting off the airplane today." Bobby Harold speaks up, "I'm leaving this room now." "Were with you Bobby we're out of here," say all the seals.

The Navy Seal team 007 arrives in the mess hall for dinner, what is served is a tossed green salad, T-bone steak, baked potato with all the timings, corn on the cob and chocolate pudding for desert. It is a very good meal but the seals are somewhat disappointed they were hoping for some Jamaican island food like spicy jerk pork or spicy jerk chicken served the island way, as a steel drum band is playing songs in the far corner of the room. As team 007 was sitting down they noticed that Lt. Darren James looked as though he had seen a ghost in the picture of himself. "Hay Governor," Mitchell says. "How did you like your picture because it sure scared the hell out of me?" Lt. James speaks up, "I am just as confused as you all about the picture it really has me thinking about my past or my future. Today is today and I am one man that does not believe in past lives so I don't have any frigging idea what the hell is going on. Let's move on we have a mission to accomplish and that is the only thing I want you bums thinking about that is an order, got it." "Team 007 says, "We got it." "After we eat lets walk down to the dock where the boats are tied up I am anxious to see our new boat." says Hunter. "Yea you should be you're the one who will be driving it, "chimes in Christopher. "To tell you the truth I believe we're all excited these new boats sound fantastic and to take our first ride."

Both seal teams are walking rather briskly towards the dock the sun is just about to set in the next hour and there is still sunlight left in the evening sky. They see the boats tied up ready to go now they start to run all excited like small children on Christmas morning. Admiral Robert McCann is waiting on the dock, "OK men calm down, calm down this is what I want accomplished on your first run. The Gatling Gun is not armed, what I want you to do is climb in take the boats out run them go full throttle, make exaggerated turns, feel the boat out get comfortable for two hours, you don't have a lot of time before it's real. Two hours later the two boats return with the most excited seal crews ever. They get off the boats as Admiral McCann is on the dock and they are screaming at the top of their lungs, "This boat is the greatest boat we have ever seen we love it, we love it." Admiral McCann is very pleased that they are pleased he says, "Tomorrow morning early say 0600 if you want you can take the boats out again for at least a two hour run and the Gatling gun will be loaded with live bullets before our 0900 meeting in the war room." The crews are stoked and promise that they will be on the dock at 0600.

Sunday morning arrives early the two crews are at the dock at 0600 ready to drive the new boats getting a better handle on the boats performance and fire the Gatling Gun. Admiral McCann is on the dock and tells the men, "You have two hours this morning now gentleman start your engines." The two Navy Seal crews turn the key and the engines come to life they know that these boats are special. The next thing that is finely noticed from the first day is how quiet the engines are they were on board and could hardly hear the engines. Hunter scream out an order, "Take your seats swabbies and buckle up if you have one and hang on tight." The boat operator on team 008 is having the same conversation with his men and says, "That goes double for you Big Bad John safety first not second the last thing you want is for you to be thrown off the boat. Now everyone is seated and hanging on to either the ropes or a metal object. Hunter slowly pushes the throttle forward moving steadily away from the dock now both boats are in open water about 300 yards from the dock.

Hunter moves the throttle two notches forward as does the other boat is keeping pace perhaps a race will take place. The throttles are moved forward until they are three quarters of the way to full on both boats are 100 feet apart moving as if in a race. Hunter screams out, "Were not full open and were moving at 45 knots." The ocean is smooth as glass this early in the morning and the boats are accelerating to their top speed with no problem. Both boats break off when they reach 55 knots then reduce their speed to make sharp turns checking out the handling, no boat has ever done what these boats are doing. The boats make hard maneuvers to starboard then cut to port the boats with the wide beam makes handling a dream. Lt. James steps up to the Gatling gun and pulls the trigger wow what a feeling he yells, "We are the king of the world no one messes with us." Hunter screams out, "Men we are at full throttle 65 knots it is like gliding on the ocean I never expected a boat could handle this great thank you navy and thank you Apex. Lt. James says, "I can't wait to kick Muslim ass and take names that will be our war cry "Kick Ass and Take Names" As team 007 arrives at the dock team 008 is already tied up. "How did it go," shouts Lt. Schneider. "'Fantastic ride best ride I have ever been on," shouts Lt. James. "I totally agree," says Lt. Schneider. "I can't wait until we are in a real fight the enemy doesn't have a chance in hell." Admiral McCann says, "OK men time to get to our meeting we have a lot to cover."

The time is 0900 on Sunday morning the coffee is served it is the best coffee in the world it is Blue Mountain Coffee of Jamaica along with donuts and sweet rolls. Admiral Robert McCann and Major General John George start today's meeting off with a prayer to keep the men safe and return with all the hostages safe and sound. Admiral McCann begins the meeting, "Now let's begin yesterday we gave the time line of 2200 we believe everyone should be at their designated stations to begin open firing on those damn terrorists. That means we work backwards in time to accomplish that goal. If the attack commences at 2200 hours then the two boats must leave the dock precisely at 1300 hours to meet up with the mother ship fifteen miles off the coast of Southern Jamaica the USS Kildare. In order to refuel and then rest for a few hours and then get you into your fighting clothes and camouflage face paint. The USS Kildare will drop you off six miles from shore and head for the mouth of the Rio-Cobra River as it enters the sea to start your journey up the river to the Muslims encampment. You are expected to enter the mouth of the river at 1900 hours and slowly sight unseen proceed to the terrorists camp. Make sure you are familiar with the river with the maps we have provided and where the look outs are about 3 miles from the camp and take them out making no noise. When you arrive at the encampment contact base the V-22 Osprey with the 10 additional Navy Seals on board will only be less than 20 minutes away when you see the V-22 Osprey begin to make its decent open fire on those evil bastards to keep them busy the Navy Seals on board will only take 2 minutes or less to disembark and engage the enemy. The AH-1Z Viper attack helicopter will be at the camp and opening fire as well with its rockets attacking first the headquarters where the Muslim leadership resides. With so much shock and awe going on the terrorists will be confused they won't know which way is up and will begin to panic they do not even think we know where they are surprise, surprise. Remember the first thing is to protect the six hostages to get them aboard the V-22 Osprey safe and sound then kill every Muslim bastard you see then set the hell fire to all the buildings. These are the pictures of the camp become familiar with each building and floor plan and the building the hostages are kept in. You must know every square inch of the encampment like the back of your hand. Go ahead and take a break be back in 30 minutes for your weapons that you choose to take with you.

As the men take a break Lt. Darren James is standing alone by himself off in the corner of the room. Ensign Jacob Blum approaches him and places a hand on Darren's shoulder and says, "Hay buddy what are you thinking about?" Darren responds, "I'm still thinking about that damn picture we saw earlier of me painted in 1700. I do not believe in time travel that is impossible but I have no answer for my picture with a lady that is supposed to be my wife." Jacob responds, "I'm with you buddy you know that I don't believe in that bull shit either. I have no answer for what we saw on the wall in the museum but this mission is too damn important to be thinking about anything else so you have to stay focused." I know your right Jacob thanks, not another word," answers Lt. James. Admiral McCann opens this session by saying. "When I originally called your military bases and spoke to your base commander I asked what weapons would you recommend on a mission like this? These are the weapons that have been recommended and are going to be issued to you for this mission. You have seen and fired the Gatling Gun on the boat already also referred to as the minigun. That gun has been mounted on helicopters, airplanes, tanks, Hummers, and other naval ships it can cut trees down, shred trucks, personal carriers, brick and stone walls from 3,500 yards it is the perfect tool to kill men and break things treat it with the utmost respect. The next weapons are your personal held guns each man will be issued these weapons with double the ammo needed. I am going to turn this part of our meeting over to Major General John George. "I thank you Admiral McCann your presentation was certainly an eye opener. Now for your personal killing weapons so you stay alive we are going into this fight with vengeance on our minds and killing in your hearts. We are presenting you men with more firepower then those frigging, evil, Muslim, Terrorists could ever imagine more then you really need but who's counting."

"These are your weapons; a Barrett M468, 6.8 semiautomatic submachine gun it has more stopping power then the Russian AK-47 and fires a bigger bullet with more kinetic energy, its barrel length is only 16 inches gas operated and designed for close in quarter battles the gun only weights 7.4 lbs. with an overall length of 35.4 inches it has no recoil and has a good kill distance of over 1,000 yards oh yea it also has a suppressor. Next weapon is a TDI Vector 45 caliber submachine gun also called a "Kriss" this little son of a bitchen gun my favorite it has no recoil and its overall length is only 24.7 inches and only weights 5.55 lbs. and its rate of fire is 1,500 rounds per minute oh and it has a folding stock so when its folded its only 16 inches long almost small enough to put in your back pocket with an over the shoulder carrying sling its very small but very deadly in as very big way firing a 45 caliber bullet. Next is a really deadly kill weapon it's the Atchisson Assault Shotgun 12 gauge with a rate of fire 350 rounds per minute the drum holds 32 rounds of death and utter destruction. A shotgun changes everything especially in the close quarters of a room room the very sound of the firing is scary as hell. The maximum effective range is 100 yards that's a football field length. Gentleman there is more I mean more fire power we were not kidding when we told you that you will have more firepower then you might need."

"The two Navy Seal teams in the boats will receive these two weapons; a Chey-Tec 408 sniper rifle one of the most advanced sniper rifles ever developed with a magazine that holds seven 50 caliber bullets with very little recoil the kill range is one and a quarter miles with the most advanced scopes. Last weapon but not least is the AT-4 anti-tank rocket firing shoulder mounted bazooka made in Sweden and used by our military because it has no blow back and can be used in confined spaces. The rocket fuse can be set to explode prior to impact, upon impact or 2 seconds after impact for the most damage to be caused with very quick reload ability. All 22 of you will carry your pistols as standard equipment that you fire every day the MK23, 45 caliber pistols. This is one of the weapons that I really like for a number of reasons it has 40% reduced recoil and has a 12 round magazine. Along with your favorite attack knives strapped to your leg sharp and deadly with an 8" long blade. Everyone will be issued our newest full body armor called Dragon Skin so far it is the best body armor that has ever been developed very light and will keep you from harm. This ends my portion of the weapons presentation good luck and God speed," says Major General John George.

The last person to speak is the Director of the CIA Tomas Matlin, "I want to personally thank every one of you brave men it is my honor to be in the same room with you all. I would like to explain the encampment to you that our spy plane took the pictures of that you have on the adjoining tables study the pictures. The football or soccer field they play soccer on is perfect for us to land on you will only be less than 2 minutes from engagement once you step off the V-22 Osprey. We couldn't have designed a more perfect place to attack it's like it was custom made for us and the river is only 45 yards away from the camp. We know that there are a total of 29 Muslim Terrorists and 6 hostages at the encampment. Fourteen friggin Muslims guard the hostages at all times, twelve Muslims walk around the camp or sit by the river or are with their leader in his building the one that is on the right side of the large building where the hostages are. Don't forget the 3 Muslims that are on watch 3 miles downriver from the camp they must be eliminated first before they can make a call to the camp. This will end my portion of the meeting and thank you all for your service the best of the best Navy Seals."

Admiral Robert McCann stands and speaks up. "Everyone check your watches so everyone is on the same time frame at this moment it is 10:45 A.M. Operation Phoenix commences at 1300 hours, familiarize yourselves with the weapons if you need to go to the firing range and shoot a few rounds for an hour or so for the men in the boats the 10 men on the V-22 Osprey can fire on the range a lot longer. The 22 Navy Seals all head for the firing range together to familiarize themselves with any weapon they have not fired. The 12 Navy Seals that are assigned to the boats return to the headquarters to get a lunch and rest for an hour or so. Lt. James sees Margo the lady who showed him the picture walking by he smiles and says, "Hello, could you please answer a question for me?" "Sure no problem," answers Margo. "I would like to know the name of the lady sitting beside me in the picture?" asks Lt. James. "Her name is Lilliannah a most beautiful name for a most beautiful lady do you agree?" "Yes I agree," says Lt. James. "That picture I'll tell you the truth scares the hell out of me." Margo responds by putting her arms around Lt. James giving him a much needed hug and says. "God speed my friend what will be will be."

All the Navy Seals and the men who organized Operation Phoenix are at the dock to say, "God speed and God be with you and bless your mission." The 12 Navy seals assigned to the two Apex Pegasus inflatable boats climb aboard take their seats. They are ready for the ride of their lives as the two Apex Pegasus boats pull slowly away from the dock with everyone waving. The weather is perfect temperature around 80 degrees the sun is high in the blue sky with only a few white puffy clouds and best of all the ocean is calm and flat no waves at all. The two Apex Pegasus boats with 12 Navy Seals on board leave the land farther and farther behind. Navy Seals and all our military personal are special men and women of duty and honor who love this country with all their heart.

They put their lives on the line when called on not knowing if they will ever return. This is a unique mission they are on to rescue 6 hostages one who is the Vice President of the United States of America and others by radical, evil, Jihadists, Muslims willing to kill them. But that is what the military does each and every day of the year and asks for no additional compensation or any recognition and no public adulation. The military is made up of volunteers who love this country there are no left wing, progressive, leftists and anti-American democrats in the military. Perhaps that is why they hate the military so much because they know that they would never volunteer or have the guts to put their life on the line for their country. The Apex boats head out to meet the mother ship the USS Kildare 15 miles out to sea for a final ronde view. The Navy Seals could hardly wait until they were safely out to sea so they could all fire the Gatlin Gun with the rotating barrels. They also fire their own weapons for a short time to get into the rhythm of battle in a few hours. Hunter is keeping the boat on a steady line as all the weapons are firing. Now Hunter instructs the men, "Put away your weapons men take a seat I'm going to open her up to top speed to see what she can do. Hunter puts the handle to its max the other Apex Pegasus boat follows about 100 feet to port they both are traveling over the water at 69 knots what a rush. Then they both slow down to make safe starboard and port turns to really become familiar with the handling of these fantastic boats. Jacob yells out, "I can see our mother ship the USS Kildare to starboard about two miles dead ahead."

In the encampment Mohammed Abdullah and his followers Ayyub, Ismail, Magyar, and Adren the men he has trusted most are sitting on a rug in the middle of the room. All the furniture is pushed to one side they are sipping tea. The day is Sunday hot as usual for this time of year in Jamaica. But not blistering hot as it is in their own countries. In fact it is so hot in their own countries most of the time that it is believed the gate to hell is there somewhere and the devil loves to vacation there. The day is going along like a lazy day afternoon no problems on the horizon. The stupid Muslims are fat dumb and happy in their belief that no one knows where they are, and that no one would ever be so stupid as to try to rescue the hostages. They also believe that the Allah supports their cause and they are perfectly in the right to be doing what they are doing and they are heroes in their own countries. Abdullah speaks and when Abdullah speaks everyone had better listen or their heads would roll, literally. "Men, today is such a boring day it is Sunday let's do something fun lets go to the hostages and beat them some more." Good idea," chimes in his followers. "Lead the way great leader we will follow." The Muslim Terrorists enter the room where the hostages are kept still sitting on the floor in the center of the room. Vice President Dick Cheney has a four inch gash on the top of his head with blood oozing down his face. Secretary of State Condoleezza Rice has a broken right shoulder where she was hit. Senator Orrin Hatch is bent over in pain from where he was jabbed by the bamboo pole and may have a damaged spleen. The son of King Oman his right hand has turned all shades of blue, black and red and is three times the size of his left hand.

These are normal ways Muslims treat infidels with no feeling, no compassion and completely void of any emotion. Abdullah walks over to the Englishman with a devious look in his eye and asks the Englishman to stand then with his bamboo pole Abdullah smashes it against the right side of his neck. Making a large welt on his neck then he smashes the bamboo pole against the left side of his neck just about breaking his neck, the Englishman falls to the floor unconscious. Then Mohammad Abdullah proceeds to the Frenchman telling him to get on his hands and knees bending over exposing his neck. Then a sword is put in Abdullah hands and everyone in the room cry's out not to cut off his head. Abdullah raises the sword to decapitate him and tears are flowing from the Frenchman as he sobs and pleads not to take his life. Abdullah then brings the sword down and just rests it on his neck cutting him slightly. All the terrorists in the room have a great big laugh at the Frenchman's expense. Then Abdullah takes hold on the bamboo pole and proceeds to beat the Frenchman on his back and his head until he passes out from pain. All the hostages are sickened by what they just witnessed and have already endured themselves these Muslims are barbaric and need to be killed. None of the hostages dare to speak out knowing the act of speaking would bring them more serious harm. Abdullah walks over the where Dick Cheney is and says, "Old man I really like the watch you gave to me it is a fine watch only Muslims should have a watch like this one it is too good for infidels I am sure it will bring me good luck." Dick Cheney smiles says, "I am sure it will bring you luck and justice believe me." The terrorists leave the building Abdullah turns and says, "These Americans what fools they are very stupid to be wearing such a beautiful watch with all the gold and diamonds on it and it is so heavy a terrorist may take it from him. I know this watch will bring me good luck for the rest of my life."

End of chapter number one

CHAPTER 2

The Navy Seals are now only about 150 yards from the mother ship and they can see a large ramp lowering down from the fan tail to allow them to drive their boats right into the ship. Hunter speaks up, "I am very confident about my handling of our boat it handles like a wet dream very exciting. Apex boat builders have out done themselves with such a wonderful designed boat it is a real winner." The two Apex boats drive right up the ramp and into the ship as Captain Jones is standing by to welcome them. "Welcome aboard men welcome to my ship," says Captain Jones. "You will find all the comforts of home aboard my ship, good chow and a nice rest area. You will find your battle clothes all laid out for you and a comfortable place to apply our war paint when you are ready. Your gas tanks will be topped off for your important mission. The time is now 1500 hours you have three hours before we drop you guys off five miles from the coast where the Rio-Cobra River meets the sea."

Time keeps going on never stops never rests tick-tock, tick-tock it's now time for the twelve Navy Seals to depart the mother ship. Their gas tanks are topped off at 100 gallons each their bellies are full with a good hearty meal and a snack is provide for each man and stowed away. They have their Dragon Skin Body Armor on and their freshly prepared camouflage clothing as well as their faces are pained for combat in green, blue, and black. The Navy Seals say their goodbyes and thank Captain Jones for his hospitality. Captain Jones responds, "God speed to you all be careful out there and kill everyone one of those miserable friggin Muslim bastards. I'll see you guys back here at this spot in about 8 hours." The ramp at the fan tail on the ship lowers down and the two Apex Pegasus boats slip into the sea the boats just to seem glide across the sea. They are exactly five miles from where the Rio-Cobra River meets the sea. They must be at the mouth of the river in one hour to meet the plan of attack the sun is still out but will be setting in one and a half hours. The Apex Pegasus boats are skimming across the water that is smooth hardly any wave action at 35 knots. The Apex Pegasus boats are painted in a camouflage color of sea blue green making them partially invisible to the naked eye. The Navy Seals are all dressed to kill even the sharks in the water give them a wide birth. The boats are about 100 yards apart neck and neck seal team 007 sees a 50' wide what appears to be a dark blue and crimson fog bank dead ahead. Not thinking that much about it Hunter gets on the two-way radio to the other seal team 008 and says, "Hay you guys do you see that weird colored fog bank dead ahead of us?" "Yea we sure do but we're staying clear you guys go for it." Hunter answers, "What are you guys scared of a fog bank you bunch of pussies see you on the other side." As seal team 007 enters the odd colored fog bank seal team 008 notices that the odd fog bank just dissipates and seal team 007 can no longer be seen they just seem to have disappeared.

Seal team 008 becomes instantly concerned where in the holy hell they went; they try to get them on the two way radio but no response. They were only 100 years to their starboard side just a few moments ago they went through an odd colored fog that is no longer there and now they're gone. Lt. John Schneider gets on the radio to base and says, "Base we have a problem seal team 007 seems to have disappeared." Admiral McCann is perplexed and says, "What in the hell do you mean disappeared how is that even possible?" Lt. Schneider responds, "We were only 100 yards apart when seal team 007 went through an odd colored fog bank and now we can't locate them. The sun is still out but where're the only boat on the water. We are all looking through our binoculars to find them but with no luck." Admiral McCann says, "We will try to raise them on our radio and get back to you in a few moments stand by." The base tries to radio seal team 007 but with no response just crackling dead air. Admiral McCann calls back to seal team 008 and says, "I don't know what happen but we can't raise seal team 007 either, so stay in the area keep looking for no longer than 15 minutes more then you must proceed with the mission alone. Seal team 008 does as ordered it keeps searching for fifteen minutes but with no luck and then proceeds on the mission alone, heading for the Rio-Cobra River entrance. The people at the base are confused we are told a boat went through an odd colored fog bank and then disappeared what the hell. Major General John George speaks up, "Hell we're nowhere near the Bermuda Triangle that might be an explanation but this is too odd to believe." Admiral McCann slams his fist on the table and shouts, "Well shit on a shingle we must precede with one less boat this mission still must be completed. I wonder what the hell else can go wrong when everything was going so right. With all the seal training unknown contingencies happen all the time not all missions go smoothly without a hitch, seal team 008 is mentally prepared and trained to proceed and that's what they must do." Lt. John Schneider tells his team, "Men I am as mystified as anyone that seal team 007 just disappeared from the sea. But we have our orders and an important mission to complete we did what we could do now the navy will have to search for them we must head for the Rio-Cobra River and continue on with Operation Phoenix.

Seal team 007 has just passed through the fog bank with the odd colors; the instruments that depend on satalights to function do not work. Christopher Kirk picks up the two way radio and tries to call seal team 008 no response and they cannot be seen. Christopher says, "What the hell they were only 100 yards off our port side before we went into the fog bank now they are nowhere to be seen. The seals try looking through their binoculars to see if seal team 008 boat can be seen, no luck. Hunter taps on the GPS no response the compass on the boat is working, the gas gage is working, the lights work, wristwatches are working, and the loud speaker works, but electronics that depend on satalights to work are not functioning like the GPS. Lt. Darren James speaks up, "I don't know what the hell happened or where seal team 008 is; I do know that we must continue heading for the entrance of the Rio-Cobra River we should meet up with seal team 008 there so we can continue on with Operation Phoenix." They keep going in the direction set by the compass to the meet up spot, the sun is just beginning to set and dusk is on the water. Bobby Harold is looking through his binoculars and spots something odd in the distance he shouts, "Everyone looks to starboard about one mile away or more get your binoculars and tell me what you see?" "Son of a bitch what the hell it looks like a dozen or so of old ships like Christopher Columbus sailed on." "Let me take a look see," says Mitchell, "Those ships are Spanish Galleons that I can identify, as you know I am an expert when it comes to the history of the 1600's the ships and the pirates of the Caribbean that is a passion of mine. I would say those ships look authentic and in good condition from this distance." "Ok big deal old ships in the water probably in some sort of boat ceremony or parade celebration," explains Lt. Darren James. "Keep on heading for our meeting point on the map." The men have to rely on the maps of the ocean and glad they have them and now they have to use their compass to find the meeting place the hard way no electronics to help in any way.

The sun has set the sky is dark but the ocean is still flat no waves and the evening is warm. As the seal team 007 continues the land topography is not the same as on their maps different in a lot of ways. They are getting closer and closer they now see more Spanish Galleons, English ships, Dutch ships and French ships all flying the colors of their country of the 15th and 16th century and a few ships flying the skull and cross bones flag. Bobby Harold says, "By my watch we are about one hour early so can we get a little closer and take a better look at these ships? I can see men on deck in their ole costumes walking around." Mitchell chimes in, "These ships and people must be celebrating one hell of a holiday they look so authentic if I didn't know better I would say we were back in time." Lt. James is getting frustrated because the land topography does not match up with any map everything looks completely different something is radically wrong and he thinks perhaps that they are lost. Hunter points the bow to where the river should be but after forty five minutes of searching the river is nowhere to be seen they are lost.

Seal team 008 arrives at the ronde-view site where the Rio-Cobra River meets the ocean and where they are to meet up with seal team 007. Jeff Ohnmeiss radio's the base and reports their position and that seal team 007 is nowhere to be seen asking for instructions. Admiral McCann answers, "You may wait for an additional 15 minutes no longer if team 007 does not show you must begin going up river alone do you understand. Do not call again until you are in position at the camp to begin firing then we will send the V-22 Osprey that will take less than 20 minutes of flight time to arrive at your position. Don't forget about the look outs three miles downriver from the camp. One last thing be careful out there I know you will succeed so kick ass and take names of those Muslim coward, bastards. God speed and God be willing and I believe he is, get the hostages and get out safe return unharmed that's an order." "Aye, aye sir," is the last response from Jeff. The Navy Seals are pumped at this point as they begin their trek up the Rio-Cobra River into harm's way alone. Slowly they proceed not wanting to bring any attention their way as they begin planning for their first encounter with the three terrorists along the river bank. The Navy Seals know that they can't drive up alongside of them and open fire that would raise a red flag and the terrorists would call the camp and the hostages would be immediately killed.

Plan A is to tie up about one quarter of a mile from the Muslim look outs. The flyover from the unmanned spy plane shot the perfect picture of where they would be located. The perfect spot along the river is found to tie up the boat two Navy Seals leave the boat with their MK23 45caliber pistols with the suppressors strapped to their right leg and their knives strapped to their left leg. Also they have with them the Barrett M468 semi auto sub machine gun with their suppressors. They start the swim up the river it is tough going because the river is flowing pretty well and they are swimming against the current. But they make progress just the same then the three terrorist can be heard singing songs along the bank of the river as though they don't have a care in the world, soon enough they will be out of this world. Their reckless and bad singing muffles the seals movements in the water just enough that they can proceed a little farther up river for a better kill shot. Two of the Muslims are sitting by the left bank of the river a third is up a tree for what he thinks is a perfect view. The two Navy Seals are now in perfect position for their kill shot they rise out of the water and open fire with their Barrett M468 semi-auto sub machine guns with the suppressors killing the two terrorists that are singing on the bank of the river making just enough noise that startles the man in the tree and he falls into the river. One of the Navy Seals grabs him and slices his neck cutting his head clean off. Then they call to the boat to report the kill is done the Apex Pegasus starts it's motor and proceeds up the river to pick up the two Navy Seals. "So far so good," says Lt. Schneider slapping them on their backs. "Let's not get over confident that will get you killed quicker than anything." Seal team 008 continues moving slowly up the river all dressed in their black, blue and green camouflage attack uniforms with their faces painted in black, green and blue war paint. They are making good time and expect to be in position by 2200 hours right on time.

The GPS has mapped out the river perfectly and the over flights by the unmanned spy plane has photographed the Muslim Terrorists right down to the last man and they had no idea they were being watched and photographed. And where the terrorists are standing in the camp and the exact number of them the Navy Seals know the layout of the encampment like the back of their hand. The camp itself is about 55 yards from the river so the Navy Seals plan to leave their boat tied up 100 yards from the camp and then proceed to swim up the river and approach the camp on land about 45 yards from the main landing point where there is a large dock. Hell has no fury to the American military when innocent hostages are taken no one screws with Americans now these Muslim Jihadists will get a boot put up their ass and twisted sideways. The Navy Seals know the layout of the camp the first building closest to the river is where the leader Mohammad and his closest followers usually are. That building usually has 5 to 6 Muslim Terrorists in it at all times sipping tea and talking about how great they all are. The building holding the hostages looking from the river is about 85 feet long 40 feet wide about 40 yards north of the first building. That is the building holding the 6 hostages with 10 to 14 Muslims guarding them at all times. Then there is another building perhaps another 15 yards north to the right side of that building this is the barracks of the Muslim Terrorists where they sleep and usually eat their meals. There are out houses scattered around for doing their business. The main ground area is about the size of a soccer field right in front of the building where the hostages are kept it is perfect the grass is kept cut. The Muslims that are guarding the encampment walk around every two hours and then there are usually two Muslims by the river by the main dock. The Muslims Terrorists feel very secure that they have covered all their bases and consider themselves smarter than any enemy could possibly ever be.

This encampment is a rest, relaxation and fishing camp for only a chosen few people on the island of Jamaica. This camp has a lot of amenities that the basic homes in Jamaica do not have. It is considered a real treat to be able to come here during the year. The camp was constructed from the surrounding forest of trees; bamboo, palm trees, and a lot of other trees native to this area. The reason for such a large open area is so the men can play their games of soccer, baseball, volleyball and even badminton. But now this camp has been turned into a camp of toucher, pain and death by radical Muslim Jihadists hell bent on creating chaos. This is what Muslims bring to every table they sit at. The Muslims believe that Allah is pleased and showing them favor and is protecting them from the infidels because he believes their cause is righteous.

The Navy Seals now move from the water to land very carefully and with such cat like skill movements no one would see them even if they were looking straight at them. Lt. John Schneider better known as Big Bad John is leading his team he spots two men on guard about 30 yards away dead ahead. One of the Muslims is leaning against a tree looking in the opposite direction smoking a cigarette. The other Muslim is taking a healthy shit sitting on a small log also looking in the opposite direction holding two large leaves in his hand. Lt. Schneider motions for two Navy Seals to come forward and take out these two unfortunate terrorists. The two Navy Seals move into position not even disturbing a twig on the ground. The Muslim leaning against the tree smoking his last cigarette he takes his last drag as the Navy Seal covers his mouth with his hand and with the other brings his 6 inch blue steel blade cutting his throat from ear to ear. Then the other Muslim taking his last shit of his short life is grunting and grunting perhaps he is constipated. But he does not hear the other Navy Seal sneak up behind him forcing his knife into his back coming out of his chest piercing his heart. "Good work men," Lt. Schneider whispers. The base is contacted and the V-22 Osprey with the 10 Navy Seals are already aboard ready to get this show on the road. And the AH-1Z Viper attack helicopter Super Cobra which is outfitted with Hellfire air to surface missiles, 8 Hydra rockets and all the ammo needed for the 20mm M197 Gatling Gun, start their engines and lift off into the night sky anxious for some action. The Navy Seals aboard the V-22 Osprey are well armed each has his MK23 Mod .45 caliber pistol strapped to his leg. Three of the Navy Seals have chosen to bring the Atchisson Assault Shotgun a deadly weapon, the other three men have chosen the TDI Vector .45 submachine gun a perfect killing weapon, four of the men are bringing the Barrett M468 6.8 semi auto submachine gun that spouts death with every pull of the trigger, and each man has on his Dragon Skin body armor.

Admiral McCann, Major General John George and all the personal that had anything to do with the planning are on the tarmac. Waving them goodbye and God speed praying for a safe attack and bringing the 6 hostages home safe and sound. They know that within 20 minutes they will engage the enemy and kill every last one of those evil, Muslim, Jihadists, bastards. Lt. Schneider has positioned his men at the two doors of the main building where the 6 hostages are kept they can be seen through the windows sitting in the middle of the room and the Muslims off to one side. Now all they are waiting for is the sound of the V-22 Osprey over head to begin the engagement. It doesn't take long the slapping of the helicopter blades on the V-22 Osprey are heard since they are listing for the sound very intensely. As the V-22 Osprey begins its descent the Navy Seals stationed at the two doors they throw into the room six flash bang grenades totally confusing the terrorists as to what in the hell is happening. At that exact moment 2 hell fire missiles slam into the headquarter building killing Mohammed Abdullah and his four most trusted terrorists. The V-22 Osprey lands and within 2 minutes 10 screaming Navy Seals come running out ready for action. The AH-1Z Super Cobra hovers over head searching for any one running into the night. The six Navy Seals enter the main building where the hostages are and seven additional Navy Seals enter from the opposite direction screaming and firing their weapons. The Muslim Terrorists all 12 in the room scramble for their AK-47 weapons that are across the room as three Navy Seals stand right in front of the hostages to protect them from harm. Then all hell breaks loose as the Atchisson Assault Shotgun and the Barrett M468 6.8 semi auto sub machine guns open up bringing death and dismemberment to all the Muslims in the room. Just the very sound of the Atchisson Assault Shotgun would scare you to death. Then two terrorists enter by a door with their AK-47 raised to fire before they can pull the trigger two Navy seals see them and open fire with their Barrett 468 semi auto submachine guns literally cutting them in half before their bodies hit the ground. Lt. Schneider screams, "Check the last building the barracks clear it out kill every one of those bastards." One of the terrorists runs into an outhouse to hide two Navy seals see him and open fire making the outhouse look like Swiss cheese. His body parts, hands, feet, blood and guts and eye balls are all mingled in with the shit.

Muslim Terrorists being the true cowards that they are three ran so fast that the hounds couldn't catch them into the jungle. No problem the pilot Bob Allen of the AH-1Z Viper attack helicopter spots them beating a path to where ever in the jungle. The pilot is wearing his night vision head gear along with the heat seeking camera the Muslims are lit up by their body heat as they try to scramble to some place safe. They are ducking behind trees under logs the AH-1Z sees them clear as if it were noon on a bright day. He is hovering above them at 200 feet like a bird of prey, like a Falcon watching a white rabbit move and dodge thinking it is getting away. Two of the scared and terrified Muslims stay together running as fast as they can, one is slower and trips and falls. Bob Allen the pilot yells out, "Your time is up." Yelling in the cockpit for his own entertainment and pulls the trigger of the Gatling gun zzzzzxxxxzzzz making a horrible deadly sound. His body parts go flying all over the place, one down two to go. The AH-1Z Viper, Super Cobra rises 50 feet higher into the night air turns right spotting the two Muslims in a praying position in a small opening. The trigger of the Gatling gun is pulled the terrorists are like Humpty Dumpty they could never be put back together again. The AH-1Z Viper, Super Cobra rises higher and reverses its direction and heads back to the terrorist's camp mission completed. The body count of these Muslim Terrorists are very important because the orders were no terrorist gets away, no one lives, no terrorist gets to vacation at camp Gitmo in Cuba. All the bodies are accounted for all 29 are dead and in various body pieces.

The Navy Seals all provide help to the hostages, helping them to stand and remove their bindings they are all smiling. Vice President Dick Cheney with tears of happiness and gratitude gives the Navy Seals his wonderful smile and his big bear hug. Dick Cheney says, "I always believe you guys were coming, I didn't know exactly when the hostages and I are all very grateful God Bless you all." Secretary of State Condoleezza Rice her dress torn and in shambles was also crying openly. She with all the love she could give thanked the Navy Seals best she could with a broken shoulder and her cuts and bruises and swollen body parts. Senator Orrin Hatch was the worst of the hostages he has a ruptured spleen and is in great pain, but he also smiles best he can and thanked the men for their bravery. The Englishman and the Frenchman dignitaries also in bad condition gave the Navy Seals their thanks. The Prince of Saudi Arabia his right hand in extremely bad condition did his very best to say thank you to the men. "OK men," yelled an order from Lt. John Schneider, "Get these wonderful, brave people on the V-22 Osprey and into a hospital as quickly as you can, move, move, move." Now the Navy Seals take a moment to reflect on the battle no one was even hit all the seals are fine all safe and sound. The 10 Navy Seals and the 6 hostages are now safely aboard the V-22 Osprey and buckled up, the blades are turning and it is lifting off the ground. Lt. Schneider calls the base to report. Admiral McCann is handed the phone, "The hostages are all safe and on their way they will all need medical attention and all Navy Seals are unharmed perfectly OK." Cries of joy for a successful battle engagement could be heard and the men at the base all thank God for answering their prayers. Admiral McCann immediately calls President Bush with the good news and he is very happy.

Lt. John Schneider gives his last order, "Men we need to burn this camp down spread the gas around and set your timers on your explosive packets for 20 minutes hell fire is about to consume this awful place." The Navy Seals are tired very tired that is what you're body does when coming down from such an adrenalin battle rush from what just occurred. Every man who just saw action would rather the Muslims did not take these hostages and this action did not have to happen. The six Navy Seals turn to see the hell fire consuming the buildings as the fire light lights up the midnight sky. The six Navy Seals from team 008 head back through the jungle to their Apex Pegasus boat to take them back to the mother ship.

Time is not the same and not the same time when you go through a portal of time, forward or back on one side it could be a few hours a day or a matter of seconds while on the other side of time it could be a day or even a week.

Seal team 007 is still searching for the Rio-Cobra River with the full intention of joining seal team 008 and continuing on with Operation Phoenix. For whatever reason they could not understand or even contemplate what the hell happened when they passed through that dark blue and crimson odd fog bank. They are now using flashlights to read a map a map that does not make any sense. The entrance of the river is supposed to be 20 miles from Kingston, Jamaica. The team approaches the exact spot on the map Mitchell says, "There is no fucken river feeding into the ocean so what in the hell are we supposed to do now, make one?" Lt. Darren James speaks up in an angry voice, "Our maps are never wrong, never and neither am I they are plotted by satellite GPS see I have it located on the map right here. I want to continue another 4 or 5 miles along the coast going north it has to be there." After the Apex boat goes an additional 5 miles up the coast they do not find what they are looking for. Bobby Harold says, "Hell look at the time its way past 2200 the time for Operation Phoenix to begin we have lost our way admit it." Lt. James instructs them to turn around to where they last saw the flickering lights and ask for directions. They approach what is supposed to be where Kingston, Jamaica is located they see the lights of a city not electric lights but flickering fire light. Mitchell franticly checks the map, now what in the hell is going on the lights are located in a completely different location of this very large harbor. There are no lights where Kingston supposed to be and so many lights at the end of the land mass that is protruding into the harbor area. They are moving along at just under 20 knots the flickering lights are coming at them it seems rather quickly. The Navy Seals are all keeping a sharp eye out for anything out of the ordinary not knowing what that might be. Then they see again the enormous amount of old style ships of the 1600's and the 1700's there must be over two hundred ships now tied up in the harbor a daunting site to behold and they all look in perfect condition.

What the Navy Seals are seeing are the lights of Port Royal, Jamaica an English port and an English strong hold the ships that are tied up in the harbor are ships of this present time, and the year is 1692. The Navy Seals are not aware at this time what they are seeing or what year it is, at least not yet. Port Royal, Jamaica was captured in 1655 on May 10th by a full contingency of English sailors when they landed at Passage Fort in Kingston Harbor and marched towards the Spanish town of Port Royal. On May 11th the Spaniards surrendered and were told to leave Jamaica. Some of them went to Cuba and others secretly went to the north side of Jamaica, Port Royal was now in English hands for the very first time.

When the British occupied Jamaica they realized that Port Royal maybe a useful place to set up a fort to discourage the Spaniards from coming into the harbor. The fort was soon established but unfortunately there wasn't really a navy to protect the harbor in Jamaica for that matter the Governor of Jamaica, D' Oyley took it upon himself to issue letters of Marque to raise a private navy of privateers. He recruited these privateers from among the pirates and buccaneers in Tortuga. The greatest stories to come from the pirates of the Caribbean come from this golden age of piracy. The privateers quickly found royal protection from their attacks on Spanish and Dutch ships that they found very helpful. The town of Port Royal quickly became full of looted gold, jewels, and other products that would be going to Spain. The town of Port Royal grew at a tremendous pace until 1692; there were approximately 6,000 people that now reside here. In fact at the time Port Royal was a large city even larger then Boston, Mass. and it was richer, alcohol was plentiful food was expensive and business was lucrative. In fact because of the influx of privateer loot in Port Royal they had a thriving trade with London and the American colonies. The people in Port Royal wore the latest fashions from London. In exchange for the fine clothing and other manufactured goods, Port Royal sent back gold, sugar, sugar cane, molasses and other raw materials. The Plantation owners and many merchants within the city were cut from a more civilized gentry, they distained the whoring and debauching of the transient privateers, pirates and buccaneers. Although Port Royal was designed to serve as a defensive fortification guarding the entrance of the large harbor it assumed a much greater importance.

As a result of its location within a well-protected harbor its flat topography with deep water close to shore, large ships could easily anchor and be serviced, loaded and unloaded. Ships' captains, merchants, and craftsman established themselves in Port Royal to take advantage of the trading and outfitting opportunities. Jamaica's economy grew and changed between 1655 and 1692 Port Royal grew faster than any town founded in the new world. And it became the most economically important English port established in the Americas. The cities 2000 buildings were packed into 61 acres of land they were primarily made of brick (a sign of wealth) and some were as tall as four stories high. During Port Royals hay day it was known throughout the known world as the richest and the wickedest city on earth. Prostitution and debauchery were rampant throughout the city, nothing was off limits, whatever a buccaneer or a pirate wanted or needed he only had to ask and it would be provided to him. It was said that there was a tavern in town for every eighty thirsty men. Prostitutes would roam the streets openly and freely selling and presenting their wares but most stayed in the many taverns.

The buccaneers and pirates had the run of the town killing's and murders and fights were a very common place it was no big thing it was accepted as a way of life there was no law an order to speak of. A number of problems in the development of cities in that era was clean water, sanitation, and healthy living due to the fact that most drinking containers and eating plates were made of pewter, which is an alloy of tin and lead and is eventually poisonous to man but that was the material of choice during the 17ᵗʰ century. The stench from terrible sanitation conditions was over powering from waste water and toilets they did not have sewer pipes at the time. Finding clean and fresh drinking water was a real challenge. The people of that era did not bathe regularly perhaps they would take a bath once in 60 to 90 days or more and would not change or wash their clothes with any regularity in the same time period. For the most part personal hygiene was not a priority or a daily standard. This description is a very common description of life in the cities and just about every city around the world, civilization was not yet civilized in the 1600's.

Not knowing what to expect the Navy Seal training took over naturally; stay aware, stay ready, be prepared and take nothing for granted. With their weapons out and ready Lt. James says to Hunter, "See that dock about 300 yards to port head for that dock three of us will depart and three of you will stay on the boat. Jacob, Christopher, and I will go ashore to learn what in the hell is going on. The rest of you guys stay on board after we disembark but take the boat away from the dock move the boat into the shadows but stay within eye site of the dock, no lights, and no flashlights stay invisible. I have a very strange feeling about this place something isn't quite right. We will be caring our MK23 mod 45 caliber pistols strapped to our legs along with our knives. I recommend that we each carry the TDI Vector Kriss Super 45 sub machinegun. Is can be carried without being seen just sling it on your back when the stock is folded it is only 16 inches long but a real killer of men if need be. Also get on your Dragon Skin body armor vests just to be safe and protected from the unknown. This place gives me the creeps." "Oh shit," says Jacob, "We still have our faces painted for combat all in blue, black and green."

Christopher speaks up, "Well hell it looks like this town is celebrating something perhaps we won't stand out at all maybe we will blend in." "Perhaps your right," adds Jacob. "All right men check your weapons," instructs Lt. James, "Hunter head for the dock and you men staying on the boat be at the ready keep your weapons handy and loaded be ready for the unknown."

Earlier today June 1st 1692 the daughter of the Governor of Jamaica Sir William Beeston, Lilliannah and her two best friends Cassandra, and Carol Kay planned a trip into Port Royal to do some shopping. There is a Governor's Ball on Saturday night and the girls needed to get the final measurements on their gowns. As well as Lilliannah needed to give her final ok on a beautiful necklace, a gold Bessel surrounding a 6 carat diamond with safaris and rubies on a 24 inch 18 carat gold chain. The jewelry merchants and the dress designers in Port Royal were some of the best in the world. So Lilliannah and her two best friends got into the carriage for the 2 hour ride into town. They said good bye to her father the Governor the carriage was driven by a trusted house servant. Little did they know that the events of today would change their lives forever?

In the town of Port Royal a pirate ship captain was plotting to do harm to the Governor's daughter Lilliannah the next time she came into town. He was aware that she needed to come to town to pick out her gown for the Governor's Ball on Saturday night. The pirate captain was mad as hell that he was not invited to the Governor's Ball. The name of the pirate captain's name was Captain John Wallace a despicable mean pirate who enjoyed cutting the limbs of his captives off with his sword. Capt. John Wallace was the leader of a very large group of pirates who were also captains of their own ships a total of ten captains along with approximately 80 men on each ship giving this very evil group of men more than 800 men that were under his command. They all belonged to the "Brethren of the Black Spot" a very evil gang of pirates all hell bent on murder, killing, stealing, robbing whatever they wanted to do. They were highly trained to attack ships that were carrying anything of value. Spanish and Dutch were the ships of choice to plunder in the seas of the Caribbean. The reason the "Brethren of the Black Spot" was formed was safety in numbers to be able to attack in numbers groups of ships of two or more at the same time. They thought that they were invincible and could do anything they wanted to do, plunder, kidnap, kill, steal and no consequences would come to them due to their organizational size.

Capt. John Wallace was also known as Black John a most evil man the most evil pirate in Port Royal that was feared by all the pirates of the day. But he was also a leader of men by torture, intimidation, and fear. What Capt. John Wallace wanted today was to kidnap the daughter of the Governor of Jamaica for a couple of reasons. One reason he was pissed that he was not invited to the Governor's Ball. Second he wanted to establish himself as the rule of law in Port Royal feared by all. His plan was to kidnap Lilliannah hold her for a ransom of 120 pounds of gold that was what she weighed. His plan was diabolical to capture her and her friends and bring them to his favorite tavern The Catt & the Fiddle a rather large tavern by the standard size of taverns in Port Royal. The Catt & the Fiddle was large enough to hold over 130 patrons plus about 60 prostitutes or more on any given night. Captain John Wallace was sure that the Governor would pay up the 120 pounds of gold within a few hours of his daughter being kidnapped. If the governor did not comply with the demands then the three ladies would be taken aboard his ship the "Red Dragon" and the governor may never see his daughter and her friends again. This action would also show to all the pirates well over 250 ships that he Captain John Wallace was in charge and ruled Port Royal no questions asked. He did not fear the wrath of the governor or the so called police in the city or the soldiers on the island. He wanted to show his power that he could do anything he desired solidifying his leadership to all the pirates, and buccaneers for all time a very bold deed indeed. As the carriage with the three unsuspecting ladies was approaching the town a pirate was on look out for them he raced his horse to the "Catt & the Fiddle" to tell Captain Wallace that in 30 minutes the three ladies would be entering Port Royal. Capt. Wallace was very pleased stood up and said, "Arrrrr, ye maties, you six bilge rats go and capture the Governor's daughter and her two hand maidens and the driver of the carriage and bring them all to me, or ye will be sleeping with Davy Jones tonight." The six pirates went to do as they were instructed for fear of their own lives.

The carriage carrying Lilliannah, Cassandra, and Carol Kay arrived in front of the dress shop. As they proceeded to get out Lilliannah out of the corner of her eye spotted six of the wildest looking pirates she had ever seen walking rather fast in her direction. Lilliannah was not too concerned because she believed she was protected from such men as these, due to the fact she was the Governor's daughter. When they got within arm's length they reached out to grab hold of the three women grabbing their arms in a very rough manner hurting and bruising them. One of the pirates said, "Ye wench's be coming with me Arrrrr, to the Catt & Fiddle Tavern." "No we won't be going any place with the likes of you toilet slime, scum." Shouts Lilliannah, "You filthy, ugly, scallywags unhand us now I say, I am the daughter of the Governor and these ladies are my best friends." "We know who ye be we be coming to get ye," says another pirate." Then the six pirates do something that no one watching thought they would ever see, the pirates were dragging the three ladies down the street. The three ladies were fighting, kicking, and screaming for someone to help them. But everyone knew you did not mess with the Brethren of the Black Spot pirates. As they entered the Catt & the Fiddle Tavern Capt. John Wallace rouse from his seat with a wicked laugh and a most freighting grin on his ugly face and said, "I be Capt. John Wallace the most feared pirate captain in all of Port Royal leader of the Brethren of the Black Spot and captain of the Red Dragon ship. I know who ye be you be the daughter of the Governor and ye are with ye two best friends. You lasses be my prisoners an ye ransom be 120 pounds of gold to be delivered by morning time or ye be coming with me aboard my ship. You, carriage driver go tell the Governor what I want Arrrrrrr and be quick about it ya lily livered bilge rat." The carriage driver runs to the carriage to hurry back to the Governor to tell him of his daughters capture and ransom of 120 pounds of gold that must be delivered by morning or he may never see his daughter and her two friends again.

The pirates do not treat the three ladies with care or respect; in fact they were abused, pushed and even hit in the face at least once to teach them an ugly lesson. "Bring to me my tinkered of grog an be ye quick about it or ye will sleep in Davy Jones locker under the sea tonight and a bowl of Salmagundi, NOW." yells Capt. Wallace. "Ye ladies want a tankard a' grog?" "Go to hell," answers Lilliannah, "All you bastard cowardly pirates, you bunch of ugly bilge rats." "I was trying to be me a gentleman," says Capt. Wallace. He laughs in a loud voice and the other 15 or so pirates standing and sitting around him laugh out loud as well.

Lt. Darren James turns to Jacob and says, "Jacob you and Christopher Kirk bring a couple of flash bang grenades. I am going to get my iron fist. (That is a piece of steel the width of your fist about 1 inch in diameter with a ball of iron on each end the size of a ping pong ball and a one inch wide steel bar covering the knuckles) That is one hell of a hand to hand weapon to strike a man in the head with it breaks bones and your hand is not harmed in anyway. "Hunter cut the power on the engines that's it now pull alongside the dock, I'll hold on to the timbers of the dock now get your two asses off the boat, Jacob now pull me up on the dock." says Lt. James., "Now Hunter follow my orders keep out of sight stay within 50 yards if you can but out of sight we'll see you guys within the hour stay ready for anything." "We're off to see the wizard," sings Christopher. "Shut the fuck up Chris," whispers Jacob Blum. "We're not here to party hell I am thinking this is not right somehow and I am on edge to tell you guys the truth." They make their way along the heavily timbered wooden dock a dock like they have never seen before. The evening is warm a quarter moon is high in the sky not giving off much light tonight but that is a good thing.

The three Navy Seals not really knowing what they are about to walk into, proceed along the very unique dock built with the heaviest timber they have ever seen. The dock of the bay is not like any dock they have ever walked on before. Up a flight of steps 22 steps to be exact looking back down to the water it was over 20 feet below because of the very low tide. As the three Navy Seals stepped on to the street the first thing they realized was there were no electric lights. Liked they assumed there would be when they first saw the town while in the harbor, only gas and oil lamps and candles so many candles. The observation that they made was the streets were not paved in black top or concrete but made of mostly dirt and some cobble stones. And then what hit them next was the smell of this town, it was quite unpleasant garbage and trash and human waste seemed to permeate the air. "What the hell kind of a town is this," asks Jacob, "It feels as though we stepped back in time way back in time." "Don't be stupid there is no such thing as stepping back in time stay with me, stay focused." Answers Darren, "There has to be a rational explanation for what we are seeing but what the hell would that be." Christopher Kirk isn't saying anything his eyes are seeing what his mind does not believe and he speaks up, "This place is unbelievable I have never been scared of anything in my life before but tonight this is different." The three Navy Seals continue walking up the street away from the dock people stop and stare and turn to one another and whisper about the three odd looking men and wonder who or what they are. The people seem quite taken back especially with the paint on their faces the color of black, green, and blue they are not from Jamaica they all agree on that fact. Christopher speaks up again, "The people that I see are all dressed like they are living in another time not dressed for some sort of a celebration. I don't believe they are pretending this looks real to me. I have been to a number of Renaissance Fairs where people dress in the period of the time like the 1700's century of England and this has a completely different feeling to it."

Enough is enough come on let's get on with it what we came for that is some information from someone who can set us straight on where the hell we are," says Lt. James, "Look for a building that we could enter and perhaps someone with some intelligence could answer a few simple questions." They proceed down the street, Jacob being the happy go lucky person he is started waving and smiling at the people passing by. A number of people respond back with a nice smile and wave saying, "Good evening." "There how about that place," shouts Christopher, "That bar across the street it looks larger than other bars I'll bet our questions could be answered in there." "The bar is on the right side of the dirt and cobble stone street, a large sign hung outside about 3 foot square with a carved picture of a cat playing a fiddle. "That sign looks friendly."

mentions Christopher. Into the bar they walked they could see a lot of people in the bar both men and women it was not very well lit, that is because candles are not the best source of light. The bar itself was rather long and it appeared that there was some room at the large bar at the far end that's where they headed hoping to talk with the bartender. The bartender watched these three odd looking men walk to the far end of the bar thinking, damn they are odd looking men with their face painted in black, blue and green colors. The bartender questioned if he even wanted to serve them at first. But to his better judgement he walked to where the three men were standing and said, "Arrrr, what be ye pleasure grog or beer?" Lt. Darren James answers, "May I ask a question or two first?" "Aye, mate ye may." answers the bartender. "I don't mean to be rude but where in the hell are we what is this town?" asks Lt. James. "Me thinks ye must be daft to ask dat question mates," answers the bartender, "Where ye think ye be?" "We were looking for the city of Kingston." says Lt. James. "Then ye be a landlubber this not be Kingston it be Port Royal," answers the bartender. "Now I need to ask ye a question who ye be, ye faces painted in green, black and blue and your clothes very odd? Do ye what a beer or grog or maybe ye be leaving me tavern?" says the bartender with a disgusted look on his face. "Ok, ok three beers if you please," answers Jacob.

The Navy Seals start to look around the bar room crowed by any bar standards it seems that the women are leaning all over the men at the bar asking them to buy them a drink. The Navy Seals take a second look the women are all ugly as hell, very skinny or very fat with missing teeth and they did not smell very good. And their hair was a real mess like they hadn't combed their hair in a year and the hair under their arms was a long as any mans. Now the men in the bar are starting to stare at the three strangers at the far end of the bar with their faces painted and wearing strange clothing. The talk in the bar is getting somewhat louder and talking about the three men in a hostel way wondering who in the hell are they, what do they want, why are they here. Lt. James realizes that his window of opportunity to get some answers is beginning to close real fast. The three beers are brought to them and Jacob takes his first sip and spits his beer out on to the floor because it is very warm. "What be ye trouble mates that's me best beer." The bartender says in a pissed off way. Lt. James speaks up, "I apologize for my men's bad manners please tell me what year this be, I mean is?" The bartender is now really in a bad mood and says, "Ye year be 1692 June 1st why ye ask? Don't ye know?" The blood drains from the three Navy Seals faces and they are almost having a panic attack. Now for the first time all day everything made sense but at the same time nothing made any sense at all. This is too much to comprehend in a moment it will take some more time. The bartender points to a wall, "See on yonder wall be number of da year and it be right ye landlubbers 1692." Now noticing the bar even more somethings started to click and make sense. The way the floor was part dirt part wooden planks no one in the bar seemed to care about the smell, so bad the seal's almost gagged when they walked in.

Their realization is brought home hard; these are not just regular people celebrating some kind of celebration out for an evening of fun and frolic these friggin men are real pirates and buccaneers. They have somehow, some way, stepped back in time, crossed the time line, they went through a time portal, whatever they are now here back in time now what the hell to do. Now the Navy Seals are leaning on the bar as their heads are spinning out of control. They can see there is no mirror behind the bar, no cash register, all the bottles behind the bar were crudely made with no labels, and no one was drinking from glasses but tankards of pewter. Now they are aware that they are the freaks in the bar, the odd balls with their odd clothing and their faces painted in odd colors, this changes everything. The bartender in the beginning looked like the freak about 6'2" tall with a large belly around 65 years old with long gray hair, full beard and some of his teeth missing and a patch over his left eye dressed in the style of an unkempt dirty pirates costume. Hell now he looks normal and so do all the other pirates, buccaneers and the prostitutes it is now the Navy Seals that look out of place in the bar. Jacob raises his hand and motions to the bartender to come back, he returns. Jacob says, "I'll tell you the truth who we are we are Navy Seals on a military mission from the United States of America we got lost in time and now we are here and that is the truth crazy as it seems. The bartender speaks up, "Arrrr ye be landlubbers ye be welcome wit ye painted faces and all." From across the tavern five pirates who have been drinking all day finally get up their courage. They get up from their chairs each uglier then the next with what appeared to be hate in their eyes started to walk towards the three Navy Seals at the bar.

The five drunken pirates had no frigging idea who they might be messing with; picking a fight with Navy Seals is not the brightest idea of the day. As they walked they huffed and puffed and raised their arms in the air towards the Navy Seals that kind of bravado always worked on the local people. The bartender out of the corner of his eye saw the five drunk pirates advancing towards the bar area with what appeared to be a fight on their minds. The Navy Seals also turned around to face the drunken pirates but they were not frightened placing their hands on a side arm and a steel fist prepared to take care of business. The bartender now looked in their direction just in time as they were only 10 feet from the Navy Seals and said in a loud commanding voice, "A vast, get ye asses back to ye seats or ye will be banned from me tavern forever ye scallywags, Arrrr these landlubbers be friends of mine." The five drunken pirates turned thinking about what the bartender said and returned to their table. Lt. James looked at the bartender with a look like he had never seen before and said, "Thank you; you just saved five pirates lives." The bartender says, "My name be Bartholomeus what ye names be?" Lt. James smiles and says, "My name is Darren and this is Jacob and Christopher nice to meet you." Bartholomeus reaches for thee tankers of grog and places them on the bar smiling best he can and says, "This grog be on me tavern, I know not where ye come from or what ye speak of time if I can help ye I will."

Hunter looks at his watch and notices that one hour has passed, no gun shots have been heard so everything should be ok. The Navy Seals are somewhat anxious wondering how long it takes to ask for directions. But they stay out of sight keeping an eye on the dock and ready for anything that may come their way. Then for some weird reason the discussion turns to ex-president Bill Clinton. Hunter says, "My Mom was on the right side of the discussion about Bill Clinton as well as his crazy lying corrupt wife Hillary. I have done my own research over the years and they have turned out to be the Bonnie and Clyde of our era. They are both pathological liars and both toxic narcissists and most likely sociopaths." Bobby Harold chimes in with what he believes, "My mom has always told me how evil they both are and how destructive to America they are. I will go so far as to say Bill Clinton should be serving time in the jail house not being in the White House. For his sexual deviancies like exposing himself to strange women he doesn't even know, and fondling and raping women and his having sex in the Oval Office that makes me mad as hell how he disrespected his position and America. Then he has had documented well over 140 women he's had sex with while being married. Bill has told many people that Hillary is bi-sexual and has had eaten more pussy then he has." Mitchell speaks up joining the conversation, "My mom has raised me right to respect women and to honor them and she would agree with everything you guys just said. Hell there are men in prison serving 10 to 20 years who have not raped and harmed women like Bill Clinton has with his unlawful deviant, perverted actions against women." "Well I suppose what your definition of is, is, Clinton's defense." adds Hunter, "That just goes to show you how he has been supported by the democrats who have no moral code, no moral center, basically no morals. Hell look at Ted Kennedy and Chris Dodd both democrat senators they have committed crimes against woman almost as bad as Bill Clinton has when it comes to abusing women." The battle ready Navy seals have a good laugh at what they were talking about.

Back at the Catt & Fiddle Tavern Lt. Darren James is watching with interest the goings on in the far corner of the tavern. Three ladies look out of place and their dresses are torn in places those pirates are treating them rather roughly. By yelling at them, pushing them down, slapping them in the face and hitting them. The three ladies are resisting the best they can and yelling for help as the pirates are having such a good time being mean to the three ladies. Lt. James calls the bartender over and asks, "Tell me about those pirates and those three ladies," Bartholomeus says, "I beg ye not ask or we be in Davy's Locker at the bottom of the sea by morn." "I don't know what that means and don't give a damn tell me what in the hell is going on." says Lt. James. "Ok but this be on ye own head not mine, dat be Capt. John Wallace better known as Black John have ye ever heard of him?" "Hell no," answers Lt. James "He be the captain of the pirate ship the Red Dragon and the leader of the "Brethren of the Black Spot" he be the most vile pirate in all of Port Royal, bad to da bone. He captured the three ladies earlier today and is holding them for ransom for 120 pounds of gold. The lady in the gold dress is the daughter of the governor of Jamaica with her two best friends. If the ransom not be paid by morn I fear the three ladies will be taken aboard the pirate's ship and we may never see them again. If ye interfere ye will die a horrible death by keelhauling ye or beat ye to death while being hung upside down by a yard arm," explains Bartholomeus the bartender shaking in his own skin.

Capt. John Wallace is beginning to take a shine to Lilliannah and her two friends and it crosses his mind he hopes that the gold ransom is not delivered. So he can take Lilliannah and Cassandra and Carol Kay to his ship and have his way with them for his own pleasure. Lilliannah jerks her arm away from the tight grip of Captain Wallace and she feels the crack of his hand across her lips as her blood begins to run down her mouth an onto her gold dress. Lt. James turns to Jacob and Christopher and says, "Those pirates have never dealt with the likes of us before, I intend to rescue the three ladies." Jacob speaks up, "Are you crazy, fucken nuts you're only going to get us all killed didn't you hear what the bartender just told you? There are well over 150 badass pirates in this bar tonight let along getting back to our boat with the three ladies in one piece." Christopher chimes in and says, "All right there are over 150 badass pirates in here and only 3 Navy Seals well that sounds to me like the odds are in our favor, I'm ready to kick some pirate ass.

Lt. James has heard enough and cannot stand by and watch what is taking place to the three ladies and do nothing. He can hear the faint cries for help by Lilliannah and her two friends and can see the look of fear and panic in their eyes even in this dim candle light. A Navy Seal would never walk away with ladies in such distress that is not the Navy

Seals way no matter the odds. Lt. James gets that look in his eye and both Jacob and Christopher know what that means they have seen it many times before; he nudges Christopher and Jacob on the shoulder to follow his lead. They can see what is taking place as well and both agree that action must take place to save the three ladies. The two Navy Seals follow their leader and say under their breath, "Oh shit here we go again." Lt. James pushes away from the bar stands up straight and tall checks his Kriss V 45 submachine gun and his MK 23 45 caliber pistol and the other Navy Seals do the same. Lt. James says, "Time to dance lets go." Lt. James, Jacob and Christopher begin the walk across the room that will change their lives forever. The Navy Seals are so well trained and know each other so well like the back of their own hand, that word commands are not necessary. Just a mere look, the flick of a hand or finger and instantly they can read the mind of one another and react as one. Lt. James walks to within three feet of Captain Wallace and looks him in the eye, with a steely look only a trained Navy Seal possesses. This unnerves Capt. Wallace he has never had any one do this to him before. Capt. Wallace says, "Who be ye an were ye come from." "None of your fucken business just hand over the three ladies to me now, or you will experience hell tonight and you may all die if that is your choice." says Lt. James with a commanding tone in his voice.

Then Capt. Wallace does a very stupid act, he pulls his blunderbuss pistol from his belt sash and fires. To Capt. Wallace's shock and dismay Lt. James is still standing before him unharmed then four more pirates do the same and pull out their blunderbuss pistols and fire at the three Navy Seals. What they do not know is the Navy Seals are wearing the latest bulletproof armor called Dragon Skin the pirates can't believe their eyes. These men should be lying on the floor covered in their own blood and dead. Now it's time to return the favor Jacob pulls his Kriss V 45 submachine gun from behind his back and begins to fire. Now blood and guts and body parts of the pirates go flying across the room as Lt. James and Christopher both begin to fire their Kriss V 45 submachine gun. Lt. James fires his weapon at Capt. John Wallace hitting him in his shoulder and leg. Bullets are flying so fast no pirate has ever experienced weapons like this before killing a number of surprised pirates where they stand. Jacob fires his weapon into the head of a pirate blowing his brains all over the shocked pirates. Lt. Darren James yells at the top of his voice, "You were warned now you will die," As the three Navy Seals continue to fire their weapons. Capt. Wallace is hit again in his leg and he cries out in pain. Lt. James reaches for the ladies who in their own right are also scared of the Navy Seals the way they are dressed with the paint on their faces. Jacob Blum comforts the ladies with his smile through his face paint, Jacob not only is a fierce and deadly fighter but he also has a way with the ladies. All the pirates are in shock and awe with what just took place with 18 or so pirates lying dead with a lot of body parts missing. The whole damn bar is stunned the ladies of the night are under the tables the bartender is also in shock. Lt. James says in a commanding voice, "We're leaving now don't try to stop us or follow us or more of you miserable bastard pirates will die tonight." The Navy Seals take the three ladies by the arm gently and walk out the front door of the tavern. Lt. James is holding on to Lilliannah, Christopher Kirk is helping Cassandra and Jacob Blum takes Carol Kay by her arm best he can and they all leave.

As soon as everyone has left the tavern Capt. Wallace is revived and he starts yelling kill those bastards now get dem bring dem to me now. Now all the pirates start to get their fighting senses back and begin yelling, and screaming and cursing and chasing after them. Lt. Darren James looks back and sees about 45 madder than hell pirates chasing after them he yells, "Get your asses moving to the docks as fast as you can and leave behind all of the flash bang grenades to go off to confuse and scare them." Hunter, Mitchell and Bobby Harold hear the noise and have heard the firing of the seals weapons Hunter starts the boat and quickly heads for the dock pulling right beside of it. The three Navy Seals quickly run down the 22 steps on the dock practically carrying the three surprised ladies with them. Mitchell and Bobby open fire with their M-468 semi-automatic submachine gun throwing out a deadly bullet fire storm that kills or wounds over half of the pirates on the top of the dock. A bloody mess to behold the remaining pirate's retreat running as fast as they can to the safety of the tavern. Those pirates that are wounded cry out in excruciating pain for help with some of their arms and legs only hanging on by bones, muscles and tendons. The dock is now a bloody mess and the stench of death is in the night air. What kind of men were these men in such odd clothing and their faces painted in black, green and blue colors. And what kind of new weapons did they possess the fire power was over whelming and never seen before where in the hell did they come from. The three ladies were helped into the Apex boat and safely buckled in they are very surprised, confused and scared in this odd little boat. Hunter pushed the throttle forward at a speed of 15 knots still in the harbor with all the pirate ships at anchor. The three ladies are scared to death at the speed they are traveling over the water without a sail. They are moving out of the harbor moving in between ships at anchor finely they are clear of the ships and out into the open sea. The time is now 2:30 A.M. early morning the moon is a quarter moon not providing much light the evening air is still warm the sea is smooth like a babies bottom not a ripple in sight. Hunter continues to push the throttle forward until they reach 50 knots. No one is following them not at this speed anyway. Lt. James speaks up, "I believe we're safe we are a good 12 miles from the harbor let's stop and introduce ourselves to these lovely ladies." The light from the moon is very dim so Hunter turns on the two 1,000,000 candle light lamps. This creates a panic with the ladies as well where does a light this bright light come from the ladies see no candles and are scared they have never have seen such bright lights like this before. The ladies are thinking with this boat moving across the water with no sails so fast, and now these bright lights and these six men with their faces painted and in such odd clothing maybe they might be better off with the pirates something they knew and understood.

The Navy Seals are looking at the beat and battered women as they try to cover up from where their dresses were ripped and torn. The can see real fear in their eyes real and honest to goodness fear. The seals realize that these women have never seen men like them before especially with their faces pained for war and their odd clothing, their weapons and now this boat and the lights. The Navy Seals finally realize how scary they must appear to these three ladies in the 1600's back in time. The three ladies are huddled close together wrapping their arms around each other for protection they are all shaking from fear with tears streaming down their faces. The Navy Seals wonder what their first move should be to alleviate their fears and show them that they are safe and with friends. Jacob approaches the ladies first and says, "Ladies you are safe and with friends I know what we must look like but when we wash this paint off our faces you will find us all to be good looking nice guys." So far the ladies are not convinced talking to themselves expressing thoughts that are about to die at the hands of these odd men. Never before in all their years have they seen a boat that goes as fast as this one and without sails how can that possibly be. Lilliannah speaks up, "Your lights where do they come from how is it possible to light up the night sky so bright?" Lt. Darren James now speaks up, "Well those lights are made possible by a battery, we are from the future we are not here to harm you but to help and protect you. We are as surprised to be on your island as you are to be on our boat. We were on a military mission from the future and for some reason we are now here and to tell you the truth we are also scared and confused." With that explanation the ladies seem to relax a little bit and stop crying and shaking. Cassandra says, "We saw you be shot by the pirates blunderbuss and nothing happened how was that possible?" Bobby Harold stands and takes off his shirt and says, "We have on special protection to protect us from bullets see I'll show you." Hunter says, "Try to wash of the paint on you faces in the sea water that may relax them a little more." The seals try to wash off the paint but it is difficult hanging over the edge of the boat Hunter finds some soap in his back pack and now the paint is coming off. The ladies believed that the color of their faces that was their real skin color it's no wonder why they were scared.

The three ladies are still concerned thinking about the weapons that they used bringing so much death so quickly to the pirates. Carol Kay speaks up, "Your weapons cannot be from this time so deadly they must be from the future like you say you are." Christopher says, "You are right we are using our weapons from the future and as you can see our boat has many mysteries for you as well. But please understand we are your friends and will bring no harm to you." With a lot of the face paint washed off the Navy Seals start to appear like regular looking men and the ladies begin to finally believe them and relax and feel that no harm will come to them. Mitchell turns to Lt. James and asks, "I need to know what you found out in town, where we are and what in the hell is going on?" Lt. James answers Mitchell's questions knowing that the other two seals need to know as well, "This is what I found out and believe, we did go back in time when we went through that odd colored fog bank how that happened I have no idea. We are in Port Royal, Jamaica the pirate capital of the Caribbean in the year 1692 and the month of June. You saw all the people dressed in their old clothing they were not in costume that was their real dress. Those pirate ships you saw anchored in the harbor they are real, those pirates chasing us trying to kill us was real. I don't want to believe in time travel never have but I have to believe in the reality of what is now and this is for real. Go ahead and ask the ladies a question perhaps their answers will convince you." Mitchell asks the ladies a question, "Can you ladies please tell me what year this is and where we are? Cassandra answers, "The year is 1692 and you are in Port Royal, Jamaica that's what it is." Hunter asks his question, "What do you think of our boat have you ever seen a boat like this before with our lights?" Carol Kay answers with a tone of fear in her voice, "No we have never seen a boat like yours before and it goes so fast really fast and has no sails how do you make it go?" "Hunter responds, "We have a jet engine in our boat the water pushes our boat to go fast." Cassandra joins the conversation, "How do you capture the sun to make light so bright with no candles?" "Hunter says, "Our lights are special but everyone in the future has lights like these in our cities and our homes and in our cars."

Lt. Darren James says, "I think we should all introduce ourselves what are names are. Lt. James begins. "We are from the time of 2005 from the United States of America we were sent to your island to help save some of our people from some really bad men. Then we went through an odd colored fog of dark blue and crimson and we have ended up here in your time. The Navy Seals all introduce themselves along with a friendly smile. The ladies introduce themselves, "I will go first my name is Lilliannah I am the daughter of the Governor of Jamaica." With what she just said Lt. James face turns chalk white remembering the picture on the wall in the museum in Jamaica and his own fear. "My name is Cassandra her best friend." "My name is Carol Kay also Lilliannah's best friend."

All the Navy seals are now convinced that they somehow gone back in time and believe their lives are now totally screwed. They are concerned that they may never see their own time again and possibly be stuck here forever. Convinced now Mitchel, Hunter, and Bobby Harold are back in time and that's what it is and now they will have to deal with it. Mitchell stands up and at the top of his voice he says, "I have figured it out what the dates mean, I remember my studies of the Caribbean during this time. We have got to get our asses to a safe place and soon today is June 2nd 1692 on June 7th at 11:50 A.M that is only five days from now. There will be the largest earthquake ever recorded in the Caribbean and Port Royal will sink into the sea the earthquake will be an 8.2. Also the largest tsunami spreading out to the sea so many islands will be affected. I am not making this up I know from what I speak it will happen and it cannot be stopped." Lt. James speaks up, "I don't doubt what Mitchell just said so let's be smart enough to be prepared for Saturday perhaps we can warn the good people of Port Royal and save some of them. But for now let's get the ladies home I am sure Lillianna's father is worried sick about his daughter's safety and her two friends so let's get going and take them home. Can any of you ladies help direct us to your home?" Carol Kay speaks up, "I know the way I have been out to sea a number of times our home is along the coast approximately 23 miles north of Port Royal. I will show you the way now that we believe you mean us no harm." You could see and feel the final curtain of fear fade away as the three ladies relax and begin to smile. Hunter turns on the ignition and the boat begins to move slowly at first, the sea is still calm and the sun is just beginning to rise in the east. The time is 0600 what a beautiful sight it is when the sun rises flooding the ocean with the fire light of the sun. The three ladies are now relaxed knowing they will be home soon they are talking to each other about this weird adventure and how grateful they are not to be held captive by Captain Wallace and his dastardly pirates. And not taken aboard the Red Dragon to become his sex slaves and die a slave. The Apex Pegasus boat is now well past the harbor where so many pirate ships are tied at anchor. The welcome sunlight sheds a new light on the Navy Seals that they are human odd looking humans but humans from the future. This is a new day, yesterday has passed, and today everyone's life has now changed forever.

End of chapter 2

CHAPTER 3

*A little true history first,
so you know a little more of the
island of Jamaica and the Caribbean.*

On the shared Anglo-French island of Saint Christophe (called "Saint Kitts by the English) the French had the upper hand. The French settlers on Saint Christophe were mostly Catholics while the unsanctioned but growing French colonial presence in the northwest Hispaniola (The future nation of Haiti) was largely made up of French Protestants who had settled without Spain's permission to escape Catholic persecution back home. France cared little what happened to the troublesome Huguenots, but the colonization of western Hispaniola allowed the French to both rid themselves of their religious minority and strike a blow against Spain—an excellent bargain from the French Crown's point of view. The ambitious Huguenots had also claimed the island of Tortuga off the northwest coast of Hispaniola and had established the settlement of Petit Gove on the island itself. Tortuga in particular was to become a pirate and privateer haven and was beloved of smugglers of all nationalities after all even the creation of the settlement had been illegal.

Dutch colonies in the Caribbean remained rare until the second third of the seventeenth century, along with the traditional privateering anchorages in the Bahamas and Florida. The Dutch West India Company settled a "factory" (commercial town) at New Amsterdam on the North American mainland in 1626 and at Curacao in 1634. This island is positioned right in the center of the Caribbean off the northern coast of Venezuela and was perfectly positioned to become a major maritime crossroads. The mid-seventeenth century in the Caribbean was again shaped by events in far-off Europe. For the Dutch Netherlands, France, Spain, and the Holy Roman Empire the Thirty Year War being fought in Germany the last great religious war in Europe had degenerated into an outbreak of famine, plague and starvation that managed to kill off one-third to one-half of the population of Germany. England having avoided any entanglement in the European mainland's wars had fallen victim to its own ruinous civil war that resulted in the short but brutal Puritan military dictatorship (1649-1660) of the Lord Protector Oliver Cromwell and his roundhead armies.

Of all the European great powers Spain was in the worst shape economically and militarily as the Thirty Years War concluded in 1648. Economic conditions had become so poor for the Spanish by the middle of the seventeenth century that a major rebellion began against the bankrupt and ineffective Habsburg government of King Philip IV (1625-1665) that was eventually put down only with bloody reprisals of the Spanish Crown; this did not make poor Philip more popular. But disasters in the Old World bred new opportunities in the New World. The Spanish Empire's colonies were badly neglected from the middle of the seventeenth century because of Spain's many woes. Freebooters, pirates, and privateers experienced after decades of European warfare, pillaged and plundered the almost defenseless Spanish settlements with ease and with little interference from the European governments back home who were too worried about their own European problems to turn much attention to their New World colonies. The non-Spanish colonies were growing and expanding across the Caribbean, fueled by a great increase in immigration as people fled from the chaos and lack of economic opportunity in Europe. While most of these new immigrants settled into the West Indies' expanding plantation economy, others took to the life of pirates and buccaneers. Meanwhile the Dutch, at last independent of Spain when the 1648 Treaty of Westphalia ended their own eighty years war (1568-1648) The Habsburgs made a fortune carrying the European trade goods needed by the new colonies. Peaceful trading was not a profitable as privateering, but it was a safer business.

By the latter half of the seventeenth century, Barbados had become the unofficial capital of the English West Indies before this position was claimed by Jamaica later in the century. Barbados was a merchant's dream port of the period. European goods were freely available, the island's sugar crop sold at premium prices, and the island's English Governor rarely sought to enforce any type of merchant regulations. The English colonies at Saint Kitts and Nevis were economically strong and now well populated as the demand for sugar in Europe increasingly drove their plantation-based economics to a record high. The English had also expanded their domination in the Caribbean and settled several new islands, including Bermuda in 1612, Antigua and Montserrat in 1632, and Eleuthera in the Bahamas island chain in 1648. Though these settlements began like all the others as relatively tiny communities that were not economically self-sufficient but in a few years grew into productive trading island communities.

The French also founded major new colonies on the sugar growing islands of Guadeloupe in 1634 and Martinique in 1635 in the Lesser Antilles chain of islands. However, the heart of the French activity in the Caribbean in the seventeenth century remained in Tortuga, the fortified haven off the coast of Hispaniola for privateers, buccaneers and out right pirates. The main French colony on the rest of Hispaniola remained the settlement of Petit Grove, which was the French toehold that would eventually develop into Haiti. The French privateers still used the tent city anchorages in the Florida Keys to plunder the Spaniards' shipping in the Florida channel, as well as to raid the shipping that sailed through the sea lanes off the northern coast of Cuba. For the Dutch in the seventeenth-century Caribbean, the island of Curacao was the equivalent of the England's port of Barbados. This large, rich well defended free port was open to the ships of all the European countries offering good prices for sugar that was exported to Europe and also large quantities of manufactured goods in return to the colonists of every nation in the New World especially the American colonies. A second Dutch controlled free port had also been developed on the island of Saint Eustatius which was settled in 1637. The constant back and forth warfare between the Dutch and the English for its possession of the island in 1660's later damaged the island's economy and desirability as a profitable port. The Dutch also had set up a settlement on the island of Saint Martin which became another haven for Dutch sugar planters and their African slave labor. In 1648 the Dutch agreed to divide the prosperous island in half with the French.

The late seventeenth and early eighteenth centuries are often considered the "Golden Age of Piracy" in the Caribbean. The military power of the Spanish Empire in the New World started to decline when King Philip IV of Spain was succeeded by King Charles the II (1665-1700) who in 1665 became the last Habsburg King of Spain at the age of four. While Spanish America in the late seventeenth century had little protection as Spain entered a phase of decline as a great power, it also suffered less from the Spanish Crown's mercantilist policies with its economy. The lack of interference, combined with as surge in output from the silver mines due to increased availability of slave labor. (The demand for sugar increased the number of slaves brought to the Caribbean) began a resurgence in the fortunes of Spanish America. England, France, and the Dutch had all become New World colonial powerhouses in their own right by 1660. Worried by the Dutch intense commercial success since the signing of the treaty of Westphalia, England launched a trade war with the Dutch. The English Parliament passed the first of its own merchant Navigation Acts (1651) and required that English colonial goods be carried only by English ships and legislated limits on trade between the English colonies and foreigners. These laws were aimed at ruining the Dutch merchant's livelihoods that depended on free trade. This trade war would lead to three outright Anglo-Dutch wars over the course of the next twenty five years.

Meanwhile, King Louis XlV of France (1642-1715) had finally assumed his majority with the death of his Regent Mother Queen Anne of Austria's chief minister, Cardinal Marzarin in 1661. The "Sun King's' aggressive foreign policy was aimed at expanding France's eastern border with the Holy Roman Empire and this led to constant warfare against shifting alliances that included England, Holland, the various German states and Spain. In short, Europe was consumed in the finial decades of the seventeenth century by constant dynastic, intrigue and warfare; this is an opportune time for pirates and privateers to engage in their bloody trade. In the Caribbean, this political environment led colonial governors to new threats from every direction. The Dutch sugar island of Saint Eustatius changed ownership ten times between 1664 and 1674 as the English and Dutch dueled for supremacy in the Caribbean islands. Consumed with the various wars in Europe, the mother countries provided few if any military reinforcements to their colonies. So the colonial governors of the Caribbean increasingly made good use of buccaneers as mercenaries and privateers to guard their colonies or carry the fight to their mother country's enemy. Surprisingly these undisciplined and greedy men of war often proved difficult for their sponsors to control. By the late seventeenth century, the great Spanish towns in the Caribbean began to prosper and Spain also began to make a slow, fitful recovery, but remained poorly defended militarily because of Spain's problems and so were sometimes easy prey for pirates and privateers.

The English presence continued to expand in the Caribbean as England itself was rising to become a great power status in Europe. Captured from Spain in 1665 the island of Jamaica had been taken over by England and its primary settlement of Port Royal and became a new English buccaneer and pirate haven in the midst of the Spanish Empire. Jamaica was slowly transformed, along with Saint Kitts, into the heart of the English presence in the Caribbean. At the same time the French lesser Antilles colonies of Guadeloupe and Martinique remained the main centers of French power in the Caribbean. These are among the richest French possessions because of their increasingly profitable sugar plantations. The French also maintained privateering strongholds around western Hispaniola. Of their settlements on the western half of Hispaniola they also founded Leganes and Port-de-Paix, sugar plantations became the primary industry for the French colonies in the Caribbean. In the Caribbean the use of privateers was especially popular. The very cost of maintaining a fleet of ships to defend the colonies was beyond national governments of the 16th and 17th centuries to financially maintain. So private vessels would be commissioned into a "Navy" with a letter of Marque, and paid with a substantial share of whatever they could capture from enemy ships and settlements, the rest would go to the crown, hence came the name privateers.

These ships would operate independently or as a fleet and if successful the rewards could be great. When Jean Fleury and his men captured Cortes' vessels in 1623 they found an incredible Aztec treasure the large majority of the treasure that they were allowed to keep. When Francis Drake captured the Spanish "Silver Train" at Nombre de Dios (Panama's Caribbean port at the time) in 1673 his crews were rich for life. This was repeated by capturing port Piet Hein in 1628 this made a profit of 12 million guilders for the Dutch West India Company. This substantial profit made privateering something of a regular line of business; wealthy businessmen or nobles would be quite willing to finance this legitimized piracy in return for a share. The sale of captured goods was boosts to colonial fortunes in the Caribbean were pirates were termed buccaneers. Roughly speaking this way of a life arrived around 1620 and remained until the effective end of piracy in the 1730's. The original buccaneers were escapes from colonies; forced to survive with little support but they were skilled in boat construction, sailing, and hunting they were rugged men of the times. The word "buccaneer" is actually from the French word "boucaner" meaning "to smoke meat" from the hunters of wild oxen, deer and pig curing the meat over an open fire. They transformed their many skills which kept them alive into piracy which they found to be more lucrative. They operated with the partial support of the non-Spanish colonies and until the late 1700's their activities were legal or partially legal and there were irregular amnesties from all nations.

Traditionally buccaneers and or pirates had a number of peculiarities. Their crews operated as a democracy; the captain was elected by the crew and they could vote to replace him, he had to be a leader and a fighter. In combat he was expected to be fighting with his men, not directing operations from a safe distance. Spoils were evenly divided into shares, when the officers had a greater number of shares; it was because they took greater risks or had special skills. Often crews would sail without wages-"on account"- and the spoils would be built up over a course of months before being divided. There was a strong "esprit de corps" among pirates. This allowed them to win sea battles they typically out manned and out fought trade vessels by a large ratio. There was also for some time a social insurance system, guaranteeing money or gold and silver for battle wounds at a worked out scale. The romantic notion of pirates burying treasure (that did happen but not often) and wearing gaudy clothes had some truth to the tales. Most pirate and buccaneer wealth was accumulated by selling of chandlery items; like ropes, sails, block and tackle and so many other items stripped and plundered from captured ships and some of the ships themselves went on the for sale block. Note also that a typical poor man had very few promising career choices at the time apart from becoming a pirate. A pirate's life was not an easy life in fact it was rather a hard life. The ships were cramped with rats and other insects were found in their food and throughout the ship and crawling over them as they tried to sleep. The sleeping quarters were usually a hammock hanging from the bulkhead. They could spend six months at sea or longer before they would dock the ship in a port. The men's hygiene was horrific the stink and stench was over whelming, disease and sickness was very common. No way to bath and that was the last thing usually on their minds. For the most part the sailing duties and work aboard a ship was back breaking work with no time to relax. But still men volunteered for this kind of a life and some men were kidnapped from taverns and forced to serve aboard pirate ships. Port Royal, Jamaica began its hay day in 1655 because of a number of reasons; There was a deep water harbor that butted up to the land, their location was perfect for raiding and attacking other ships that were haling cargo, the law there really wasn't much of that, and there were safety in numbers of like thinking men.

Bios of Navy Seal team 007

Lt. Darren James was born in 1977 in the city of Glendale, California. Both of his parents were good patents and always encouraged him in whatever he wanted to do. He went to the Navy Academy class of class of 2001 he stands 5' 10" weighs in at 185 lbs. When he entered the Naval Academy in Annapolis, Md. He did not know what direction his navy career would take him, but he was very glad to be a part of the navy. After graduation and receiving his commission he was assigned to an attack landing ship where he met a number of Navy Seals impressed with who they were and the adventures they were involved with especially the clandestine assignments. Darren James knew that he would sign up to become a Navy Seal hoping he would be able to pass the rigorous training. He was accepted at the U.S. Navy Seal Training facility on Coronado Island in San Diego Ca. A true leader of men well-liked and respected by those who served with him, he also served two tours of duty in Iraq.

Christopher Kirk, was born in the year of 1979 in the city of Pasadena, Ca. he also had two wonderful parents the loved him with all their heart. He stands 6' weighs in at 196 lbs. all muscle due to his loving to work out. He is also a talented artist and went to Stanford University on a scholarship in art to receive his masters. He always envisioned himself to be a great artist. But stuff happens and not all plans work out as first planned. Making no money with his art he joined the Navy to see more of the world then Pasadena and Glendale CA. In the navy he found a completely new life he found a home, new buddies and working with weapons and becoming a weapons expert. He was now rated to second class gunners mate but he was looking for more, more adventure in his life. He had always enjoyed the water and read a number of books about the Navy Seals he found himself volunteering for the Navy Seals and to his amazement he was accepted, he graduated in the top 10% of his class.

Christopher will never talk about it but he received the coveted Navy Cross for his heroic actions while serving in Iraq.

Jacob Blum born in 1979, in a small town in Northern Calif. Clovis. He stands 5'10" weighed in at 181 lbs. This man when he was only three years old knew what he wanted to be, in the Army played with his army toy soldiers constantly 24/7. When he was still a little boy he would salute anyone in a military uniform that he saw even police men. He also had a way with girls in school and they all seemed to like him as well. He possessed a charismatic smile and charm about him and friendly nature he was very handsome as well. How he decided to join the navy no one really knows but one day he came home and told his surprised mom and dad he joined the navy right out of high school and that was that. Jacob was a champion swimmer like his mother in school, strong headed and smart as he could be. All of his friends knew that you better not get on his bad side. Jacob was always adventurous, wanting to try new things like sky diving, scuba diving just to name a few. Not interested in just sitting on a ship, he made friends with a couple of Navy Seals while on the navy base in San Diego. Their stories and adventures intrigued Jacob since he was now rated second class he would qualify to apply. He was accepted and he will tell you the training to become a Navy Seal was the hardest thing he had ever done but also the most rewarding. Jacob has 9 kills to his credit while serving in Iraq, a quiet man but could turn deadly when necessary.

Hunter was born in 1978 in the city of Folsom, Calif. he stands 5'11" and weighs in at 180 lbs. He has been a star athlete in high school and Davis University participating in water polo, and wrestling. He also developed a genuine interest in operating racecars, airplanes, and speed boats and excelled in his ability to operate and fix any moving vehicle. After college he was wondering what he was going to do for adventure and self-filament. He picked up a book at Barns and Noble book store about the Navy Seals this really open his eyes to his next adventure. He joined the navy and became rated within two years then applied for the Navy Seals in North Island, San Diego CA. and graduated with flying colors. A handsome man with a quick charming smile and blond hair he fit right into the Navy Seal team organization. He also served with honor and professional dedication in Afghanistan.

Mitchell Davies was born in the year of 1978 in the city of Covina, CA. he stands 6' 1" weighs in at 198 lbs. He is an exceptionally bright man and gifted athlete in high school he got a football scholarship to Arizona State University along with a grade point average of 4.2. He played four years as a tight end setting many school honors on the football team. His major in college was International Law with a minor in history he chose the time line of the 1600's in the Caribbean, West Indies studies. He is a great patriot loving America as his mom and dad always taught him his mother was a member of the California, Tea Party standing for American honor and respect with little government interference. He always had a desire to serve his country with honor the more he read about the Navy Seals the more he wanted to become one. He joined the Navy and when he was qualified as a third class petty officer he joined the Navy Seals and this became his passion he moved through the ranks rather quickly and became a Warrant Officer. He was sent to Iraq where he served with honor and distinction receiving the coveted Medal of Honor for his brave service in the face of battle saving 7 of his men putting his own life in danger.

Bobby Harold was born in the year 1977, in the city of Folsom, California he stands 6'2" weighs in at 198 lbs. all muscle he competed in body building contests while in high school. As a young man he also competed in Golden Gloves boxing and did very well as a light heavy weigh, with 25 fights and nineteen were knockouts and six were by decision no losses. He was very head strong and was fortunate to have two wonderful parents that understood him and supported him but took no back talk. Bobby Harold's grandfather was always a political inspiration as a Republican Conservative to always love your country and to never give up. He had served in the Viet Nam War as a Navy Seal and shared many war stories with him. After high school and attending college at San Jose State University at the insistence of his father he graduated with honors but then joined the navy unexpectedly. He received his second class gunners mate classification then volunteered for the Navy

Seals. He has proven to himself and to everyone else that he was born to be a Navy Seal.

As the morning sunlight fills the sky with its welcome rays of daylight, the seals could see clearly see how battered and bruised the three ladies were from their treatment on their arms and faces it was shocking. Lt. Darren James could see how very beautiful Lilliannah was even with the beating she now displayed. She was the most beautiful lady Darren had ever laid eyes on. Now Lt. James has an awakening moment of realization he remembers that the lady's name and she herself was the lady sitting beside him in the picture on the museum wall back in Jamaica a few days ago and wonders how this will all play out. Darren also remembers the last words of Margo the lady who showed him the picture said, "God speed my friend what will be will be." Did she know something or were her words just profound. "Oh my God," Lt. James thinks to himself, "This can't be true this is Outer Limits stuff, unbelievable but realizes that he must keep his emotions in check and will just have to see how this thing plays itself out." Time travel is not something that you just bring up in a conversation especially when you are right in the middle of it. The little Darren knows about time travel which isn't much he also realizes the people of this time would never be able to comprehend the idea or be able to understand. So there will not be any more talk about time travel it will never be discussed again, not by him or any of his men. Carol Kay and Cassandra are shown the map of Jamaica since they indicated that they knew the area. They were able to understand the lay of the island and indicated where the Governor's compound is where home is located not very far away now. The two ladies say that they will be home within the hour just keep going on this course.

There is no sign of any pirate ships even on the horizon, the navy seals do not need any encounter with any more pirates today not with the ladies on board. Hunter can see where they are on the map in relationship to where Port Royal is even though Port Royal is no longer on any present day map. Everyone relaxes and feels safe in the new day; Hunter puts the throttle forward until they are cursing at 18 knots per hour over a calm sea. Just in case Bobby Harold and Jacob are keeping a sharp eye open through their binoculars for any signs of a sailing ship. Lt. James asks Lilliannah to come and sit beside him; she complies and moves to the seat beside him, Lt. James does his very best to show his very best smile even though some of his war paint is still not totally cleaned off. For some strange unexplained reason he now appears to be a friendly man to her, and she is thinking that she would like to get to know him better. Lt. James is just making friendly small talk asking her about her life in Jamaica. Lilliannah seems pleased to answer his friendly questions. Christopher stands up and moves over to sit beside Cassandra trying to be less threating then he seemed to be a few hours ago. He is doing his best to smile a friendly smile still knowing that his war paint is still mostly covering his face. Chris is trying not to show how nervous he is to be sitting beside such a beautiful lady but she seems to be responding in a positive way to Christopher's advances.

Jacob does not want to be shown up by his seal teams advances to the ladies. He believes himself to be the most charming of all the seals and a real ladies man he approaches Carol Kay and they seem to hit it off together friendly is as friendly does. The boat ride is turning out to be a very enjoyable leisurely ride along the coast of Jamaica. Considering last night and what took place with the fire fights that they got into and not knowing if they were going to get back to their boat alive because of so many hostile pirates in the tavern their minds were still reeling from it all. Just the mere thought of what the ladies were going through when they were held captive by the pirates was just as mind boggling for them and hard to relive in their minds. As the Apex Pegasus boat goes around a land mass within 300 yards of shore Lilliannah stands up and points and screams out load. "There that is my home to the left do you see it? I never thought that I would ever see my home again; the two ladies stand and scream with joy as well. Hunter sees her home and with caution drives the boat to the dock; the boat is tied and secured as everyone disembarks. Her father the Governor and his help come running to the dock as fast as they can arms out stretched with tears flowing from their eyes everyone is so happy again.

In the chaos in the Catt & Fiddle Tavern aftermath of last night the tavern is in pandemonium, bodies lying all around 22 pirates met their death and another 9 were seriously injured. The blood splatter was on a number of walls and on the ceiling, body parts like arms, hands, legs, fingers and internal organs were now being picked up by the employees of the tavern and the blood wiped clean from everywhere. They were getting the tavern ready for business tonight. This mayhem was created by weapons no pirate had ever seen before or ever imagined ever existed. What manner of men were they with their faces painted in colors of green, blue and black and wearing odd clothing where in the hell did they come from. Now the sun light was filtering into the tavern and with the morning sunlight you can see so much better then candlelight now the mess in the tavern was really horrifying. And to think only three men did all this chaos with their new weapons and got away unbelievable. Capt. John Wallace is screaming revenge at the top of his voice for everyone to hear. "What ye men be, who be ye, an from where ye come from. Ye men be sleeping with Davey Jones at the botm'o' da sea with body parts missing I give ye me word soon revenge be mine." This is not the way this day was supposed to go, the pirates were to be paid 120 pounds of gold and then set the ladies free all there planning has now gone to straight to hell. The reputation that Capt. Wallace was supposed to show the town and his fellow pirates how smart he was and the true leader of all the pirates and the Brethren of the Black Spot. This has now gone away with a hail of bullets and the death of his own men with a hardy Hi-O-Silver from men the likes he's never seen before. Capt. Wallace is standing in the blood of his men covering his black boots and clothing with the stench of death all around and he was wounded in his shoulder and leg. He knows that his reputation is at stake now he looks foolish to everyone, scary and weird thoughts are filling his head he now secretly wishes he never decided to capture the three ladies to make his bones.

One of the pirates that was running after the three men with the three ladies who escaped with no wounds walks into the Catt & Fiddle Tavern and walks to where Capt. Wallace is standing and says, "Ye men jumped into a boat da likes I'd never seen before, tit' was black and blue close to da water. It went so fast with no sails were seen faster den any boat I'd ever seen it went across da water so fast an no noise were made. I am afraid of ye men with the painted faces and 24 men lie dead on da docks. Captain John Wallace is so damn mad and angry at the pirate admitting he is afraid of these odd men he pulls his cutlass from his sash and plunges it into the pirates belly and then he screams out, "Ye better be afraid of me ye scurvy cur, for ye know what I do." No one had ever stood in the face of Capt. Wallace before or beat him in a fight like the three weird men of last night. Capt. John Wallace knows he must defeat these weird men, kill them all, his honor and reputation as a pirate captain and the leader of the Brethren of the Black Spot must take place or he will surely be replaced and put to death by the code of the pirates. He must not appear defeated or frightened by what he experienced so getting control of his decision making abilities is important to being a leader. Capt. Wallace makes sure that all men who are in need of medical attention be taken to the doctor even those left on the dock. Deep down inside he is consumed at what just happened the weapons the fast firing weapons that created so much death and destruction. He also remembers that he personally shot one of the men with his blunderbuss and nothing happened to him and other pirates fired as well and nothing happened to them. "What ye be ye kind of men?" He thinks, "Now what of da boat be moving over da water faster than any boat ever wit no sails." Capt. Wallace will only admit this to himself, "But ye be afraid." "That's it," Capt. Wallace says, "I am right these are Devil men that what ye be called Devil men for the pit of hell." Capt. Wallace takes one last look around the tavern remembering only last night, they were celebrating capturing three wenches, drinking grog and beer, now so many of his men are dead or seriously wounded. Capt. Wallace is cursing all the way to the dock to go aboard his ship the Red Dragon. He shouts out an order to his first mate, "Gather up ye other 9 captains Brethren of the Black Spot all of them come to me ship and be quick about it Arrrrr." Even though Capt. Wallace was wounded he would not let his men see he was hurt or in pain. Capt. Wallace also says, "Bring da doctor to me cabin on me ship by high noon, themes be me orders."

The whole town of Port Royal is abuzz with the news of what happened last night with the three men dressed in such odd clothing and painted faces rescued the daughter of the governor William Beeston and her two best friends and defeated Capt. John Wallace and killing a lot of bad and evil pirates. The town's people are also concerned about the daughter of the governor and her two friends will they ever be seen again. The town is mad at the fact that Captain John Wallace captured the three ladies and held them for ransom to be paid by morning that kind act of unlawfulness will not stand. The taking of Governor Beeston's daughter could have brought the royal guard into town and there would have been a lot more bloodshed and unrest. But now the town's people worry what happened to Lilliannah and her two friends taken by these odd men with painted faces aboard their little boat. Are these odd men out to steal our women and our people to take them back to where they came from? A boat like they have never seen before low in the water also painted a black, blue and green color and moves on the water so very fast with no sails what madder of boat is it, fear is the number one emotions of the new day. The death and destruction of the pirates and killing with weapons unheard of and killing so many in only a moment or two sent them into a new fear. Unknown fear is far greater then fears that you know about and are familiar with by ten fold.

All of the 9 captains of the various ships that belong to the Brethren of the Black Spot have received orders to arrive on Capt. Wallace's ship the Red Dragon for a very important meeting with two exceptions. These two captains were out to sea doing pirates business Capt. Benjamin Steenwinkel of the ship the Devils Servant and Capt. Peterman Grandstaff of the ship the Mary Margaret they are both out on patrol seeking Spanish and Dutch ships laden with jewels, silver bars or gold coin of the realm. For the pirate captains are aware of some ships movements from Panama this month with good cargo to steal and they intend to get them some. These are the 7 captains that showed up for the meeting; Capt. Bartholomew Threepwood, Capt. Enrique Barbossa, Capt. Ceaser Demantie, Capt. Bellamy McVaine, Capt. Guy Percy, Capt. Hector Browerman, and Capt. Murray Tweemain the badest of the bad captain pirates are assembled on the Red Dragon wondering what in the hell last night was all about and what did it all mean. Who were these men, how did they get here, what manner of men have so much fire power. The speed of their boat went in between the large ships so fast and then they were gone out to sea in an instant of time. Baffling just baffling no answers and the boat had no sails so what made it go.

The Captains all gathered in Capt. Wallace's cabin to understand what happened and what revenge they are going to get. Capt. Wallace spoke first, "Shiver me timbers, ye know me and me men was attacked by what I call the Devil Men from the pits of hell, last eve. Me know not how dam weapons work, not seen such guns before just fire, fire, fire and nor reload. Me and me men shot dem first with our blunderbuss in dar chest not a thing happened to dem dar just stand dare. We must take revenge dis can't not stand or we be thought weak." At that moment the pirates have spies and lookouts all over the island of Jamaica and the word is that the Devil Men are at the governor's mansion and compound with the three lasses there be a total of six Devil men, and this information is now given to Capt. Wallace. He speaks up again in a very angry voice, "I knows were de Devil Men are at Governor Beeston's home me plan is to go there and capture us one or two Devil Men tomorrows eve. We capture us one or two Devil Men and bring dem aboard me ship a good pirates welcome will await dem." The captains make their plans best they can everyone knows what he must do and their plan be a good one. If they can capture a Devil man he will tell of his secrets and then the pirates can kill all of the Devil Men and capture their weapons. These odd weapons will make them superior fighters to all the Caribbean pirates and the whole world will fear them.

Only a great pirate captain like Capt. Wallace could think of such a good plan. (They have no frigging idea whom they are messing with) The plan that they all agreed on was. Capt. Bartholomew Threepwood and Capt. Enrique Barbossa and Capt. Guy Percy will take their ships to lay off the land just west of Governor's William Beeston mansion and compound. Then two landing boats will go ashore with 20 men lay low hide along the shore line and when they see one or more Devil Men hopefully alone walking along the seashore. Capture them and bring them to Captain Wallace he will get the information and answers we needs to deal with the Devil Men and destroy them all. Capt. Wallace shows the captains his wounds by removing his billowing red long sleeve shirt, an what a wound they saw a hole in his shoulder larger than they had ever seen and a hole clean out of his back no bullet stuck in the flesh. And then he points to his leg where there is a bullet hole as well. As the captains are gasping the doctor that was summoned enters the captain's cabin, "Ok ye captains of the Brethren of the Black Spot time to go, I have me work to do."

All the captains leave they make plans to go to town to the Catt & Fiddle Tavern to have a few pints of beer and grog and some crackle fruit (chicken eggs) cured ham and potatoes. They want to see for themselves the tavern where all the chaos took place and possibly talk with some of the men who were wounded. All the captains walk into the Catt & Fiddle Tavern together and what a daunting sight it is. One of the captains Capt. Bellamy McVaine walks right up to the bartender and says, "Tell me mate what ye know bout de' Devil Men of last night who'd killed me mates. I hear ye were friends yo'em, speak up or ye be hanging from me yardarm by midnight. The bartender is well aware of his predicament and what it would mean to defy a pirate captain. Before the very obvious and nervous bartender could answer, Capt. McVaine says, "What ye name be bartender?" "Me name be Jeremy Bartholomeus," answers the bartender with fear in his voice. And with good reason Jeremy Bartholomeus had never seen Capt. Bellamy McVaine before today and he had just threatened to hang him if he didn't answer his questions. Capt. Bellamy McVaine is a very large and threating looking man standing 6'5" and weighing in at over 360 stone with a full black beard and one cold blue eye the other eye covered with a patch. A man the likes of him would scare any man and send chills run down their spine if he is directly asking questions of you. Jeremy Bartholomeus speaks up, "Ye men ye call the Devil Men were only in me tavern for one and a half hours maybe two hours at de most. They told me de were from a country far to the north called the United States of America, de told me de were Navy Seals sent on a special mission but de were lost. De asked me where de were and seem lost and what year it be, when I told deem it were 1692 dee was berry surprised." "Thank ye," says Capt. McVaine, "I know not were dat land be maybe someone know, dis whole ting be puzzling.

"One more ting, "says Jeremy, "De weapons be small, small pistols were strapped to da legs and the weapon that fired and fired and keep on firing was also small and be an odd shape dat was strapped to da back." "I tank ye again," says Capt. McVaine. He walks over to the tables were the other captain were sitting and sits himself down and tells them what the bartender just told him. No one at the table had ever heard of the United States of America this must be a wondrous land with so many weapons, and boats. "Perhaps we should tell Capt. Wallace about this land so we get info from a prisoner when we capture him," says Capt. Enrique Barbossa. Now that it's lunch time the pirate captains order crackle fruit (chicken eggs) ham & potatoes others order Salmagundi (It's a popular dish of chopped beef meat, fish, chicken, pig, turtle eggs, anchovies, onions, grapes, cabbage seasoned with salt, pepper, garlic, oil, vinegar served in a very large bowl) Jeremy Bartholomeus approaches the table of the pirates and speaks up, "I remember a important ting me wanted to tell ye." "Go ahead speak up mate we don't bite Arrrrr," The pirates say then have a hardy belly laugh. "When de Devil Men be at me bar, I told em' not to go and bother Capt. Wallace, but they say dey had to do something to save the wenches." "Dat be good to know," said Capt. Threepwood, "Over dar at dat table in the far corner be four prostitutes dat stood close to Capt. John Wallace when he be attacked, maybe dey know someting," says Jeremy. Capt. Bellamy McVaine the largest pirate stands up and walks in a very intimating way towards the four prostitutes and speaks in a loud angry voice. "Ye wenches know any info to tell me what be happing last night?" The wenches all shaking from fear one says in a low voice, "Capt. Wallace asked the Devil Men who ye be, they said none of ye fucken business, then the captain fired his pistol and then four of his men fired their pistols and ye Devil Men dey stood there not hurt but should be dead. Den dey fired der weapons and all da hell broke loose in de room." Capt. McVaine returns to the table and tells them what the wenches just told him they are shocked that a man would curse in such a way at Captain Wallace and then fire dar weapons wit so many pirates in da tavern. The pirates all agree the Devil Men and only three of them have no fear they are very dangerous to all the pirates in the Caribbean and must die. The doctor treating Capt. Wallace's shoulder tells him that if the wound does not begin to heal in a good way within the month then he may have to remove the captain's arm. Capt. Wallace Curses and screams with that news, "No not me arm, not me arm, I need me arm, ye must save me arm, I will kill da man who took me arm me vengeance be great."

Now the Navy Seals have arrived at Governor Sir William Beeston's mansion and compound to the delight of Lilliannah, Cassandra, and Carol Kay the three ladies began to cry with so much emotion built up over their ordeal. The three ladies let all their emotions completely out and cry uncontrollably from the pure joy of being home again and that they are alive and well. The guards of the governor's mansion alert the governor that his daughter and her two friends are home standing by the dock and walking towards the house. Governor Beeston could hardly believe what he just heard and with great joy began running towards the boat dock to welcome his daughter and her two friend home again. Knowing full well that yesterday they were being held captive and in the clutches of Capt. John Wallace and his band of pirate thugs. Ever since he received the ransom letter the governor was concerned for his daughter's safety and a real possibility that he may never see his beloved daughter again. The governor was ready and willing to pay the ransom the demand of 120 pounds of gold. Then when they were safely back home he was going to send out the royal guard to kill Capt. Wallace and the entire pirates associated with the Brethren of the Black Spot knowing that would bring instability and chaos to Port Royal. The pirates led by Capt. Wallace have shown they have no regard for law and order and no respect for the governor and do not fear him or his royal guards. This is the power and control the pirates in the town of Port Royal and the Caribbean have in the 1700's. The ladies are crying, hugging, cheering and laughing out of pure joy and the release from fear. The Governor Sir William Beeston and about a dozen of his guards are now seeing for the first time six of the strangest looking men they have ever laid eyes on. They are walking towards the governor as they now see the strangest water craft tied up to the dock. Some of the guards not understanding what they are looking at begin to get ready to fire their pistols pointing their guns at the strange men.

Lilliannah sees what is taking place and raises her arms and is waving her hands and shouts, "These strange men saved our lives because of them we are here safe at home please welcome them with open arms the Jamaican way by extending your hand not your guns." The guards were relieved because these men did not look like any men they had ever seen before and had no real interest is fighting with them. "Daddy, I want you to meet the bravest group of men in the world a group of men like you have never met before, these men are like no other men I have ever known. I will tell you more about our adventure later this evening after we have had a chance to rest a little and get cleaned up. Governor Beeston extends his hand of friendship as well as the Royal Guards providing protection for the governor. They welcome the strangest men they have ever seen in their lives by their looks with still some green, black and blue on their faces and the strange water craft they exited from. Governor Beeston smiles and says, "Welcome men I am really looking forward to hearing your story this evening."

Everyone begins the long walk up to the governor's mansion at the top of the incline, a 20 room mansion large and pure white a three story home like no other any Navy seals have ever seen before. They approach the very large front porch with a dozen large, tall white pillars going from top to bottom. As they approach the large magnificent house Lt. Darren James stops and says to the governor, "Please let me introduce myself and my men to you then this evening we can relay a story, one like you have never heard before and most likely will never hear again. My name is Lt. Darren James this is Hunter and the one standing to Hunters left is Jacob Blum, then Christopher Kirk, and standing behind him is Bobby Harold and the man to your far right is Mitchell Davies, these are my men I am proud to serve with them and they are also my best friends.

One last statement that I want to say now is, we are Navy Seals from a country far to the north called the United States of America. If you are interested we will do our best to explain best we can what is going on but we are still in shock ourselves." Governor Beeston says, "Yes I am always interested in a good adventure story and I thank you all from the bottom of my heart for bringing my daughter and her two friends home safe to me. Now you will be shown to your rooms by the staff where you can rest up for perhaps for or five hours or longer and take a warm bath and get cleaned up. Your clothes will be washed and pressed along with some of our clothing from Jamaica if you so wish to ware our type of relaxing clothing. The time is 9:00 A.M. I would like so much to see you all in my study at 6:00 P.M. Lt. James says, "Governor I and my men want to thank you so much for your generous hospitality and sharing your fantastic home with us. We only wish that we could have met your daughter and her two friends under better circumstances and friendlier surroundings." "I am really anxious to hear about your adventure story this evening," says the governor, "Have a peaceful rest and relaxation you all look as though you need it, it must have been a hard day's night." The Navy Seals enter their rooms each one having a large welcoming bed with clean white sheets and a large bath tub that soon would be filled with fresh warm water.

Now the time is about 4:30 P.M. the Navy Seals are all rested cleaned up and relaxed three of the seals have chosen to put on the Jamaica clothing; white cotton pants with a string tie around the waist with a colored cotton pull over shirt with long sleeves with a deep vee at the neck and comfortable sandals. The other three seals have chosen to put their freshly cleaned and pressed original clothing back on either way they all look a lot different especially with all the paint on their faces washed off. They find themselves walking around and admiring this large fantastic house and the grounds some even take a walk to the water's edge to relax. One by one the Navy Seals find their way into the study, which also serves as a game room. The study has a bar area with over stuffed leather chairs plush rugs on the floor along with beautiful pictures painting of landscapes of Jamaica by local artists and a large natural stone fireplace in the far corner. This is a manly room where men can talk freely and let their hair down about anything that is on a man's mind. There is nothing feminine about this wonderful room. As the Navy Seals enter they all seem to have the same reaction, damn now this is what I call a great study. Feeling good, cleaned up and rested they are finely able to relax on this Monday evening with the clock striking 6:00 P.M. a nice cool evening breeze enters through the large open windows facing the sea. For the first time in many a day the Navy Seals could smell the sweet salt air without having to wonder if they were going to die in the next few hours. All of the Navy Seals are now gathered in the great study, a house servant is filling drink orders, rum was the primary drink served straight the beer was warm and tasted like piss (That's what warm beer is all about) Jacob asked the house servant serving the drinks if they had any fruit juices on hand? He responded in a positive manner, "Limes, lemons, papaya and coconut." Next Jacob asked, "If they had or knew what ice was?" "Yes," was the answer, Then Jacob says, "Please bring me and my friends glasses filled with ice and your fruit juices with some sugar and rum. The house servant had never even thought of such a combination of drinks before but he did as suggested. He tasted one of the drink combinations and liked it very much then he served all the Navy Seals with their drinks.

Now Lilliannah, Cassandra and Carol Kay enter the room refreshed in clean dresses and looking like new ladies with their makeup covering some of their cuts and bruises. The three ladies took a look at the cleaned up Navy Seals and were very presently surprised as how handsome they all were taking a seat on a couch. Jacob then asks the house servant, "Please bring the ladies the same drink that they are drinking." The ladies are a little puzzled because they have no idea what the men are drinking. When the drinks are served they taste for the first time a combination of fruit juices and rum with some sugar on ice and they declare what a wonderful drink this is. The time is now 6:30 P.M. the governor Sir William Beeston enters his study looks around and is pleased that everyone is here and appears to be relaxed all freshened up and clean. "Daddy," says Lilliannah, "You have to try this wonderful drink that these men just made up." "Wow, now I really like this drink," says the governor, "We will be eating dinner with in the hour we usually have dinner around this time, I hope you're all hungry." "Starved, famished, we haven't had a filling meal in days," says Lt. James. "We are having tonight for dinner a Jamaican meal I know you will love it like I love this new drink," say the governor, "Now please do tell me about your adventure Lilliannah how you met these strange men."

Lilliannah begins, "We just arrived in front of the dress store to get our dresses finished for the ball last Saturday when 6 or 8 or more ugly pirates grabbed us by our arms and dragged us through the streets to the Catt & Fiddle Tavern. There Capt. John Wallace was waiting he started yelling at us for no reason and then he and his men were all slapping us on our arms and on our faces. Then they threw us to the floor and told us to stay like dogs and shut up, than he told the carriage drive to deliver his ransom note to you, did you receive it father?" "Yes I did and when I read it my blood ran cold from fear of what might become of you. I was prepared to send the ransom to them then when you were safe the Royal Guards would bring justice on their heads." "Then listen to this father, later in the evening as we were being held captive not one person even looked our way of offered any help to us. We really felt that we were not going to live much longer. Then in walks these three strange men they walked straight to the far end of the long bar, their faces were the color of green, blue and black and had on the weirdest clothes we had ever seen. They just stood at the bar talking with the bartender for such a long time, never looking our way either so what were we to think to tell you the truth they scared us as much as the pirates never seeing the likes of them before. All of a sudden they were standing in front of Captain Wallace and demanding he let us go and were saying some real angry words. Then Lt. James did something I thought I would never see he took another step or two really getting close to Capt. Wallace and called him some nasty names. I don't remember the names but I remember the look in Capt. John Wallace's eyes it was a look of disbelief and fear. Then the pirates fired their guns hitting the three men in their chests and nothing happened to them that really surprised the pirates and also scared them and they just stood there smiling." "Daughter please don't make things up how could they not be injured?" asks the governor. Lt. James speaks up, "That is true we were wearing special protective vests so bullets would not harm us called Dragon Skin. Mitchell goes to his room and retrieves his Dragon Skin bullet proof vest and returns to show the governor. "I would never believe what you said my daughter if I hadn't just seen it with my own eyes. Oh my God what other wonders do you men possess," asks the governor. "In due time we will show you things beyond your world,' answers Bobby Harold. "Go on my dear please continue with your story," says the governor. Just then the head chef of the mansion enters the study and makes an announcement that everyone was anxious to hear that dinner is served.

Everyone files into the dining room for a delicious Jamaican dinner; of jerk chicken and pork with fresh vegetables and rice and plenty of delicious tasty wine served with dinner. Everyone begins to eat this delicious meal the governor is still anxious to hear his daughter's story and asks her to continue. "Yes father, but you have always made a rule to never talk while eating," says Lilliannah. "Damn my rule I am too interested to hear about your adventure, please continue," says the governor. "Ok, so after Capt. Wallace and his pirates fired their guns with no effect these three strange men took out their guns that were behind their backs and begin to fire, and fire and fire never stopping to reload. The bodies of the pirates were dying all around us body parts were flying in the room arms, legs, heads, hands they died where they stood not having time to get away. Even Captain Wallace was hit in the arm or shoulder I'm not sure, tables were turned over the people not involved ran for their lives, blood was all over the ceiling the walls the floor it was a bloody mess," answers Lilliannah. "Go on girl tell me more this is so interesting and exciting," says the governor. "Then what I remember is the three strange men grabbed us and we all ran out the door, with a lot of pirates chasing after us. Then the strange men all threw cans on the ground and they made loud noises and a lot of smoke that confused the pirates they didn't know what to do, that gave us more time to get to the docks. When we got to the dock this very strange little boat was waiting for us we all got in it was so close to the water, that is tired up at our dock right now. Then there were three more men already in the boat they possessed weapons like we haven't seen before and they opened fire on the pirates following us. Their weapons fired and fired and fired never stopping killing a lot of pirates and wounding so many more blood was all over the docks it was a horrific scene. Then the strangest thing of all happened this weird little boat just went fast very fast in-between the pirate's ships anchored in the harbor. It has no sails then out to sea we went so fast I have never been in a boat that went this fast before we were so scared, perhaps they will give you a ride in their boat tomorrow." We were very scared of the six strange men for a long time; it took us more than an hour before we relaxed just a little bit. It was after they began to wash the paint off their faces we could tell they had white skin like our own. They were so kind to us and spoke in soft, nice voices then we began to trust that they were not going to harm us." Lilliannah looks over at Lt. Darren James and gives him her very best smile and says, "After we began to feel safe and relaxed then all three of us really began to like these men they tried to be so charming."

"We were very grateful that they put their lives in jeopardy, in harm's way to save us when no one else in town would lift a finger. When these strange men offered to take us home that was a wonderful feeling and also we were very great full and excited. Hunter drove the boat and Mitchell who could read the sea charts brought us home and here we are." "Daughter that is the scariest and at the same time the most adventures story I have ever heard in all my 55 years," says the governor. "Ok gentleman or perhaps I should call you great and worldly seaman, or perhaps just strange men, whatever I welcome you into my home and thank you again from the bottom of my heart for saving my daughter and her two best friends.

Now what I would like to hear is your story of adventure how you got here and from where you came." Lt. James begins to speak, "Our story is complicated because we are still not sure how we got here, although I will do my best to provide some answers since you asked. As I said before we are U.S. Navy Seals that were sent on an important mission to Jamaica to save some of our important people that were captured by very bad men. Our country is far to the north called the United States of America from a different time in the future. I know how crazy that sounds it took me some time to except the truth. In fact when we first were walking the streets of Port Royal we thought that all the people were in costume celebrating some kind of holiday not realizing we had gone back in time. We never believed that time travel was possible but we are now living proof of that fact. This is the truth as what happened we were cursing on the ocean along with another boat to complete our mission. When all of a sudden a large fog bank appeared before us it was dark blue in the center and crimson color all around we didn't think anything about it and went into the fog. When we got through the fog everything changed all of our navigation instruments our GPS instruments connected to our satalights did not work. And we could not contact the other boat or our home base we searched for them but never found them then we saw the lights of the town decided to ask someone where in the hell we were it turned out it was Port Royal and we were told that the year was 1692 unbelievable. We were talking with the bartender of the Catt & Fiddle and I noticed three ladies being badly treated well we had to put a stop to that and save them from what we didn't know. That is our story believe it or not." The governor smiles and says, "I knew your story was going to be odd very odd I will have to think on it. But it appears that your mission is all about helping others that are in harm's way. One more drink then we must turn in and we will pursue or conversation in the morning, that special drink you guys made with rum and fruit, sugar and ice would be a perfect way to end this day.

Tuesday morning and it's early at the governor's mansion it is already in a flurry of activity, the sun is smiling down on the day a cool ocean breeze of sweet salt air is gently moving throughout the mansion. Lilliannah, Cassandra, and Carol Kay it seems they were up half the night talking, laughing and discussing the handsome Navy Seals and who was interested in whom. Lillianna has made it clear she is attracted to Lt. Darren James because she thought him to be everything a real man should be, strong, handsome and he protects ladies. Cassandra said that she was interested in Bobby Harold for he was a little aloof and didn't seem to care if she gave him her best smile or not. Cassandra said that she found him to be the most exciting man she had ever seen. Carol Kay was interested in pursuing Jacob Blum a very friendly man with a friendly smile and he was so funny. Jacob was the first man to get the ladies to relax and feel that everything would be alright and also being good looking didn't hurt. This evening there will be a grand dinner party and invitations have already gone out to many of the governor's friends and political associates to commence at 7:00 P.M. at the governor's mansion and compound tonight. The party will be for fun and a fabulous Jamaican cookout with tasty and spicy Jamaican food, and to meet the men who saved his daughter and her two friends. And to meet the most interesting and strangest men they would ever meet in their life time.

Mitchell comes into the study room to sit and ponder just what in the hell is going on what does it all mean, how did it happen and more important how do they get back to their own time if ever. Mitchell considers himself to be not only the most intelligent and learned man on this adventure but also the most paramagnetic. He thinks to himself that time travel is not possible but yet here we are back in time June 1692. Governor Sir William Beeston enters the study from the outside doors he was taking an early walk along the water's edge like he usually does in the early morning. But today he was also pondering what he heard last night regarding time travel could that be possible. "Good morning governor," says Mitchell with a smile from a comfortable brown chair. "A wonderful good morning to you," answers the governor. "Governor I have an important question to ask you, do you happen to have a calendar about?" "Yes I believe I do in the drawer of my desk, "answers the governor, "Please do tell me of your interest in the calendar?" Mitchell takes a long look at the calendar and studies the dates then he sits down in a hard way like he had just seen a ghost. "What be your trouble," says the governor.

Mitchell ponders his answer for a long moment searching for just the right words to say. "Governor please believe me when I tell you this, just as you have seen us, very strange men with strange powerful weapons and a boat that goes very fast across the water. I know things that are in the past history because I have studied Caribbean past history in college, now I am from the future. You must believe me thousands of lives depend on heading my words. On this coming Saturday at 11:45 the largest earthquake ever to hit the island of Jamaica and Port Royal will sink into the sea. Then a tsunami title wave (A very large and powerful wave) will go out into the ocean and impact many other islands in the Caribbean killing hundreds and hundreds of people. I do not tell you this to scare you but perhaps prepare you and your people for Saturday it is coming it cannot be stopped. There is nothing that can be done to stop this awful event just get as many people to safety as you can." The governor says, "That is very startling news perhaps I can make a difference with the people that will be here at my party tonight. I will make an announcement to let the people aware of what you told me and they will tell others I believe most of the people will believe what I say. There will always be skeptics who do not believe in future warnings but I believe what you say I really do. We do have a few days to prepare and if for some reason you are wrong then no harm was done. Now for this morning can I get a ride on your grand and strange boat and see you weapons fire that would really please me." "Yes, I believe that can be arranged as soon as all of my buddies have come down for breakfast we will convince and shock you with what we have and who we are," says Mitchell.

Still early in the morning on Tuesday the rest of the Navy Seals enter the dining room for their breakfast. Mitchell tells his buddies that he has informed the governor of the impending earthquake that will occur on Saturday at exactly 11:45 without fail it will be an 8.2 earthquake no earthquake will ever occur in the Caribbean this large again. And that a grand party is going to take place tonight so the governors friends and political partners can meet us, he said he would inform his guests tonight about the earthquake I only hope they believe him because it is coming. Mitchell continues talking, "Not much more we can do, but the governor would like to take a ride on our boat this morning and see our weapons fire. I told him after breakfast that we would accommodate his wishes." Lt. Darren James speaks up, "Well I don't see us doing anything more we don't rule this island and we don't make policy there are a few days left before Saturday, so let's make the best of it." Just then the three ladies came walking into the dining room all smiles and looking right at the three seals they have their eyes on the three seals they have chosen to get to know better. Lilliannah sees a chair unoccupied beside Lt. James and sits right down without asking if it would be ok to sit there. Cassandra does the same thing finding a seat beside Bobby Harold giving him her most inviting smile. And Carol Kay is setting beside Jacob and places her hand on his and giving him a great smile. The rest of the seals can sense what is taking place and excuse themselves from the table since they have finished breakfast of what the people call crackle fruit (chicken eggs) with bacon and plenty of fresh fruit juice and wonderful Jamaican coffee. The three seals stand up and say to the governor, "Do we ever have some amazing things to show you more wonderful then you could ever imagine. So first things first let's get down to the magic boat," says Hunter. Down to the dock they go Hunter, Mitchell and Christopher along with governor Beeson.

"Sit down buckle up we hope you enjoy the ride, governor, says Hunter, "I am about to turn on the engines, everyone set and buckled up?" "Yes," comes the answer. Ok then the lines are untied bow facing the open sea and the throttle forward ho," yells Hunter. And with the flick of Hunter's wrist the Apex Pegasus inflatable boat moves across the calm water of the sea. Ten knots, twenty knots, now speeding along at thirty knots the Navy Seals are watching the facial expressions of the governor, and they are really enjoying what they see. The governor is absolutely petrified, he has never ever gone so fast over water and neither has anyone else in this time. He is holding onto his seat cushion as though it would save him as well as holding onto a metal support. Out into the open sea the sea is calm no white caps and today the air is warm and the salt air is wonderful to taste and feel against their faces. Today they have no agenda, no one to fight with; just enjoying the calm serenity of the moment and it is wonderful. The only thought that they have is how in the hell will they get back to their own time if ever. Hunter pulls the throttle back, the Apex Pegasus boat comes to a dead stop in the water they are about 10 miles from shore. "Well governor how are you enjoying the ride?" asks Mitchell. "Let me catch my breath," says the governor, "Fantastic far beyond anything in my world, your world must be so wonderful does it have a lot of interesting and odd unique things?" "Our world shall we say is light years ahead of your world just 314 years to be exact," says Christopher,

"Would you like to see what makes this boat go so fast?" "You bet I would," says the governor. "This is what we call an engine it is powered by a fuel called gasoline, these engines are called jet engines like the engines that power our jet airplanes that fly in the sky." "What are jet airplanes?" asks the governor. "Not today perhaps we can explain that at another time," injects Christopher. "Well men I am shocked and amazed beyond my wildest dreams, now could you show me how your weapons fire, I am somewhat of an expert on our firearms," says the governor. "We have a number of weapons on board we can show you a few, see that gun at the bow lets show that one to you first," says Christopher, "It's called a Minigun it is a multi-barreled Gatling-gun that fires this bullet I am holding in my hand 6000 of these bullets in one minute, stand back I'll fire it now." VRRRRRRRRRRRRRRRRRR was the sound the gun made firing for only 3 seconds. "Well governor what do you think of our gun? What if a pirate ship had one of these guns?" asks Christopher. "Oh my God that would be the very end of us all, they would rule the seas I have never seen anything like this gun before," says the governor.

"Take a look at this gun it is a Barrett M468 semi- automatic gas-operated submachinegun, its rate of fire is 200 rounds per minute with a 30 bullet magazine. This is the gun that was used to mow down the pirates on the dock the other night the pirates could not believe what was happing to them. I'll show you, step back BRRRRRRRR, BRRRRRRRRRRR, BRRRRRRRRRRRRR. Now this is one of our favorite guns that is issued to us it is a real killing weapon, we like it because it is small and light weight, proclaims Mitchell. "Take a look at our sidearm that we carry strapped our leg, it is a MK-23- 45 caliber pistol it can fire even if it fell in the water would you like to fire my pistol?" asks Hunter. "Oh yes I would really like to fire your pistol." Hunter instructs the governor, "Point it out to sea, hold your hand steady, there will be a kick, and now pull the trigger." FFF-FFF-FFF the pistol fires and the governor can hardly control himself with what he experienced and the power. "What an amazing weapon this gun is," proclaims the governor, "These weapons must never fall into the hands of the pirates promise me that," begs the governor. "We promise that will never happen," say the Navy Seals. "Take a good look at our armor vests called Dragon Skin, no bullet can pass through it and harm us, try it on if you like this is what we were wearing in town," says Hunter. "Wow this is so neat, what else can you show me," proclaims the governor.

Lt. James and the other two seals are finishing breakfast along with the three ladies who are making eyes at the Navy Seals. "Will you come with us and sit outside in the garden overlooking the sea?" ask the ladies. The seals have nothing better planed they agree to go to the garden and it is truly a beautiful garden. The garden is overlooking the ocean with so many beautiful flowers in bloom all giving off their fragrant smells. With the palm trees swaying in the gentle morning breeze, the seals are thinking this is what heaven must be like. Lilliannah, Cassandra and Carol Kay do not intend to waste this early morning romantic feeling, so they are smiling their best smiles, giggling at anything the seals may have said, and touching their arms and hands with light sensual touches. Lt. James and Jacob Blum are interested and going along with the program they like the beautiful ladies and the attention they were receiving. Bobby Harold just wasn't getting with the program and he did not show much interest in Cassandra he seemed preoccupied with other thoughts. Thoughts of his wife and his little girl back in another time and if he would ever see them again. He meant no harm in not showing interest in Cassandra for she was a very beautiful lady. "Cassandra, I have something I need to explain, " says Bobby, "My two buddies are not married but I am I have a beautiful wife and beautiful baby daughter in another time back home that I miss very much I hope you understand." "Thank you for sharing your story with me I was beginning to think that there must be something wrong with me," answers Cassandra. "No believe me I think that you are a most beautiful lady and if I wasn't married I would want to jump your bones." says Bobby. "What did you say and what does that mean?" asks Cassandra. Bobby realizing what he just said and was somewhat embarrassed and did his best to apologize he explained that was what people just said in our time.

Meanwhile Lt. James and Lilliannah were wondering off to be alone and to get to know each other better. Lt. James is smitten by the beauty of Lilliannah and her courage; he is very attracted to her and encouraged her forwardness. He was fully aware of the picture of the two of them in the museum that hung on the wall and the explanation that went with the picture in his time, and is willing to see how all of this is going to play out. Lt. James turns to Lilliannah and takes her in his arms placing his hand on the small of her back to bring her closer. He bends his face to hers touching her lips with a soft, sweet, passionate kiss a feeling of true passion erupts in Darren as though this is the first lady he has ever kissed in his life. Lilliannah feeling the same passion was kissing back just as hard as she could, lifting her right foot off the ground and holding on for dear life, for she in all her 25 years had never experienced a feeling like this before and in her mind she was never going to let this man go. Now holding hands they walked looking at the ocean, the romantic ocean with the sweet smell of salt air and passion they turned to kiss and kiss some more as they walked together. Jacob and Carol Kay were also enjoying their time together; Jacob with his sense of humor and ease of making friends completely took Carol Kay by surprise as to what a great and wonderful guy he was and how easy he was to talk to about anything. Jacob was really interested in Carol Kay's life her dreams and how she saw her future. Carol Kay had never before met a man who was really interested in her and her life and she relished in the feeling. They also held hands as they walked along the beach watching the waves of the blue, green sea caress the white sand. Jacob stops and turns to face Carol Kay and says, "You know us Navy men really need a kiss now and then to sooth our lonely soul." Carol Kay understands and complies with a sensual soft kiss on Jacob's lips and a loving hug, now they are really enjoying each other's company.

End of chapter 3

CHAPTER 4

More true history about the real pirates of the
Caribbean that will tantalize your mind and your soul.

The pirates and buccaneers that worked there trade in the Caribbean were luckier than most men who sailed their wooden ships throughout the world in search for trade goods, gold, silver, treasure and adventure. Because of the temped weather, warm, sometimes hot but never freezing cold, cold weather was the most feared of all. Like the worst weather in the world going around the Horn of South America in winter, where the gale winds could reach sixty plus miles per hour and the angry seas would reach thirty to fifty feet high with white caps. The rain would freeze upon contact of the sails and the wooden masts making them top heavy and if the ice was not chopped or broken off with axes the ship would tip either to starboard or port at forty five degree angles or more and sink into the fridged sea and all hands would be lost. Some ships that met their peril at the bottom of the world could have as many as 200 men on board their merchant ship or pirate ship seeking new adventures in the different seas around the world. Sailing the Horn of South America was only for the fool hardy or picking a better time of year like summer when the weather may be somewhat better but the weather at the horn is always tricky and dangerous. I personally sailed around the Horn of South America on April 9, 1960 on the USS Shangri la an Essex class aircraft carrier when I was in the Navy. The temperature was very cold the wind was blowing at 40 to 50 miles per hour and the swell of the waves were at 30 to 40 feet high but no white caps. When you walked on the hanger deck you could see the sea above the deck. I can only imagine how terrifying sailing around the Horn in a wooden sailing ship would have been.

The wooden sailing ships of the time were damp, dark, cheerless places at best reeking with the stench of bilge water and rotten meat. Whatever the weather a wooden ship leaked; its planks could seldom be caulked so thoroughly that they would let no water in. In heavy weather, seas beat down the hatchways; so that the lower decks were awash and once wet the inside of a ship was always difficult to dry out properly. The men suffered badly from cramps, colds and sickness made worse by the lack of dry clothes and by the labor of hauling ropes and sails and manning pumps. When he went below, a sailor or pirate had only forecastle to go to; there in the wretched candlelit gloom he might if lucky to share a sopping blanket with a shipmate. The pirates, buccaneers, sailors and seaman who sailed the Caribbean were luckier than most, because they were able to drop anchor in a nearby port of call and dry out their belongings and clothing before they had to sail again, for the most part they enjoyed warm and dry weather.

To man all the cannons and be able to board and over power their pray, a pirate ship would carry a crew two to three times larger than any merchant ship on the high seas. May a time a pirate ship would have 200 men jammed onto a ship hardly longer than 120 feet by 40 feet at the beam. Men slept packed side by side on the steerage floor, or if so lucky had a cloth hammock strung across a couple of beams or to the bulkhead. All crews did their very best to combat pestilence. Pirates and sailors alike would wash down the decks with vinegar and salt water. Pirates would even swab the decks with plundered French brandy or Spanish wine that is if they had an enormous stock and the mood was just right. Below decks, the usual work on all ships bar none was to fumigate with pans of burning pitch and brimstone. But nothing could stop the accumulation of filth and the infestation of vermin during a long voyage from one to three months sometimes more. There were nooks and crannies that could never be cleaned or dried. The refuse that collected in the bottom of the hull, became a breeding ground for cockroaches, rats, worms, and the rats scurrying by the hundreds. It was not unusual for a captain, merchant or pirate to lose half of his men to disease during a voyage. Typhus and typhoid were endemic on board any ship. The men also fell sick to scurvy, caused by a diet lacking in fresh fruit, especially oranges, lemons, and limes with its abundant vitamin C, they suffered horribly as well from dysentery, yellow fever and malaria. But among the most retched and feared disease was venereal disease by far. And it was such a curse that crews boarding a captured ship were often more interested in searching for and ransacking, medicine chests or cabinets for mercurial compounds to treat their syphilis and other peter burning and itching venereal diseases' then searching for gold.

What a life this was considering that most pirates and buccaneers and seaman choose the profession of serving aboard a ship rather than finding work in a town. The ordinary food was universally terribly atrocious. The water stank, the meat and fish were more rotten then fresh, the biscuits were infested with large black headed weevil maggots. The men would only bring themselves to eat in the dark, so they would not be able to see what they were biting into. But the good part was at least seaman and pirates have a reasonable expectation of something to eat, no matter how vile or objectionable the food was. For pirates, thirst and starvation were constant companions. The irregular nature of pirate cruises with their sudden changes of course, and their hazardous haunts in very remote corners of distant oceans would put the men on desperately short rations. By the very nature of choosing to be men of the sea, pirates suffered prolonged agonies of just plain boredom, mainly relieved by playing dice and cards, or shooting off guns when they could afford the ammunition. Drink, was their greatest comfort; grog, wine, beer and in particular rum from the West Indies. Believe it or not some pirates of those who could read found comfort and solace in reading of the Bible and prayer books. At best, the community of pirates was a kind of a guild with no ideological ambition. At its worst it was pure anarchy and was treated accordingly.

The pirate captain therefore had no constitutional authority and was entitled to no special privileges aside from the double share of any bounty. A pirate captain's cabin had one very important privilege, and that was a dry bed he did not have to share with any other pirate. Only in battle did a pirate captain become what he was commissioned to do and that was to lead his men into battle in an engagement, and he better not show fear or be timed of a battle plan. He must be in the forefront of the engagement never standing behind of his men shouting orders only then is a pirate captain a captain. A captain's power is absolute uncontrollable in chase or in battle, drubbing, cutting or even shooting anybody who does not obey his command. The pirates naturally sought out a captain who was judged to be brave, fearless and particularly competent for the job. The one man who is superior in his knowledge of the sea, and sea battles tactics and boldness, a man who is pistol proof and does not fear death. If pirates would not follow tyrannical captains, they certainly would not follow or abide incompetent or unlucky ones either. While many captains kept their appointments for year's captains who were not up to the code were disposed of rather quickly and that usually meant death by throwing them over the side of the ship, hanging or shooting them. The pirates were only too well aware of the trouble a bad captain could create, the worst that a bad captain could create was choosing a ship that could not be boarded or taken, a ship that would not surrender and perhaps the pirates would lose the battle and or all be killed.

Next to the captain the most important man on the ship was the quartermaster, he was the ship's magistrate and empowered to punish minor offences like quarreling or not looking after weapons properly or doing his assigned duty aboard the ship. Serious offences would have to be tried by a jury. He was the only man on a pirate ship who was allowed to administer flogging, though so detested was this form of punishment, that it was only allowed when sanctioned by a majority of the crew. The quartermaster was also the first man to board a merchant ship taken in battle. He was responsible for the selection and division of the bounty and in charge of the ship's boat on any particularly difficult or dangerous enterprise. The quartermaster was subject to the will of the majority of the pirates on board any ship. He was chosen by the majority and he could be deposed by it as well. The other officers on a pirate ship were sometimes chosen by the crew but more often appointed by the captain and the quartermaster. There was a first lieutenant who had no particular function except to assume command if the captain were killed. The sailing master was very important he was in charge of the navigation and the setting of the sails. The boatswain was responsible for the ships maintenance, ships tackle, and the stores and the day to day working of the ship. The chief gunner he was in charge of the ordnance, gunnery training and the gun crews when the ship was in a battle. Then if the ship was lucky enough to have a doctor on board that was primo, but most of the time they were kidnapped from a town when the ship was in port or taken in war a real prize for a pirate ship. The doctor on board a pirate ship spent the majority of his time treating venereal diseases among the pirate crew. But when it came to treating main causes of death in tropic waters, such as yellow fever malaria, dysentery, scurvy he was virtually helpless. During a battle the doctor would be required to dress wounds and perform amputations. If there was no doctor on board the head carpenter stood in for him because the tools were vertically the same. The most popular of the ship's specialists were the members of the pirate band. These men were mostly captured and taken from other ships in battle they were called on to play a jig or a hornpipe at a pirate dance on board and to serenade the pirates when they were eating. But the practical purpose was to play nautical tunes and aggressive war tunes on drums and trumpets to demoralize the enemy when they were at war.

The type of ships that were the ships of choice for pirates were usually smaller ships built to be fast to catch merchant ships with the advantage the amount of cannons to be one dozen evenly placed on both sides of the ship. The type of ships were a schooner with speeds of up to 11 knots, weighing in at about 90 to 100 ton and she could carry a crew of 75 men, she also had a shallow draft about five feet allowing the pirates to navigate shoal waters and hide in remote coves. The largest of the pirate ships suitable as the flagship of a pirate fleet and the flagship of the Brethren of the Black Spot was a three-masted, square-rigger it was not as swift as a schooner but very intimidating for her size. She would usually weigh in a 350 ton and 180 feet in length, she was valued for her seaworthiness for long sea voyages. Hosting a crew of 150 to 200 pirates and usually mounted over 30 cannon, plus a numerous swivel guns. This ship would usually standoff of the battle and let the smaller, faster pirate ships engage, then she would come over the horizon and end any resistance that a merchant maybe thinking of engaging in battle. Her large cargo capacity made her an excellent transport for the collected bounty and swag of a pirate flotilla. Greatly favored by smugglers and pirates was a near perfect ship for the pirates, a sloop usually the fastest ship in the pirates arsenal exceeding well over 14 knots because of her rapier-like bowsprit, she was able to mount a rather large sailing canvases and with a square topsail this gave her an extra measure of speed. Her draft was deeper than a schooner or brigantine she drew eight feet in the water weighting in at 140 ton she would have a complement of crew at 75 to 95 pirates and mounted usually 14 cannons 7 cannons on each side. A sloop could still maneuver in the channels and the sounds where brigands would hide. But the work horse of the day the primary ship that most of the pirates favored was the brigantine, chosen well as a combat ship. She was basically a two-masted vessel that carried on her mainmast either square or fore-and-aft sails which made her immensely versatile, the square sails drove her the fastest in quartering winds. This ship is 90 feet long weighting in at 165 tons and mounted 12 cannons with a crew of 100 or more depending on the mission.

Captain Benjamin Steenwinkel has a ship by the name of the Devils Servant that is in desperate need of repair, his ship is a smaller ship it is a schooner old by time of use at sea over 15 years. The ship was in a battle about a month ago and suffered three direct cannon hits, eight pounders each at the water line causing extensive damage. A lot of operating damage was done to the speed of the ship the Devils Servant by torpedo worms that infest the wooden hall below the water line the worm's tunnel through wooden hulls robbing the vessels of speed and eventually its seaworthiness. Barnacles that attach themselves in the thousands to the bottom of the ship also are robbing it of its seaworthiness and speed.

Capt. Steenwinkel is on a hunt for another pirate ship to commandeer and change ships in exchange for his own, and also take over the bounty and cargo of the new ship a win, win, win for Capt. Steenwinkel. What he knew he needed to do was not to damage the new ship but make it surrender without firing a shot. Capt. Steenwinkel and Capt. Peterman Grandstaff of the good ship the Mary Margaret are sailing in tandem searching the Caribbean seas for a new ship to replace the old and tired ship the Devils Servant. Their plan was simple in its conception to scare and intimidate the crew of the ship they choose to surrender. The two pirate ships keep a lookout for any ship on the horizon that would meet their needs without any concern for its crew.

"Thar she be," shouts out a pirate look out sitting in the crow's nest on the ship the Devils Servant. The ship on the horizon is a perfect prize a three-masted, square rigged ship. A 280 ton merchant ship flying a Spanish flag, which possibly meant that their cargo, would be precious metals and stones. The ship lay off the horizon about 5 miles, so the pirates had time to make their plans to capture the ship. Capt. Steenwinkel developed a genius of a plan, he ordered a dozen of his men to dress up in lasses dresses and clothing and other pirates to dress in merchant clothing to make believe that they were in distress and needed assistance. The ship flew a distress flag and fired a shot in the air to get the attention of the merchant ship, to slow down and stop dead on the water. The other pirate ship the Mary Margaret stayed back off the horizon out of sight, but could see that the pirate ship the Devils Servant had spotted her quarry using flag signals. As the ship the Devils Servant sailed closer she could count the merchant seamen on board that amounted to less than 45 seamen even though the ship had 18 cannons but did not open the gun ports because she believed that she was in no danger from a ship in distress. The pirate ship pulled along the starboard side of the merchant ship, and soon as the lines were secured 80 pirates quickly boarded the prize totally surprising the entire merchant seaman aboard. Then the other pirate ship the Mary Margaret quickly came over the horizon flying the pirate flag of the skull and cross bones and the flag of the Brethren of the Black Spot. The two pirate ships bringing total fear for to lives of the captured merchant Spanish vessel. Four merchant seamen made the mistake of reaching for their weapons and pointed blunderbuss rifles at the pirates, the pirates quickly overpowered the four seamen firing a pistol killing one of the seamen with a bullet to his face. Than Capt. Steenwinkel made all the merchant seamen sit on the deck as five of the pirates went about searching the ship for medical supplies. Primarily to treat venereal diseases for his men then after they found the medical supplies they continued to search for the bounty, the gold, silver and precious stones.

What they found even surprised the pirates, treasure beyond any ones belief it was truly the mother lode. This unsuspecting merchant ship with a very light crew was caring in its locked hold, $450,000 in gold and silver currency, silks, and porcelain and other cloth goods worth another $355,000 in valued treasure. Last but not least diamonds so many diamonds that each pirates share would be 15 diamonds per man. The pirates under the command of Capt. Benjamin Steenwinkel have scored the biggest bounty of their lives ever. They commandeered a ship that they intended to call their own not even considering that the merchant ship would be carrying such a large amount of valuables. What the pirates did next was unconscionable and just pure evil. The Spanish seaman never really put up a fight and also came to what they thought was to help and rescue a ship in distress. Capt. Steenwinkel said to the captain of the merchant ship, "Today be an excellent day for all of ye to die, ye captain will watch hims crew be whipped with the cat o' nine tails until ye cry for death to take ye. First hang de four men whom reached for de weapons by pulling dem bodies by ye necks and ye feet do da dance of death. Now sew dem mouths shut of de captain and him officers with a sail needle and thread." As the men are being flogged to death and cry out in excruciating pain the pirates are having the times of their lives enjoying the death before their eyes. Capt. Steenwinkel and Capt. Peterman Grandstaff are observing the death and pain that they have ordered and laughing so hard their sides are hurting then made orders that lead weights be tied to all the merchant seaman's legs and in their state of dyeing and death be thrown overboard to join Davy Jones ship at the bottom of the sea. Now that the merchant seamen have been disposed of, all hands remove their belongings from their ole ship and bring them aboard the new Devils Revenge and anything else of value, all weapons and ammunition and any stores of food worth saving, this be a good ship for us cheered the pirates. Then Capt. Steenwinkel ordered that his old ship be set on fire and then cut her loose and when it is 25 yards away fire the 9 cannons on the starboard side to sink his ole ship and send her to her watery grave. As the two pirate ships the new Devils Revenge and the Mary Margaret gave the order to sail away the drums and horns and singing from the pirate ships could be heard all the way to hell.

With their new ship, plenty of fresh food and fantastic treasure, the two captains plan to return to Port Royal, Jamaica with their bounty and if any other ship be seen on their return, my God have mercy on their souls, for the pirates give no mercy only war and death. Luck seems to be on the side of the two pirate ships a ship is seen three days later from their last encounter. A pirate in the crow's nest of the Mary Margaret shouts, "Ahoy a merchant ship be seen off the port bow at the very edge of the horizon." All hands scurry on deck to have a look see at what this unlucky merchant ship be. It is a Dutch ship fresh from Curacao an island in the southern hemisphere of the Caribbean. It is a flat bottom ship a very common merchant ship, 80 feet in length and it is about 250 ton a slow but steady ship and easy to sail. This type of ship is well known to all the pirates a sure kill because it only carried a crew of 21 men and only a few cannons. The cargo is primarily sugar, tea, and other exotic prized spices and was encountered many times in the Caribbean with great success. The pirates were all jumping for joy for what they were about to do to this hapless Dutch ship caught in the open water. The captain of the Dutch ship also spotted the two pirate ships sailing at full sail towards him and flying their pirate flags the skull and cross bones and the Brethren of the Black Spot a red flag with a black spot in the middle. The pirates are having fun playing with their pray knowing the fear that they are causing and what their intentions were going to be when the prey was caught, just like a pack of jackals chasing a scared rabbit.

This type of ship is called a flute and the ship design was adapted by the English and the French as well to hall large amounts of spice cargo. This is not the kind of ship that the pirates would want to sail, slow and only with a small amount of cannons only ten cannon that would only fire an 8 lb. cannon ball. On the two pirate ships there are about 220 men pirates seeking blood as a vampire needs blood to survive, pirates need to spill blood to feel alive. Also between the two pirate ships are over 40 cannons and 20 cannons could fire a 20 lb. iron cannon ball at a distance of 2,500 yards. The Devils Servant was running on the port side of the Dutch merchant ship and the Mary Margaret was coming fast on the starboard side. The pirate ships are within one mile and closing fast, the musicians are hard at work earning their keep. They are beating there drums with a war and battle rhythm that sounded like the devil himself was playing and the horns were blaring a mean tone of certain death while the rest of the pirates were screaming war chants and cries of certain torture to be bestowed upon the poor innocent merchant seaman. They knew that there was nothing they could do to stop the pirates a white flag of surrender would not be honored and would show their weakness making the pirates even more intent to torture them. So they loaded there cannons readied there blunderbuss rifles and pistols to make the best stand they could to defend themselves. Now the pirates seemed to slow there attack to back off just outside of the Dutch Merchant ships cannon range as if they were toying with them and they were as the merchant cannon balls all fell short and into the sea. The pirates know that there was nothing worse than the knowledge of immanent death the kind of death someone feels standing on the gallows waiting for the trap door to drop. Now the pirates make their move and open fire with their cannons blasting into the sail masts cutting them in to and firing their weapons. The pirates are excellent marksmen and able to kill half of the merchant seaman before they even board the ship. The rest of the merchant seaman are now scared to death and flustered and not trained in battle raised their hands to show the pirates they were unarmed, perhaps just perhaps the pirates would show mercy. The Mary Margaret slammed her bow into the amidships of the merchant ship with such a jolt that no merchant seaman was able to stand upright.

Pirates rushed onto the ship from the Mary Margaret over 100 pirates now surround 11 scared merchant seamen all pissing in their pants from fear. Just then the Devils Servant pirate ship pulled up along the port side and another 75 pirates jumping aboard with their boarding axes held high and screaming. Capt. Peterman Grandstaff lashes out his orders, "Me turn to murder these son-of-a dog bastards to makes dem scream and cry as ye arms an legs be cut from dar bodies." All the pirates let out a blood curdling joyous screams for the fun they are about to witness. Capt. Grandstaff yells, "Take dat man hiding in da corner first, cut him legs away and den see if he can do a gig for us." A pirate raises his cutlass and whacks away at the poor seaman's legs just below his knees five or six times before his legs are severed with his blood flowing freely on the deck. "Dance for us ye bilge rat, dance," the pirates keep yelling. The pirates were having so much fun at the expense of the merchant seaman they had forgotten to begin their search for medical supplies. Now 8 pirates begin their search and find some medical medicine for their venereal diseases and also search the ship for their bounty. They discover to their delight the ship's cargo hold has tons of sugar, tea and other spices.

A number of pirates are unloading the Dutch merchant ship of its cargo to the two pirate ships. The torture continues with some of the remaining Dutch seaman cutting arms and legs from their bodies at the pirates delight and entertainment. They grabbed one poor seaman who was crying and hung him upside down from a broken mast and then proceeded to beat him until his eyes fell from his head and he died a horrible death. The rest of the pirates are now in a fever pitch of excitement, with horror, pain and suffering that they are causing. The remaining merchant seaman four to be exact could only hope for a quick death not a lingering torturing death. All the cargo has been transferred to the pirate ships including the medical supplies that were found. Capt. Grandstaff raises his arms and yells, "Enough is enough, we have found good bounty on board this ship and I will show mercy to the remaining four seamen. If any of ye scallywags wish to join us and become pirates stand up." Two men stand up and were quickly taken to the pirate ship the Devils Servant. "Now ye two men that refuse to stand wit us shall die, tie der legs wit de iron weight and throw dem worthless bilge rats into da sea Arrrr." Capt. Grandstaff gives the order to sail and when the pirate ship the Devils Servant is out safely out of range he orders the cannons fire at the water line to sink the Dutch ship. After the pirate ships began to sail away and the merchant ship has been sent to the bottom of the deep blue sea all the pirates feel that they have had a good, fun and profitable day and point the bows of their ships heading toward Port Royal, Jamaica their home port.

The reason that the Brethren of the Black Spot was formed was to have a number of ships able to attack any merchant ship or any other ship as a fighting group and succeed giving no quarter, and having their organizations name send absolute fear and terror throughout the Caribbean. Whether they were at anchor in port or out to sea their name meant fear and death to all. They even attacked any town on any island in the Caribbean for fun and profit that they choose. The pirates knew that intimidation was a primary fear factor and was always a pirates first and foremost weapon. Capt. John Wallace was the man who thought up the idea to form this formidable group of pirates, the first three pirate captains to join the group were chosen by Capt. John Wallace himself then the rest of the seven pirate captains had to be elected by the first three captains who were members. In order to even be considered for membership into the Brethren of the Black Spot you must have proven yourself and your crew in 7 battles over the last two years. You must possess no fear and be ruthless and willing and able to take on the merchant ships capturing cargo and treasure and have already captured at least $250,000 in booty. All members are to share in 25% of each captured bounty and treasure with all the other members. A black spot was a terrifying symbol to many for many years among the pirates a black spot on a piece of parchment paper meant certain death to any one or any ship that it was presented to. The Brethren of the Black Spot was the most feared pirate organization in the history of the known world at this time.

The pirates of the Brethren of the Black Spot are getting their plans together to kidnap and or kill the Navy Seals (Devil Men) at tonight's party held at the governor's mansion. Their plan is to have two ships just off the coast of the governor's compound to transport any Navy Seals they are able to capture. But now their plans have changed somewhat they now plan to send four pirates to the governors party tonight and perhaps they can arrange the kidnapping somehow. Four pirates have been chosen to attend the party tonight getting them cleaned up with descent clothing and not smelling or looking like bulge rats will be a real challenge. The barber must shave and cut their hair the pirates who were chosen and to make them look somewhat civilized anything for the cause they agree to. The plan is simple in its conception the four pirates attending the party will mingle with the regular guests, if they can get one or two Navy Seals alone knock him out and get him to the row boats waiting at the shore. They plan on having about a dozen pirates on shore waiting hidden to strike out and capture any Navy Seals walking along the water's edge tonight. Capt. Barboosa and Capt. Threepwood are planning on sending one boat each to shore with six to ten men on each boat. The pirate captains are pleased with their plans and feel that their plans are quite good now they must get Capt. Wallace approval. Capt. Wallace is very pleased with their plans and believes that they will succeed and capture at least one Navy Seal. (Devil Man) Timing is everything so the pirates leave in the two ships so they make the 25 mile journey up the coast from Port Royal to the governor's compound. They must go to shore with the four men who will attend the party in two landing boats with six pirates each to wait along the shoreline to capture any of the Navy Seals (Devil Men)

"Well governor that will have to be all of our weapon demonstrations for today, perhaps another day we will be able to show you a few more of our weapons," says Mitchell Davies. Hunter speaks up, "Would you like to see firsthand the control panel of this boat governor? These are the gages that tell me about the operation of the boat; how fast we are going, the direction, how much fuel we have in the tank, how deep the water is, and if there might be a problem with the engine." "Fascinating and very interesting the people in your country and time must be so smart to be able to build such a boat and your weapons," explains the governor. "Yes, that is very true but consider the people 300 years earlier then today they would be amazed at your inventions and how modern you would appear to them, it is all relative in time," says Mitchell. "I'm sorry but I don't really understand what you just said," speaks the governor. "Not important pay me no attention I was just thinking out loud," says Mitchell. Hunter starts up the engine and says, "I think it's about time to return to your dock governor, what say you." "Good idea, in fact that is an excellent idea, I have so many things to do before my grand party tonight I got so wrapped up in your fantastic boat and weapons I completely forgot about the time." speaks the governor. "Buckle up and secure yourselves, I'm going to really open the Apex Pegasus up to maximum speed to see how she handles," says Hunter. As the Apex Pegasus boat moves along the water toping speeds of just over 60 knots even a seal or two finds it hard to believe how fast this boat can really go. The poor governor is holding on for dear life it looks like all the blood has drained out of his face he is almost reaching panic mode hoping they reach his dock real soon. "There she is," Yells Christopher Kirk, "Your home just off in the distance we will be there in just a few short minutes," The governor opens his eyes to really see if he is close to home he does his best not to show panic or fear. Standing on the dock the women welcome them back are Lilliannah, Cassandra and Carol Kay, and Lt. James is holding Lilliannah's hand, along with Jacob and Bobby Harold standing on the dock.

The grand party has begun as many of the guests drive up in front of the mansion in their finest carriages and fancy party clothing. It is early evening around 7:30 P.M. the sun will be setting into the sea within the hour. The governor invited seventy eight couples who were friends and political allies everyone is having a great time. One unexpected surprise for the party is Mitchell and Hunter were able to hook up the loud speakers from the Apex boat and were playing music from Mitchell's ipod's music from the 50's and the 60's good ole rock and roll music. That was the only music that Mitchell recorded because that was the only music he liked. Everyone could not believe what they were listing to and hearing just what kinds of music it is pray tell us? The Navy Seals were looking over the crowd in the large back yard facing the water they could see people swaying to the odd loud music and smiling. Heck there were people attempting to move their feet to the rhythm of the music a couple or two were even trying to dance to the music. Four of the Navy Seals were wearing the native clothes from Jamaica two of the seals wore their Navy Seal clothing that was laid out for them four of the seals just wanted to fit in but all the seals were packing their side arms. The governor was bringing people up to the Navy Seals to introduce them; the people were all gracious and pleasant to talk with but a little standoffish due to the strange feeling the strange people represented. One of the big hits at the party was the new drink that the seals made on the first day they arrived; the rum, coconut, lemon, lime sugar and ice drink. It was so popular that the people were not paying any attention as to how much they were consuming glass after glass.

Lilliannah was dressed in her best black and silver party dress and she looked stunning, with her long jet black hair just passed her shoulders, lips like bright red roses, her blue eyes seemed to sparkle and shine in the full moon light. Lt. Darren James could not take his eyes off of her, never in his life had he met such a beautiful and stunning lady and she in turn only wanted to be by Lt. James side. Jacob and Carol Kay were off somewhere laughing and talking and most possibly kissing, enjoying each other's company. Cassandra was standing beside a large palm tree looking out over the ocean all by herself when Christopher Kirk walked up and said, "Hello may I join you in your thoughts, I have been watching you all night from afar and to tell you the truth I'm a little scared to talk with you." "Now why would you a strong, tall, handsome man who I believe is not scared of anyone be afraid to talk with little ole me," asks Cassandra. "Because you are so beautiful and I think the most beautiful lady at this grand party tonight, and beautiful women such as yourself have always scared me just a little," answers Christopher. "Thank you, thank you so very much you are so very kind." Cassandra lights up the night with her bright smile. They are both thinking in their own minds that this is good and they could become very good friends possibly with benefits.

The four pirates dressed to impress and all cleaned up were really enjoying themselves perhaps a little too much they had never been to such a swell party before with all the important dressed up people of Jamaica. The food was absolutely wonderful tasting they had never eaten such wonderful food like this in their lives before. The food was set out on long tables so everyone could take as much food as they desired. The four pirates were taking and eating the wonderful tasty food like there was no tomorrow. They were meeting and greeting the important people of the island and having the best time of their lives. Hell they had forgotten all about their mission and why they were here, in part due to the rum, beer and wine that was flowing like a waterfall in spring time. In fact that drink that the seals made up was really a very big hit with the pirates; they could not stop drinking this wonderful concoction. The four of them found a large dark grassy area under a few palm trees in the garden area and they were now passed out cold to the world from the food, drink and interesting odd music the celebration was just too damn much for them.

The Navy Seals asked if it was alright to carry their side arms hidden under their shirts and the governor granted them permission. The Navy Seals were always on alert and tried to be prepared for the unknown even at such a lavish party. Their intentions would never be to fire first or to start any trouble but that night at the Catt & Fiddle Tavern had put them on edge. "Good people of Port Royal I have an announcement to make," speaks the governor as he stands on a table in the center of the large yard as his guests gather round. "Gather around me please this information is important and could possibly save your lives and your loved ones in Port Royal." The crowd of party goers gathers around to hear what the governor has to say and they get quiet. When Governor Sir William Beeston speaks everyone listens to his words of wisdom, he is known as a serious person who loves the people of Jamaica and watches out for their best interest. "Ladies and gentleman of Port Royal, I have it on the best authority of a terrible event that will take place this Saturday at 11:45 A.M. in the late morning. In the city limits of Port Royal a terrible earthquake will take place followed by a gigantic ocean wave that will sink Port Royal into the sea and devastate many cities on many islands in the Caribbean. I recommend that you all leave the city and go into the hills at least 15 miles from Port Royal where you will be safe. Take what important personal possessions you can but do not dilly dally by bringing everything you own." It seems as though the party was over with this horrible news the happy party time was over, the people were silent for what seemed a long time. Then the crowd started to chatter amongst themselves in earnest and fear was one feeling, how will they survive how many may die what will become of Port Royal. Then an undercurrent of words and thinking started to emerge from the crowd. How in the hell did the governor know the future, was he telling the truth, a disbelief in what the governor said started to emerge from the crowd. He is a wise and important man his words have been believed but this is it possible that he could be wrong what would be his motivation in telling a lie so bold and terrible, is now what they are thinking. What takes place is that half the crowd believes him the other half does not believe his words. The governor is still standing on the table in the middle of the crowd and says, "I can do no more than I have done please believe me and tell others of the impending disaster to save their lives on Saturday morning, as of this moment my grand party is over, my hope is that you all had a grand time."

Cassandra and Christopher were down on the beach walking along the water's edge they did not hear the announcement although Chris already knew of the impending disaster to come. They were walking hand in hand enjoying each other's company looking at each other in the full moon in the warm Jamaican night and the warm sand beneath their feet. They were far away from the mansion, the trees and underbrush was getting quite thick, neither one of them were paying any attention to the area but then decided they should go back. Then six pirates stepped out from the underbrush and were blocking their way back to the governor's mansion. Then another ten pirates stepped into full view and declared, "If ye be a Devil man surrender peacefully and the wench can return to the mansion in peace." Cassandra holds on tight to Christopher's arm and says to him, "They lie, we are both going to be taken and then that will be the end of our lives if they get us aboard a pirate's ship." Christopher is well aware of the trouble they are in and that the pirates will kill them both if and when they can. The pirates do not see the MK23 .45 caliber pistol under his military shirt and are not aware of the danger that they are in; Chris also has his knife strapped to his left thigh under his pant leg. Chris says to Cassandra, "When I start firing my pistol lay flat on the ground then get up dodge the pirates blocking your way and get to the mansion to get help, I will fire at the pirates blocking your way first." Christopher pulls his pistol and opens fire on the pirates blocking Cassandra's way. The pirates are very surprised as bullets slam into three of the pirate's heads blowing brains and their skulls all over the pristine beach sand. Cassandra gets up and starts to run and is quick enough to dodge the two pirates trying to block her way. They begin to chase her, Chris fires again his bullets hitting two of them in their backs knocking then to the sand now there is only one pirate left chasing after Cassandra, as the rest of the pirates charge Chris he fires his last bullet but reloads his pistol quickly and kills three more pirates as they charge him. The pirate chasing Cassandra gets close enough to grab her dress and swings his club hitting her on her right shoulder and her head causing a bloody gash as her blood is running down on to her dress. This makes Cassandra angrier then she has ever been at the pirates remembering what they did to her and her friends the other night. She stops, turns and surprises the pirate then she yells out at the top of her voice NOOOOOOOOOOOOOOO then she reaches down picks up a handful of sand and throws it in the pirate's eyes. Then she kicks the pirate in the perfect place right between his legs, he yells and crumples to the sand giving Cassandra ample time to get away. Cassandra continues running and is screaming for help.

Seven of the pirates now jumped on Christopher and are hitting him with their clubs; he is able to grab his knife with his left hand bringing it up into one of the pirate's belly gutting him and his intestines fall on the sand. Then Chris is able to move his knife again stabbing a pirate in his left eye and pushes his knife into his brain killing him. The pirates never thought that this Devil Man could fight so damn hard and kill so many pirates all by himself. They had some stupid idea that he would just give up and come with them with such a large amount of pirates capturing him. He is fighting as he was trained to fight, give no quarter and fight till all your enemies lay dead or are dyeing or until they surrender regardless of the odds. Christopher kicks his right leg catching a pirate on his shin bone breaking it. The pirates are able to take Chris to the sand the five that are left and still able to fight hold him down and two of them club Chris on the head knocking him out, now they are able to tie him with ropes and drag him to their boat unconscious. Cassandra's cries for help were heard by a number of mansion guards and come to her aid and are summing others still at the party for help. Lt. James comes running and calls for the other Navy Seals to come running, everyone is gathered around Cassandra, she cries out that the pirates have taken Christopher to their ships. Because of his brave actions she was able to get away and there are a number of dead and dying pirates on the beach. "Let's go men down to the beach to where the pirates have taken Chris," yells Lt. James. The seals arrive at the beach they can see a row boat rowing as fast as it can back to a ship that is also coming towards them.

The Navy Seals are able to quickly assess the damage that Chris has left behind eight pirates lay dead from gun shots two from Chris's knife two are wounded and one has a broken leg they determine that he put up one hell of a Navy Seal fight. Three of the pirates left behind are wounded the Navy Seals grabs them and asks not in a nice way where are they taking their buddy but they refuse to answer saying that they don't know anything. Jacob notices that a pirate has a broken leg; we do not have time to properly interrogate these men Jacob jumps on his leg and makes his leg bone protrude from the skin. The pirate screams out with a most horrendous sound, withering and crying in absolute pain. Jacob says, "Now answer our questions or I will jump on your friggin leg again." He withers in pain for the moment Bobby Harold puts his pistol to the head of another pirate and shouts, ""Now you tell us where they are taking our buddy you have five seconds to answer our questions." The pirate hesitates for five seconds and Bobby Harold says, "Your time is up." pulls the trigger splattering his brains all over the third pirate who is absolutely now scared to death. The pirate with the broken leg speaks up, "I will tell ye what ye want to know, Capt. John Wallace gave da odor to capture a Devil Man tonight to being him to ye ship the Red Dragon to question him about who ye be and da weapons dat ye have and whar ye come from so we can kill ye." "Why do you call us the Devil Men?" asks Jacob. "Because of ye green, black and blue faces an ye weapons ye must be from hell," answers the petrified pirate.

Lt. James says to a guard, "You take these two pirate bastards until we return we have more important business to attend to right now, all Navy Seals to our boat. We are on a mission to save Christopher Kirk now move, move." The angry Navy Seals get aboard buckle up they know this will be a bumpy ride tonight even though the ocean is calm and a full moon is out to light up their way. Hunter pushes the throttle full forward and the Apex Pegasus boat responds moving across the water at full speed. They can see in the distance the two pirate ships moving as fast as they can at 10 knots and the Apex Pegasus boat is moving at 60 knots. They approach the three ships now only 1,200 yards away, Lt. James says, "Hunter slow us down to a slow speed we have to locate which boat Chris is on so we can plan our attack." The seals get out their night scopes with night vision and are able to see Christopher tied to a mast on the third ship furthest out to sea. The Navy Seals are pretty sure they cannot be seen as they are so close to the water in a black and blue camouflaged boat in the darkness of the night. "I want those bastard pirates to know better than to fuck with Navy Seals," declares Lt. James, "We will create so fucking much death and chaos and destruction the pirates will gladly give Chris up."

"Ok we're still far out to sea no land in site plenty of time to take and destroy the three ships and rescue Chris," explains Lt. James, "First things first we won't go around that pirate ship in front of us we will go through that fucken ship, sink her and kill everyone aboard then attack the next ship and the ship they have Chris on." "God damn good plan I like it, let's dance," says Bobby The Apex Pegasus boat is so low in the water and in the darkness even with the full moon we will be in a stealth mode. The pirates for some strange stupid reasoning believe they have gotten clean away even though they lost a few pirates on the beach so what. The crazy pirates are celebrating what they believe was a successful capture of a Devil Man. They are all singing songs of victory blowing their horns and pounding on their drums and having one or two, too many victory drinks of rum, even the man on watch in the crow's nest he couldn't even stand up he was so drunk. "This is my plan," says Lt. James. "We get within 700 yards still far enough that they cannot see us; I believe we will not be taking any fire. We will fire off three or four of our hell fire missiles we will light up that pirate ship from their starboard side like the fourth of July. Mitchell you're on the rocket launcher AT4 whatever it takes three or four rockets should do the trick, Bobby you're on the Mini gun the Gatling gun and whatever is moving in the water is your target. Jacob you take the Barrett M468 Semi-Auto sub machine gun and do the same thing anything moving in the water kill it."

I chose the have the Atchisson Shot gun at my ready. Ok were at 700 yards, Mitchell set the missiles to explode 2 seconds after penetration of the hull, that will get the most bang for our buck and hit the ship at the stern first, right into the captain's cabin then at the water line. Lt. James gives the order, "Fire, fire the first missile hits perfectly creating a huge unexpected explosion the second missile hits at the water line creating a massive hole in the side and the ass end of the ship and the whole ass end stern explodes. Now Mitchell reloads and fires his third missile at the bow at the water line and then too amidships at the water line the whole damn ship seems to explode as water rushes in and within two minutes it begins to sink. The pirates are stunned what in the hell is going on what is happing to our ship they all scream in a panic. "Now Hunter go to their port side quickly Mitchell fire another missile too amidships." The missile also strikes the gun powder room and a huge explosion takes place. Bobby Harold opens up with the Minigun the Gatling gun aiming at the two masts cutting them in half and they fall into the ocean with a terrible sound and he sprays the upper deck when he see any pirates looking over the side.

The sound of the explosions reverberates across the ocean the other pirate ship knows what hell is coming their way. It seems that the screams of the pirates are so loud that they are louder than the explosions, the ship lists to port the pirates are jumping and more explosions are taking place and the pirate's ship sinks into the sea. There are a lot of pirates clinging to any wood they can find. "Hunter get in closer, until we are within fifty yards, slowly, that's it closer now Hunter light them up with our two 1,000,000 candle power lights." orders Lt. James. If the pirates weren't in awe of what just took place, now they are thinking how are the Devil men able to create this light? It looks like these men can control the sun in the middle of the night. Pirate heads are bobbing in the dark water and now the pirates are in total fear they are confused, scared and mesmerized by what is happing to them. Lt. James survey's the sea area with no feelings or remorse for what they are about to do. If you have the enemy in your gun sites pull the trigger, they started this war and we're going to finish it. Lt. Darren James yells out his next order, "Mitchell fire away and every Navy Seal fires his weapon at the bobbing heads in the water. But they are not bobbing any more, BRRRRRRRRRRRR, BRRRRRRRR, BRRRRRRRR is the deadly sound the weapons are making as the pirates die and their blood covers the sea. Then silence floats across the water, Lt. James declares, "Davey Jones you have your hands full tonight, sleep well at the bottom of the sea you pirate bastards." "Hunter, move out you see the next enemy ship near the far horizon and he sees us as well so he knows that hell will be knocking on his door soon." orders Lt. James. Hunter is at the helm of the boat in a loud voice yells, "Thar be pirate blood in da water tonight Arrrr, High O' Pegasus, up, up and away." Hunter puts the boats throttle in full forward mode.

Capt. Bartholomew Threepwood of the pirates ship the Queen Ann's Revenge is looking back at the dark sea where Capt. Barbossa was sailing his ship the Sadie Rose just short a while ago. "Hell hath no fury like what ye just saw," declares Capt. Threepwood, "I never thought there could be such explosions an da sinking of da ship da Sadie Rose so fast, ye Devil men are from hell I knows it an me are afraid, Boswain, and commander of da guns get your cannons ready to fire on me order. You on da look out stay alive let me know if ye sees anything moving in da water towards me boat." Moments later the lookout spots a small black object moving across the water at speeds he never imagined. He was mesmerized by the speed and movements, cress crossing on the water, not having the best spy glasses he could not make out men in the black object so he just keeps on watching. Then he yells out, "I see me a small black object in ye yonder water, I don't know what it be but ye be ready." On board the Apex Pegasus boat Lt. James asks Jacob, "Tell me what you see?" Jacob responds, "I see two ships the one closest to us seems to be slowing down and turning broadside to us." "That means they have spotted us and are preparing to fight but we are still outside their cannon range," speaks up Bobby, "I also believe that Christopher is on the farthest ship away from us, this ship is willing to fight us so the other ship can sail away." Lt. James screams, "They will never get away from us never." Capt.Threepwood orders, "All guns fire on the starboard side." A broadside of iron cannon balls fall harmlessly into the ocean just making splashes 1,000 yards short of the Navy Seals boat. "Are they crazy to be firing like that into the sea so far away from us," asks Jacob, "They are letting us know the distance their weapons can fire." "Perhaps for another reason that is all they know, thinking that the cannonballs will scare us away, showing us their best fire power," answers Mitchell. Capt. Threepwood says, "Reload prepare to fire again I think we showed them our deadly fire power, they should turn away from us after we fire again, now fire give them our best deadly shot." Again the iron cannon balls fall into the sea so far away that the splash of the sea water didn't even reach the Navy Seals in the Apex boat.

"These so called bad ass pirate bastards have no idea how bad we really are and the hell and destruction we will bring to them in a few moments," says Lt. James, "Hunter we will approach and fire on this ship the same way we destroyed the first pirate ship tonight." "It is possible that they really can't see us and are firing their cannons wildly hoping to hit something," says Hunter, "The way I can maneuver our Apex boat no cannon fire can ever hit us with a direct hit." "I want those bastardly pirates to know our wrath and the death an chaos we will create by messing with us," declares Lt. James, "Our mission is to create tonight so much friggin death and destruction on the pirates they will gladly give Christopher back to us unharmed that is our mission. President Bush does not negotiate with Muslim terrorists and we don't negotiate with pirates." Capt. Threepwood hears his look out yell, "I don't see ye dark object perhaps dey turned away to leave da area." Capt. Threepwood yells back, "Keep ye sharp eye open anyway matte." Lt. James has ordered Hunter to go full speed to get in front of the ship and come at them at their bow. The pirate look out keeps looking towards the stern not at the bow thinking if they are around they would be coming at the stern behind the boat. Lt. James orders Mitchell to fire at the bow with two missiles at their water line now when they are less than 800 Yards away on his command. This will allow the sea to rush in faster as the ship is moving forward. "We are now at 800 yards away from the bow Mitchell take aim and fire." The first missile hits the bow perfectly and explodes, the second missile is fired both missiles create one hell of an explosion literally destroying the bow of the ship. The pirate ship larches forward then stops dead in the water. The Apex boat them moves to the port side and Jacob opens fire with the Mini gun the Gatling gun cutting the forward sail mast in half it falls with a sickening sound onto the deck and chaos reigns supreme. Then Jacob swings the Mini gun across the deck killing any pirate stupid enough to be looking over the side.

The pirates thought that they were prepared to fight but not in this life time did they ever expect a bow attack the pirates did not know what hit them. The pirate ship lost sight of the black object in the water some time ago. Lt. James tells Hunter, "Go to the starboard side now so Mitchell can fire three more missiles into the side really finishing her off. As Mitchell prepares to fire he sees pirates looking out of one of the gun port holes and he fires his first missile directly into the gun port exploding with such force it must have hit a powder magazine as well. Then Mitchell fires two more missiles at the water line on the starboard side the ship begins to tilt on its side causing a lot of the pirates to fall into the water. Jacob keeps firing the Mini gun creating a relentless barrage of bullets killing the pirates standing on the deck. The Queen's Ann's Revenge pirate ship slips below the waves joining Davey Jones at the bottom of the sea, she didn't want to go down but wanted to sail the Caribbean forever. Pirates are hanging onto anything that floats most have injuries some are still ok. The Apex boat moves in amongst the pirates and Lt. James yells out, "Is your captain still alive, I want to talk with him now?" Capt. Threepwood yells out, "I be ye captain." "Good now tell me where my man Christopher is?" yells Lt. James. "He be on yonder ship de Red Pearl that ship be in da far distance to the horizon." Lt. James orders Hunter to back out and light these bastard pirates up." Hunter slowly backs up and flips on the two 1,000,000 candle power lights they can now see all the pirates in the water and the sea of blood surrounding them. The Navy Seals open fire with their deadly weapons sending the rest of the rat bastard pirates to the bottom of the sea along with their ship. Hunter can barely see the other ship that has Christopher Kirk prisoner, than he takes a look at the fuel gage turns to Lt. James and proclaims, "Our fuel is too low to pursue the last ship, we have just enough fuel to get back to the governor's mansion, the last thing we need is to be stuck out here bobbing helplessly in the sea with no fuel. The cursing and swearing of the unrealized desire to pursue the last ship to rescue Chris can be heard throughout the sea of the Caribbean. They have to turn back towards the governor's mansion and fight the good fight another day.

Capt. Enrique Barbossa pulls his ship the Red Pearl into Port Royal Harbor, in the early morning of June 4th Wednesday with the precious cargo of Christopher Kirk (Devil Man) tied to the forward sailing mast of the ship. Capt. Barbossa is still reeling from what he witnessed at a distance the destruction and demise of the two ships the Sadie Rose and the Devils Servant in the dark full moon sky last night. The destruction was at the hands of the Devil men never before and hopefully never again will he have to do battle with the Devil men. The explosions were huge going high in the sky and so many of them what horrible kinds of weapons could the Devil men possess to create such horror on the water and in the midnight sky. The two ships were sunk is a short period of time, the worst part was hearing the screams of pain and suffering from the pirates so far across the water. The screams are still ringing in Capt. Barbossa's ears and all the pirates aboard his ship the concern can be seen on all of their faces of fear and dread never wanting to do battle with the Devil men in a boat that no one can see. The pirates untie

Christopher from his bindings from the sail mast but have learned their lesson to keep his hands and feet securely tied. They drag him across the deck and throw him in a row boat he is to be taken to stand judgement in the presence of Capt. John Wallace on his ship the Red Dragon anchored in Port Royal harbor 300 yards away. The pirates are taunting him telling him of the great pain he is about to suffer. Christopher Kirk is frightened but no pirate can detect his fear, he appears calm and acts as though he is enjoying the row boat ride.

The pirate row boat ties up beside the Red Dragon and Capt. John Wallace is watching them with a look of anger and hatred on his face sending a feeling of fear to everyone he is looking at. Capt. Wallace screams out, "Bring ye Devil Man to me cabin an let have ye sum fun, Arrrr.

Brethren of the Black Spot

The ten pirate captains that formed the Brethren of the Black Spot and sailed from their home port of Port Royal, Jamaica, what and who were they.

Capt. John Wallace aka Black Jack a man born in Wales, England in the year of 1639 standing 6' tall weighing in at 255 lbs. He has flaming red hair down to his shoulders with a large red mustache he has piercing blue eyes that could look right through a person not just at him. Capt. Wallace is a man with a quick unforgiving temper, willing and able to lash out at anyone that dare disagree with him. He was also able to lead men into battle showing no fear of anybody he was a pirate's, kind of pirate winning all of his battles and capturing large amounts of bounty and treasure making the pirates who sailed with him rich. Capt. John Wallace was very much feared by his crew and any man whom he confronted. Death and torture was always front and center he so love to hear men cry out in suffering pain. He was a brilliant tactician in battle and a great leader. The name of his ship is the Red Dragon; it is a Square-Rigger with a crew of 210.

Capt. Benjamin Steenwinkel a man born in Wales, England in the year of 1652 standing 5'6" tall weighing in at 290 lbs. with light brown hair usually kept in a ponytail, clean shaven with brown beady eyes. He is not very good looking, his face is pocked marked and has very bad breath and teeth, six of his front teeth are missing from gum disease and fights. Capt. Steenwinkel was lucky in that he never lost a battle and he had been voted to his leadership role for the past five years. He is the type of man who liked to torture his prisoners and delighted in their cries of pain and fear. He was a weasel of a man that no one trusted or liked very much so his men would stay away from confronting him. The name of his ship is the Devils Servant the type of a ship; it's a sloop with a crew of 87 men.

Capt. Raymond Grandstaff a man born in the Bahamas in the year of 1658, standing 5'7" tall and weighing is at 195 lbs. with blond hair that he kept long just below his ears which were rather large clean shaven with green eyes. A handsome man by any mark of a man who always dressed in colored silks and loved to wear a large hat. This captain was a good captain to his men and was well liked, a fearless leader taking the lead to be the first to board any ship in battle and a fair man to his crew. Although Capt. Grandstaff did have a cold and disconnected attitude from any feeling towards any men unlucky enough to be captured by him. The name of his ship is; the Mary Margaret the type of ship is a Schooner with a crew of 78.

Capt. Bartholomew Threepwood a man born in the North of England in the year of 1646, standing 5'2" tall weighing in at 130 lbs. with dark brown hair cut short on his head with a goatee for a beard he was an ugly short man. He was mean to the bone and hated all men that were taller than he was which meant his entire crew. No one understands why he has been voted to be captain of his ship for over 11 years, perhaps because he also had no fear of any enemy in battle and was always the first to step foot on the enemy's deck. A Capt. That did give 100% of himself and believed in taking good care of his crew even though they were taller than he was. The name of his ship is; Queen Ann's Revenge the type of ship is a sloop with a crew of 82.

Capt. Enrique Barbossa a man born in Spain in the year of 1651 standing 5'9" and weighing in at 200 lbs. with jet black hair falling to his shoulders, with eyes the color of coal. He was a striking man, good looking at one time but not since his last battle, he now wears a large black patch where his right eye used to be covering a gaping hole on his face with a large scar coming between his eyes down his nose across his lips, disfiguring his lips in a permanent sad grin stopping at his chin. Capt. Barbossa has sworn revenge to any merchant ship that he sees in the Caribbean. His battle plan is to create havoc and chaos to any merchant seaman that he captures. His men have sworn complete loyalty to him and will fight to the death for Capt. Barbossa's revenge. The name of his ship is; the Black Pearl, the type of ship is a Brigantine with a crew of 126 men.

Capt. Caesar Demantie a man born in Italy of royal blood in the year of 1664 standing 5'8" and weighing in at 175 lbs. black curly hair and wavy not short not real long either, eyes were a sea blue green. Capt. Demantie was a very unique captain to say the least, more interested in chasing the ladies, lasses and the prostitutes in Port Royal and many other ports of call they dropped anchor in then chasing merchant ships. Capt. Demantie was all for fun and fun for all his pirate crew was not rich but they had a lot of fun and good times. It was very important that a large supply of medicine was kept on board to treat venereal disease. The rum, beer, grog flowed on his ship 24/7 and they got plenty of prostitutes willing to sail with them on their voyages. The last thing Capt. Demantie wanted to do was to harm others, when he would go to battle he would use deception and fear, get the bounty and the treasure and any medicine they could find but leave every merchant standing without harm. Merchant seamen have been known to wave him good fortune when he sailed away. The name of his ship is; the Italian Stallion the type of ship is a schooner with a crew of 88.

Capt. Bellamy McVaine a man born in Scotland in the year of 1666 a very large behemoth of a man standing 6'5" tall weighs in at 366 lbs. of mussel and bone. He was a man the pirates knew well, a genital man to his friends and crew as long as they did as they were told. He sported a full black and gray beard and long hair as though it were a flag of honor his trade mark. He had a patch over his left eye and a jagged battle scar from his left eye down his cheek, his right eye was the color black that could scare the living hell out of any man who dare look him in that eye. His birth date was a perfect fit to his life, that marked him as the devil's own child all of his life, and he relished that role. He was the most fearsome of all the pirates he would rather be in a battle then in a tavern, fighting and killing was what he believed he was born to do. His pirate crew never gave him one bit of trouble or complained about anything his orders were law, when Capt. McVaine was happy every pirate was happy too. The name of his ship is; the Anne Bonney the type of a ship was a Square-Rigger with a crew of 212.

Capt. Guy Percy a man born in Ireland in the year of 1661 a slim man standing 5'6" tall weighing in at 158 lbs. with bad teeth in fact he only had ten teeth left that he was born with. He spoke with a lisp and would have the Quarter Master speak for him when he wanted orders given to his crew. He lost his left leg below the knee from a sword battle and walked on a peg for a leg for the last 9 years. Even though he may have looked and appeared harmless he really wasn't. Like most pirates he was as evil as they came and his crew feared his wrath when he got mad. A cunning hunter of merchant ships at sea he knew how to bring a merchant ship to surrender without getting any of his own men harmed in battle, that is the primary reason he was voted to be captain of his ship for the last 10 years. The name of his ship is; the Sadie Rose the type of ship is a Brigantine with a crew of 101.

Capt. Hector Browerman a man born in Jamaica in the year of 1651 a man of mixed decent his mother was a black house slave his father a Spanish land owner and sugar producer. He was an average man standing 5'9" tall weighing in at 155 lbs. with a darker skin then most pirates but never the less he was well respected by everyone he ever came in contact with. A man of daring courage in battle he has been voted in as captain for the last 8 years without one dissenting vote. He gave no quarter and took no quarter, a man totally devoid of compassion to those merchant seaman he captured in battle. Capt. Browerman was sought after for his advice and console by other pirate captains on just about any problem. The name of his ship is; the Half Moon the type of ship is a Brigantine with a crew of 102.

Capt. Maury Tweemain a man born in France in the year 1650 a man of many interests and stands 6' tall weighing in at 230 lbs. a good sized man but missing his left arm that was blown off at the elbow by a cannon ball. This fact has a lot to do with his attitude towards taking revenge on merchant ships and seaman unlucky enough to be in his sights. When he would order an attack he would have the head of a past enemy tied to a bow sprint as it dangled in the air it struck absolute panic in merchant ships. A ruthless captain but fair on his judgement calls with his own crew. One of his many interests was to design and sew clothing for his men a rather odd interest considering he was so ruthless. It seemed as though he could smell a merchant ship even over the horizon and he was more right then wrong. The name of his ship is; the Demon Dog the type of ship is a Square-Rigger with a crew of 199 men.

The pirates drag Christopher not letting him walk to Capt. Wallace's cabin just to humiliate him and cause him more intense pain. Chris is placed in a chair no one speaks to him just yet by orders of Capt. Wallace until three more pirate captains arrive they are just staring at him with evil eyes to intimidate him. Their thinking is somewhat not ready for prime time any longer they think they are scaring him to freely talk when he's told to. There are now a total of six pirate captains in the cabin anxious to hear what they will learn from the Devil man and what his tale is. Capt. Wallace speaks up, "Tell me first of Capt. Guy Percy and his ship the Sadie Rose and Capt. Bartholomew and his ship Queen Ann's Revenge for me sent three ships to capture this Devil man, Capt. Barbossa where are they do tell of ye adventure." Capt. Barbossa with fear in his voice says, "We landed 20 men from two row boats, four men joined the grand party all dressed up but we never saw them again perhaps they were captured ye don't know. The rest of de men hid out along da shore line to capture one or more Devil men as da walked along the sea shore. Then one of the Devil men was walking with a beautiful wench holding hands I instructed six of me men to surround them cutting them off from any escape to go back to the grand party at de governor's house." "Dat be good thinking and planning go on." says Capt. Wallace. "Den we showed ourselves and told da Devil man to surrender, he had a pistol under his shirt and opened fire on the six pirate's closet to the mansion killing three of dem and den wounding two in da back, his gun never run out of bullets. Den da wench runs back to da party at da mansion for help, den she turn and kicks me man in him balls she be now screaming for help and da mansion guards hear her and start to help da wench. Me an me men rushed the Devil man he fires him gun and kills three more of me men we get him on da ground but he fights like a mad lion and takes him knife and stabs one man in da belly the other man in the eye they both die, and he kicks another of me men an breaks him leg. Finely we were able to knock him out and tie him up and get him on a row boat to me ship.

Capt. Wallace is starting to show his anger and disappointment at what he thought was the cowardly actions of the pirates, one Devil man killed and injured so many pirates. Was he such a fierce fighter or were the pirates such poor fighters or were the pirates acting in a cowardly way? Whatever the reasoning Capt. Wallace was not pleased and he showed it by the scowl on his face and the anger in his eyes at Capt. Barbossa, Capt. Barbossa could tell that he could be in a lot of trouble. "Continue wit ye tale," said Capt. Wallace, "Continue by telling ye how heroic you be an der men of the other two ships were in battle." Capt. Barbossa knew how heroic he was and what happened to the two ships and his fear of the truth made him petrified, but he decided to tell a true tale, because Capt. Wallace had his way of finding out what the truth would be, if ye lie ye die. Capt. Barbossa continues, "We three ships be sailing away wit da Devil man, me ship and Capt. Threepwood ship were further out to sea. Capt. Percy was lagging behind, him ship not as fast as ours or he couldn't catch the wind just right. I knew dat to accomplish de mission we was to bring back at least one Devil man." "Ye bet ye sweet ass, ye best return wit a Devil man," said Capt. Wallace, "Go on, go on I not a stopping ye tale." Capt. Barbossa is very nervous but continues, "Den out of da dark night wit a full moon I see as well as me men see

Capt. Percy's ship the Sadie Rose explode alike we nares seen before, big explosions high into da sky dat's all me see. Capt. Threepwood and me keep sailing as fast as we can now we be far from the Sadie Rose. Me men an me look back at the Queen Ann's Revenge and me see da same ting a happing, explosion after explosion but we see no udder boat with the Devil men just Capt. Threepwood's ship sinking just like the Sadie Rose, dem me sail extra fast until we reach the harbor of Port Royal dat be da truth." explains Capt. Barbossa. With a look of real fear and trepidation on his face as his hands are shaking uncontrollably he tells his story.

Capt. Wallace looks real hard at Christopher (Devil man) to see if he can see any fear in his face, no fear is registered on Christopher's face and that really pisses the pirate captains off. Capt. Wallace gives an order, "Raise da anchor, lower de sails we is taking a short voyage to sea." The ship the Red Dragon leaves the safety of Port Royal heading out to sea until the ship reaches 8 miles from land, then the orders are given to lower the sails and just float at sea. Now Capt. Wallace grabs Chris by his throat raising him off the chair and is starting to choke the life out of him, then he slams him back in the chair. Capt. Wallace is red faced from rage and puts his face up against Chris's face and begins to scream, "Ye tell me what's me wants to know; ye tell me from where ye came, why ye is here, an the powerful weapons that ye possess, I will not keep a asking ye before I bring terrible pain and punishment to ye. Chris sits up straight in the chair and looks Capt. Wallace in the eye and begins to speak, "May I please have a drink of water before I begin? I will tell you the truth we have nothing to hide but I don't believe you can handle the truth so here goes nothing. We are United States Navy Seals trained in war fare the best trained specials forces in our entire military our country is called America it is way to the north of your island. We were sent to Jamaica to rescue some of our people that were kidnapped by very bad men. Then for some unexplained reason we found ourselves back in your time over 300 years from our time of 2006 that is the truth." Capt. Wallace looks very puzzled and turns to the other captains and asks, "Do ye know from what ye be talking about?" Every pirate in the cabin shrugs his shoulders and has a puzzled look on their faces. Christopher speaks up, "Take a look at my pistol it is like no other pistol you have ever seen it is from 300 years in the future."

Capt. Wallace turns to Capt. Barbossa and says, "Where ye Devil man pistol be?" Capt. Barbossa answers, "Me don't know, it must have fallen in da sand and we didn't pick it up." Capt. Wallace is now madder than he has ever been because he should be holding the Devil man's gun in his hand. Capt. Wallace is so damn mad he is ready to kill someone especially Capt. Barbossa for his incompetence. He turns back to Chris and if looks could kill Chris would be dead right now. Capt. Wallace declares in a mad as hell voice, "Me don't know what ye say Devil man none of me captains know what ye say, no one understands ye, ye talk gibberish now I bring pain to ye then ye will say something me will believe or ye will surly die. You Devil man will go to ye watery grave and be sleeping with Davey Jones before the sun sets if ye don't speak da truth Arrrrr." Chris speaks up, "I told you that you couldn't handle the truth but I will try again to tell you my story." Christopher is well aware of his predicament that the pirates could never believe his story because the story is even hard for Chris to believe. The pirate's minds are not able to grasp time travel it is beyond their imagination, education and understanding in the year 1692. Christopher internalizes that he is about to die and is preparing himself for death the only thing that could save him is his buddies showing up right now.

Christopher Kirk begins again to try best he can to convince the pirates of his crazy unbelievable journey, "I already told you we come from the United States of America the year in our time is 2006 the year right now in Jamaica is 1692. Somehow we traveled through a portal of time I really don't understand it either but here I am. There is what is referred to as a body of water called the Devil's Triangle in the ocean although Jamaica is far below the Devils Triangle but strange very strange things happen there. Unexplained things happen there all the time most people believe in the unexplainable but I never did until a few days ago. But I have to believe what is taking place in your time I know this is not just a dream, before I continue will you tell me why do you call us Devil men?" Capt. Wallace speaks up, "Ye are called Devil men because ye are when I first saw ye, ye faces were painted black, green and blue and ye were wearing da weirdest clothing me ever see an ye walked and talked odd. Then ye used weapons we never see before dat killed so many of me men and wounded more, me was wounded in me shoulder and the doctor tells me I may lose me arm, you must come from hell so we call ye the Devil men." "Well according to your understanding of us you're not far off we do bring hell when we fight you already found that out. Shall I continue?" All the pirates are now mesmerized by Christopher's story even Capt. Wallace, and can't wait to hear more tales and stories they all yell out for the Devil man to tell them more and orders a large glass of water to be served to Chris.

Chris speaks again, "Ok I will tell you all this we have so many, many amazing things in our time that I know it will be impossible for you to understand. We have electric lights our cities are lit up like daylight even at night and even our homes and our buildings. We have a city called New York where the buildings are very tall one is 1,000 feet tall your buildings are barley 40' tall they are very small. We have sailing ships that can carry thousands of people at one time that are hundreds times bigger than your biggest ship they do not use sails but are powered by large engines. We have airplanes, objects that fly in the sky with hundreds of people on board. We can cross the oceans from Jamaica to England in a matter of 8 hours flying through the air. Our cities do not stink of raw sewage like Port Royal does. We have so much more then you could ever imagine in the future. One very important thing that my country did is we sent a spaceship to the moon and we have had men walk on the moon in 1969. We are Navy Seals the roughest, toughest, meanest and best well prepared bunch of sons of a bitchen fighting men in the world and if you want to live you had better let me go back to my men. You have already witnessed our wrath and our destruction power if you harm me, may God have mercy on your souls because the Navy Seals will not, you all will be sent to hell." All the pirates are sitting, standing or leaning against bulkheads and posts with their mouths wide open in amazement at what Christopher was saying.

Capt. John Wallace yells at the top of his voice, "Here ye hear ye no more bull crap, no more crazy talk this is a story made up from this man's crazy mind, no man can walk on da moon dat be crazy talk. He be a witch man from hell the devil's own who can cast spells on ye all." That seemed to bring them out of their stupor of listing to the wild and crazy stories told by a Devil man now back to reality. Hang him, hang the Devil man until he be dead that be the pirates cry for justice and revenge. Capt. Wallace yells out, "You Devil man have chosen to tell me lies not da truth, I told ye that ye would feel ye pirates pain and revenge for what ye have done, do ye know what keelhauling be?" Chris answers, "No I do not." "Ye will soon know very soon, men the Devil man knows not wat keelhauling be, do we have any volunteers to show him what it be?" asks Capt. Wallace.

All the pirates standing around their faces turn white from fright that they be chosen they all looked the other way trying to hide the fear in their faces. They know what keelhauling is it is a punishment worse than death itself and most men die from the experience as well. A man is dragged with a rope tied to his feet and hands beneath the ship, exposing his flesh to the causations of sea life that have built up over the years on the bottom of the ship. The causations are thick mollusks and barnacles that are razor sharp that will cut into a man's flesh making cuts and sores that most times take years to heal. The body disfigurement to a man's flesh is hideous he is never the same again. Most times the causations are from 6" to 9" sometimes more built up on the bottom of the ship. Capt. Wallace shouts out, "I don't hear ye; I don't hear ye volunteering to be keelhauled today so I will pick me a man. A man who would rather run then fights who is incompetent in his duties. I choose a man that has disgraced the good name of the Brethren of the Black Spot a man in my opinion that deserves this punishment Capt. Enrique Barbossa will be keelhauled first, to show the Devil man what it is all about. Shouts of joy ring out on the ship from the pirates knowing that they were not chosen, oh what a relief it is not to be chosen. "Strip off him shirt dem his pants now tie the rope to him hands and to him feet. Now ye men knows what to do throws him over board, raise the sails so we move forward and drag him from the bow to the stern of me ship. Capt. Barbossa is screaming and crying out loud for mercy reminding them he is a captain in good standing this is not fair not right at all. But his pleas go unanswered because a pirate knows if he would say anything he would either be taking his place or be keelhauled next.

Capt. Barbossa is tossed over the bow and men position themselves on the port and starboard sides of the ship pulling him from the bow to the stern. They are dragging his exposed body and flesh to the underside of the ship cutting into his back, arms chest, face, and whatever is exposed as he twists and turns under the ship. He pops out from the bottom of the ship at the stern as his head breaks the water he is not recognizable to anyone. His blood is coming from the holes in his body and head where his right eye and nose used to be and his right ear is missing as well. Capt. Barbossa is pulled up onto the deck of the ship even the most hardened pirates pull back and cringe at the gruesome sight of what used to be a whole man, some men even throw up. His skin on his back is cut so deeply that his ribs show threw as well as the ribs in his chest. His arms and legs are bloody stubs of what they used to be. Capt. Wallace shouts out his order, "Salt him down, so ye pain increases then throw him in da hold where the rats be living, check on him in the morning if he lives so be it, if he be dead throw him body overboard.

Capt. Wallace turns to Christopher with an exceptional evil smile, rubbing his hands together and says, "Devil man now ye knows what keelhauling be, take a good look at Capt. Barbossa as he lays before ye on de deck, now it be ye turn to be keelhauled, men prepare him, tie his hands and legs together. Revenge be mine Arrrr, for the pirates you and your Devil men have killed. Do ye have any last words?" Christopher looks up from the deck as he is prone on the deck with his legs and arms tied together as says, "You and all your miserable pirates of the Brethren of the Black Spot are domed to die at the hands of my buddies the Navy Seals in a day or two. Davey Jones is getting a welcoming party together ready to welcome all you fucken sadistic bastards." "Throw him overboard let da keelhauling begin," screams Capt. Wallace. Then a terrible splash is heard as Chris is thrown into the sea at the bow of the ship and the pirates are pulling on the ropes on the port and starboard walking back towards the stern singing songs all the way. The time takes about 6 minutes and then Christopher pops up at the stern, his face is a terrible mess his nose is missing as well as his left ear and the sea around him is a bloody mess. He is pulled upon the deck and again the hardened pirates pull back at the gruesome sight as nine pirates throw up over the side. His body skin is hanging from his appendages and his right hand is hanging from his arm by a single bone, Christopher is still conscious but says nothing. Capt. Wallace is gleeful at what he sees and says, "Good work men ye keelhauled the Devil man real good, now salt him down an tie him to da forward sail mast. So we can hear him when he cries out in pain and when we return to port and let everyone see the Devil man tied to da mast. Dis will let everyone know why to fear the Brethren of the Black Spot as we rule the seas. As the pirate ship the Red Dragon pulls into port clearing the harbor of Port Royal in the early afternoon pirates and seaman from other ships alike are shocked at what they see, the cruelty on display of Capt. Wallace's barbarism is now etched in everyone's mind forever.

Capt. Wallace makes an announcement, "We go to town to da Catt & Fiddle to celebrate our fine day's work to have drinks and food. All the captains and a lot of pirate crews head into town to celebrate, singing songs of battle and war songs, proud of keelhauling two men today, getting what they deserved. As the pirates gather in the tavern sitting at long wooden tables drinking and eating and celebrating, Capt. McVaine leans on the table and asks Capt. Wallace, "What is to become of the Devil man? Let's make some bounty wit him." "Now that be good thinking, what do ye have in mind ARRRRRRR?" asks Capt. Wallace. "We send a messenger to da governor's mansion demanding a large ransom be 200 lbs. of gold in return for da Devil man. The other Devil men can meet us at sea tonight one mile off the Jamaican Point a well-known place. Then we spring our trap with all of our Brethren of the Black Spot be there out at sea and we capture and kill the Devil men and take their weapons, explains Capt. McVaine. "Now dat be a great plan me like it, you pirate take dis note to da governor's mansion give it to da governor and steal a fast horse ride fast go now, says Capt. Wallace. All the pirates are gathering close at the wooden table to make their plans of killing da Devil Men tonight.

They order more and more rounds of grog, rum and beer and make their plans as Christopher is baking in the hot afternoon sun tied to the forward mast after he was keelhauled.

End of chapter 4

CHAPTER 5

When the Navy Seals arrived back at the dock of the governor's mansion after their night of mayhem, death and destruction of the two pirate ships, Hunter checks the gas gage and discovers there is less than five gallons of fuel left in the tank. All the Navy Seals wonder now what will they be able to do to get Christopher back. Everyone is so tired and it is now early morning about 4:00 A.M. they all head for their bed to rest and prepare for tomorrow. Lt. Darren James is just falling off to sleep from the night of death and mayhem they gave to the pirates. He turns on his right side opening one eye at a time and there is Lilliannah lying beside him with nothing on but a smile, touching him with tender loving care on his face she says to Lt. James, "I love you with all my heart, you are the most important man in my life, I have never met anyone like you before; strong, intelligent, brave, loving and handsome." Lt. James loves what he is hearing as he fell in love with Lilliannah the first time he saw the picture of the two of them on the museum wall in Jamaica what now seems like a life time ago. Lt. James whispers, "I love you with all my heart for I have never met anyone in my life like you before." Lt. James places his hand to the back of Lillianna head bringing her lips to his for what was a hard, long and passionate deep kiss. Now they move into position to make love in the early morning light.

Carol Kay is also mesmerized by Jacob, but is not as bold at showing her feelings for him; she waits outside of his door hoping he will wake up soon and join her for a walk along the sea shore. The time is about 1:30

P.M. on Wednesday the tired seals are just beginning to stir and wake up and to get out of bed to face a new day. The servants have been cleaning up the party mess from last night since early morning. They find four rather strange men asleep on the grass under the trees in the garden. The servants wake them up and tell them to get going leave the property before they are arrested by the mansion guards. They start to walk but their legs are like jello because they are still somewhat drunk and have not rested all that well on the grass, they are escorted off the property by the governor's guards and sent on their way. Governor Beeston has been sitting at his desk he has been sitting at his desk since the sun rose in the early morning sky, pondering the problem of the potential earth quake that is supposed to take place on Saturday at 11:45 A.M. how to possibly warn more people of this impending doom. Mitchell walks into the study and notices the governor at his desk and says, "Good afternoon governor." "Good afternoon to you Mitchell, please come here sit by my desk I need to talk with you about that possible earthquake." You seem distraught governor how may I help?" asks Mitchell. "Again please tell me if you could be wrong about the earthquake, is it possible that it may not happen?" asks the governor. "No I am very sorry it is written in all the history books that I have studied, perhaps that is why I am here in your time to warn the people of Port Royal," responds Mitchell, "To save as many lives as I possibly can from this impending doom. I need you to believe me when I say we are from another time, you have seen and experienced the evidence of our boat and our weapons what more do you need?" "I know you're right and I do believe as hard as it is but to get my mind around such a thing as a major earthquake is not easy to do," explains the governor. Mitchell says, "I do understand if you can think of anything that we can do to help in anyway please don't hesitate to ask."

Jacob comes walking into the study with Carol Kay at his side holding hands. He thinks that Carol Kay is a beautiful lady and being friends with her can have its friendly rewards with benefits. But his mind is still occupied at what happened last night and desperately wants to talk about it with the other seals. Then Hunter enters the study and sees the governor sitting at his desk approaches and asks, "Governor can you please tell me what is the alcohol content of your rum?" "We make two kinds of rums one for the ladies and the girly men at only 98 proof the other rum is made for real men at 180 proof, why do you ask?" asks the governor. "How much of the 180 proof rum do you have on hand?" asks Hunter. "Well I really don't exactly know, perhaps a number of barrels at 50 gallons each, would you like to go to the cellar with me and see?" asks the governor. "Let's go you may have just solved a major problem for us," says Hunter with an excited sound in his voice. The two men enter the cellar and Hunter can see there are a lot of 180 proof rum barrels on hand perhaps 300 gallons or more. Hunter speaks up," Governor may we use about 100 gallons of your rum to see if it works to fuel our boat?" The governor says, "By all means if it will work I am happy to assist you." Hunter takes two buckets holding 6 gallons each and walks briskly to the Apex Pegasus boat hoping and praying that what he is thinking will work. Is it possible that this rum could be our new fuel he was told that the specially developed jet engines would run on a number of different kinds of fuels?

The Navy Seals that were in the study follow Hunter down to the boat dock very interested in what his is doing. They are confused what in the world he is doing with two buckets of rum of 6 gallons each. They are all aware that the Apex boat was out of fuel and they were screwed, perhaps never to get Chris back again. Hunter proceeds to pour the 12 gallons of rum into the gas tank to the utter amazement of the seals standing by questioning has he lost his mind? Hunter turns to everyone on the dock and says, "You all cross your fingers." Then Hunter steps onto the boat and waits for about five minutes for the new fuel to register on the gas gage then he takes out his key inserts it and turns the key the jet engines come to life the Navy Seals are dumbfounded but so very happy. Hunter speaks in a loud voice, "Still keep your fingers crossed because the engines are still performing with the gas that was in the fuel line, and give me another ten minutes of running to see if the engines continues to run or sputters to a stop because of the rum." All the seals are now watching their watches; five minutes, now seven minutes, now ten minutes and the engines are still running smoothly. The seals are all ecstatic with joy and very pleased the jet engines are still running. Mitchell says, "You son of a gun how did you arrive at your decision to use rum as a fuel?" Hunter responds, "Well I remembered what the engineer at the base told me about these fantastic newly developed jet engines. He was so proud of the fact this new jet engine technology was other fuel friendly and would operate on any liquid that would burn. Alcohol with a high proof rating of over 125 proof will burn so I had nothing to lose but everything to gain to use rum as our new fuel it is 180 proof. All the Navy Seals shook his hand and patted Hunter on his back they were so happy telling him he was a genius. Hunter says, "I'm still not satisfied until I take her out for a trial run to see how she performs on the open sea. So if you will I need at least another 24 gallons of the high grade rum will you guys please get it for me." Everyone lends a helping hand for the little amount needed for the trial run. Then Lt. James joins them at the dock and asks, "What in the hell are you guys doing?" The seals all smile and Jacob explains "Were refueling the Apex Pegasus boat Hunter figured out what could be the new fuel to make her go."

Then Lt. James literally jumps for joy knowing they are back in action again. Hunter yells out, "Everyone on board who's going on board, buckle up we're going for a test run." The Navy Seals all climb aboard even Lilliannah, Cassandra and Carol Kay step aboard for the test run. Hunter pushes the throttle forward just a little to see the Apex's reaction to the forward movement, fine so far then a little more and a little more until the boat is speeding along at 50 knots on the smooth blue green ocean of the Caribbean. Hunter shouts again for joy his shouts could be heard back at the governor's mansion what a fantastic performance the new fuel, rum is. The Navy Seals are all stoked, now they can continue their search for Christopher and then possibly search for that mysterious fog bank in the ocean if it ever might exist again. When the Apex Pegasus boat returns to the dock they can see the governor standing on the dock with a worried look on his face. He says nothing but presents the note to Lt. James that was just delivered. Lt James shouts for joy, "Christopher is still alive but the pirates want 200 lbs. of gold for his return. We are to meet the pirates at midnight at the Jamaican Point were the exchange will take place. Do you know where the Jamaican Point is governor?" "Yes I sure do I'll show you on a map in my office follow me," says the governor. The Navy Seals are studying the map they can see a flaw in the pirates planning. There is a tall point of land jetting out into the ocean and a coastal inlet behind the tall land point. The pirate boats will be less than one mile away still in range of their sniper rifle and scope to see what is going on. What they see is a perfect hiding place for a pirate ship or two to hide in the coastal inlet a perfect place for an ambush. Lt. Darren James speaks up, "We will not be bringing any gold but we will bring hell and destruction to the pirates and then rescue Christopher in return to save the pirate ships that are left from sinking. Bobby Harold speaks up, "Those ignorant pirates have no idea how to defeat us and what we are all about and how much hell we will bring to the party tonight. Before morning there will be a lot of pirates swimming with Davey Jones at the bottom of the sea.

All the pirate captains of the Brethren of the Black Spot are gathered at the Catt & Fiddle Tavern they are planning what they believe to be the demise of the Devil men and the capturing of their weapons. One basic but very important rule of war that they should have remembered but didn't is; drinking rum and grog and beer all day puts the best battle plans in jeopardy. The basic plan is to have three ships at anchor at the meeting place less than one mile out from the Jamaican Point, two ships will be able to hide close to shore where they can't be seen in the coastal inlet and the last three ships will be just out of sight near the horizon. Everyone will be watching out for any sign of that little boat and when they see it and the gold has been exchanged and the signal is given all eight pirate ships will converge and attack with full force with all cannons blasting away. They believe in their drunken stupor that the eight pirate ships with cannons firing no little boat can survive that kind of fire power and before the little boat is eventually sunk the Devil men will surrender their weapons to save their lives, but then they will all be killed. Capt. John Wallace with his ship the Red Dragon, Capt. Benjamin Steenwinkel with his ship the Devils Servant and Capt. Raymond Grandstaff with his ship the Mary Margaret will be the three ships at anchor slightly less than 1 mile off the Jamaican Point with the Devil man Christopher tied to the mast of the Red Dragon if he is still alive. The plan is that the Devil men in their little boat will give up the gold to the Red Dragon first then the signal will be given for all the pirate ships will sail in firing their cannons and the Devil men will be so scared that they will surrender to all of the pirates fire power. Never before has so much pirate fire power ever been used to capture such a little boat with only five men aboard. Little do the pirates realize who and what they are fighting but they will soon learn the fighting tactics of the Navy Seals.

Capt. Hector Browerman with his ship the Half Moon and Capt. Maury Tweemain of the ship the Demon Dog will be hidden in the shadows of the coastal inlet will be poised to attack. Capt. Caesar Demantie of the ship the Italian Stallion, Capt. Bellamy McVaine with his ship the Anne Bonney and the ship the Black Pearl with its temporary captain Juan Lopez McGill will be about five miles away at the edge of the horizon. All told the complete complement of men will be over 750 vicious blood thirsty pirates firing more than 76 cannons some with 10 pounder cannon balls and then all the pirates with their blunderbuss pistols and cutlass swords on a mission of revenge to kill just five men in a little boat. They believe that the Devil men have no chance in hell of winning tonight against such a vicious over whelming force of mean bad ass pirates. Another big mistake they made was staying a little longer drinking more rum, beer and grog and celebrating their victory before the battle even began. A lot of the pirates who were not directly involved with the battle plans but were at the Catt & Fiddle Tavern were celebrating just the same and having a damn good time. They were all spending their coins on lap dances with the prostitutes and watching the wenches doing there wood pole dances indifferent stages of undress. Some of these so called women of the night were; so ugly that they would have scared Dracula away, over weight by a lot, they never ever thought about shaving anything, teeth were missing, they had very bad personal hygiene, the stench was awful, clothing was hardly ever washed and the worst thing of all the wenches chewed tobacco and spit any Damn place they wanted to. (Bill Clinton, would have been right in the middle enjoying himself) These are just some of the reasons what made Port Royal, Jamaica the wickedest city in the world, in 1692. Loose women plenty of drink, gold, silver and precious jewels were all about and there were a lot of places for the pirates to sell any of their booty. A pirate could get just about anything he wanted and desired. Plus the location was perfect to attack merchant ships in the Caribbean islands from.

The meeting over the battle plans set and agreed on the pirates headed back aboard their own ships, it is now early evening about 7:00 P.M. the sun is about to set by 8:00 P.M. Upon arriving at his ship Capt. Wallace went right up to Christopher who was left out in the hot day's sun to bake after the horrible punishment he received, he discovered that Christopher was dead; he died a horrible, agonizing death not making a sound that no man should endure. Capt. Wallace smiling looked Chris in the face and said, "See what ye get messing wit a pirate ye get ye dead ye do." The odor was given to leave Chris's body tied to the main mast for all to see but prop him up so he looks alive, so the Devil men later tonight will think he is still alive at least until the ransom is paid, then the captain laughs out loud. The Navy Seals know that this will most likely be the last battle with the pirates because of the impending earthquake that will change Port Royal and its harbor forever. The Navy Seals have spent the rest of the day checking and cleaning their weapons and making sure the Apex Pegasus boat is cleaned, gas tank topped off with rum and ready to go into another battle that will take place at midnight tonight. But right this minute Lt. James and Lilliannah are walking in the garden holding hands and holding onto each other. Concerned that battles cause injury and death they are praying to God that no harm comes to any Navy Seal and they get Christopher back safe.

The dinner bell is ringing calling all those interested in another fantastic supper of chicken marinated in a white wine sauce all day with a verity of hot peppers and fresh vegetables straight from the garden and a special Spanish rice dish to die for, please come to the dining room. As the five Navy Seals along with the three ladies and the governor find their places at the table a since of dread and fear fills the room for what is to come tonight. Lt. Darren James stands and lifts his glass of wine and proclaims, "Good people of Jamaica we thank you from the bottom of our hearts for your wonderful hospitality and the opportunity to become your friends. Please do not fret for our safety tonight, we are prepared and well trained to engage in battle with these pirates, to take care of business and win and bring Christopher back safe. So let's have a happy fantastic Jamaican supper filled with joy and laughter." With that said the gloom in the room dissipates and everyone begins to enjoy the supper experience together. Lilliannah sitting next to Lt. James places her hand on his right thigh giving it a slight squeeze along with a loving fantastic smile of things to come later after dinner. The governor is still contemplating the events to come for his island and his people that he loves on Saturday. Bobby Harold notices that the governor is in deep thought and says, "Tomorrow I will volunteer to go into town along with a couple of your guards that know the way and the town and the people I need to talk with to warn them of the earthquake. The governor's eyes light up and a smile appears on his face and he says, "That is a great idea thank you for your service I am sure that will save a lot of precious lives. Now gentlemen please step into my study and we will really study the map as to where you will meet the pirates tonight." The governor and the seals gather round a large round table and the large map is laid out. The governor explains, "Here on the map is your present position and where you will meet up with the pirates to make the exchange less than a mile from the Jamaican Point. Gentlemen look closely at the terrain and the shore line, you will see two inlets where ships can hide with a shallow draft and ambush you unexpectedly. What you need to know is the area and be prepared for anything those damn pirates may do, their words are no good."

With that the governor leaves the Navy Seals alone to make their battle plans knowing he has done want he can. The Navy Seals are really studying the map figuring out the best plan of attack to surprise the damn pirates with shock and awe to kill as many as they can and get Christopher back. Lt. James speaks, "Surprise shock and awe is what we do best the three pirate ships that will gather as this spot on the map one of the ships will have Chris on it I'll bet that Capt. Wallace will have him on his ship the Red Dragon. Here look at this point of land it looks to be about 200 feet high a perfect place to see the whole area from. I want Mitchell at the top with your night vision binocular glasses and your communicator to let us know what is happening along with the 50 caliber sniper rifle. From that advantage you should be able to spot Chris letting us know if he is all right. We do not know how many pirate ships will be on hand but you can bet on a lot more than three. This inlet behind the high point of land looks like the perfect place to spring their trap on us but we will be ready. I believe we need to leave now a few hours early to get into position and become familiar with the area. We need to win this one for Christopher what say you." "We all agree let's get to the dance," shouts Bobby Harold. The seals leave the study believing they have made very good battle plans and Lilliannah is waiting for Lt. James and she says, "Let's go to your room and make love honey." Lt. James responds, "That will have to wait for another time my love, right now were getting ready to leave for the battle with the pirates and to get Chris back." Lilliannah is not happy with his answer but she understands and wonders when the war with the pirates will end. "Walk with me to the dock my love to say goodbye and wish us all God speed in our mission," says Darren. The governor and the other two ladies join the seals on the dock as well Carol Kay gives Jacob a long and loving kiss. "I love you with all my heart," says Lilliannah and Darren reasons, "I love you with all my heart see you soon." The Navy Seals are strapped in ready for battle with the pirates again. The weapons are all locked and loaded their faces are painted battle ready black, green and blue with their Dragon Armor Vests on over their battle dress fatigues they now all looked like Devil men from hell and that is what they will bring to the dance.

Governor Beeston, Lilliannah, Carol Kay, and Cassandra all stand on the dock waving goodbye to five of the strangest men they have ever met in their lives but they have come to love them all. The trip will take just under an hour to reach Jamaican Point it is still early but the Navy Seals always plan well ahead never waiting to be in position at the last moment. As they near the Jamaican Point it is very clear that their plans will work perfectly the water inlets that are shown on the map were perfectly detailed. A perfect ambush for the pirates but now the ambush will be all Navy Seals. The Apex boat pulls up to a rocky shore line just below the point that is about 200 feet high. Lt. James speaks up, "Mitchell I want you at the top of the point with your night vision binoculars and your communicator set on this channel take your .408 Chey Tec sniper rifle that has a ranger of over one mile with the 50 caliber bullets. Now you can take out a number of unsuspecting pirates and hell they won't even know what's killing them. Mitchell scrambles from the Apex Pegasus boat up the rocky cliff just like a mountain goat. The Apex boat moves to the shore line anxiously awaiting for the information that Mitchell will be able to provide them about the pirate's position and able to locate Christopher Kirk to see if he is ok.

The pirates are now just waking up from their afternoon drinking stupor, weaving as they walked up on deck to take their position of command. "Up anchor, drop the main sails, make sail, bow to port," are all the captains orders. The eight pirate ships slowly begin to make their journey out of the safety of the harbor it is a spectacle. The sea is calm no waves without any white caps appearing the full moon is high in the sky like a beacon lighting their way to battle, they have no idea what is awaiting them in battle with the Navy Seals. The pirates see the full moon as a good omen and believe that Davey Jones is also wishing them good luck. So what do the pirates do they strike up the band and sing battle songs as they sail away out to sea. Capt. John Wallace is convinced his battle plan is perfect in every way as he stands at the helm of his ship the Red Dragon smiling leading the way. The rest of the pirate captains are feeling very good about their chances for success tonight. They are thinking about how they will be feared by all pirates in the Caribbean when they have the Devil men's weapons in their control, and what a brilliant leader Capt. Wallace is and that he will being them on so many more victories.

Mitchell has reached the top of the point 200 feet above the water and has a clear view of the entire area also a perfect rock formation that he can use to control his firing from. Mitchell scans the ocean again and can see ships on the horizon sailing in his direction but not wanting to make a false alarm he waits until he is certain that these ships are the pirate ships that have kidnapped Chris and is seeking a war with the Navy Seals. Mitchell now confirms that these ships are the pirate ships he is looking out for, he calls down to Lt. James and tells him that there are eight ships moving his way. He continues to observe and detects deceptive movements three of the ships are breaking off and heading to open waters as he continues to watch the three ships drop sails right at the point of the horizon and turn so their bows are facing west. Mitchell is on his communicator reporting any movement two other ships are headed towards the shoreline to sit in shallow waters just behind the Jamaican Point near where the Apex Pegasus boat is sitting. Mitchell says, "I can see the other two ships but they can't see you you're hidden perfectly within 300 yards of their position, your right behind those large stone boulders and out of sight. Now I can see three ships coming close to the point even closer then they said they would be they are now within 800 yards of my position, the ships are all turning their bows to point towards Port Royal and sitting only 60 yards apart they are now dropping their sails and dropping anchor it looks like they are waiting for you guys to show up. I can see men scurrying about working with their cannons loading them and getting ready to fire; their only firing position is either at starboard or port so they have that side pointed at you they think you're coming from."

Mitchell says, "Just one minute I think I can see Christopher, yes I do he is tied to the main mast on the Red Dragon wait there is something very wrong, about Chris. I can see him clearly God Damn it, son of a bitch Chris is dead they are untying him oh fuck half of his face is missing his body looks like it came out of a meat grinder. He is being dragged to the forward mast at the bow he is not moving at all any movement what so ever he is dead weight. Oh God his back is shredded skin is hanging from his back and his right hand is only attached by a single bone to his wrist. I don't know what they did to kill Chris but I'm getting my pound of flesh from these evil, bastard, pirates tonight." Lt. James says, "I agree but do not fire your weapon unless I give the order, is that clear?" "Yes sir, clear sir," answers Mitchell. "We have one more hour until midnight our scheduled ronde view we will wait until fifteen minutes past midnight before we attack, that way the pirates will be a little antsy and on edge wondering if we are going to show or not," answers Lt. Darren James. Time seems to pass ever so slowly when you have your finger on the trigger. Jacob is at the Mini gun the Gatling gun that can fire 3,000 rounds per minute, Bobby Harold is holding the AT4 missile and rocket launcher with the missiles set to explode after 2 seconds of hitting the target to crate the most collateral damage, Lt. James has his assault sub machine gun weapon at the ready.

Lt. James explains, "This is the plan we bring our boat out from behind these rocks when it is time to attack point our bow at the two pirates ships hiding in the water inlet just ahead of us then turn on our two 1,000,000 candle light search lights and turn on our loud speaker full force playing the 50's rock and roll songs. When they see our lights and hear our music of Elvis, Little Richard and Jerry Lee Lewis they will surely panic not knowing what the hell to expect or what in the hell is coming at them. We will blow the hell out of their two ships that are hiding and killing as many pirates as quickly as we can then move on to the three pirates ships waiting for us in the open water and destroy them as well. When Mitchell sees our search lights go on he will engage with his sniper rifle killing Capt. John Wallace first and then the other two captains that will leave them leader less and more likely to panic and then he will fire at will. They call us Devil men we will earn that name tonight and send them all to hell. We wouldn't be here if they hadn't captured Christopher the pirates have brought this war on themselves and now they have killed Chris so we are free to kill every last fucken evil pirate bastard you guys see."

Lt. James is looking at his watch and says to Mitchell, "Five more minutes to go are you ready?" Mitchell responds, "I was born ready." Hunter starts the engines and slowly pulls out from behind the rocks pointing the bow directly at the two pirate ships who think they are in hiding to ambush the Navy Seals. Lt. James shouts, "Kill em all." Hunter turns on the two 1,000,000 candle light search lights and also turns on the loud speakers with the first song by Elvis, Hound Dog the Navy Seals can see the pirates scrambling about not knowing what the hell is going on. Bobby Harold fires the AT4 missile launcher and a missile hits the first ship blowing it all to hell then he reloads and fires at the second ship blowing it all to hell. In the meantime Jacob is firing the Mini gun the Gatling gun at the men he sees running about BRRRRRRRRRR, BRRRRRRRRR, BRRRRRRR and BRRRRRRR, cutting their bodies into little pieces these dumb ass pirates are now no threat to anyone they are all either dead or dying and their boats are sinking.

The pirates on the three ships sitting 800 yards off shore are stunned by the explosions taking place on their two ships that were hiding in the water inlet. Everyone turned to see what is taking place then they see this little boat with two very bright odd lights coming out of the inlet water way with some sort of music being played heading their way this was not expected or planned for. For another moment the pirates are too interested at what it is and do nothing. Then this little boat goes so fast no pirate has ever seen a boat go this fast before especially without a sail. Now the music or whatever they hear is noise never the less they are mesmerized and distracted. The little boat goes around to where their guns are not prepared to fire and the little boat is firing some sort of a gun as it passes by the three ships it is the Mini gun the Gatling gun firing BRRRRRRRR, BRRRRRRRRRRRRR, BRRRRRRRR, and BRRRRRRR and pirates are being killed and dropping like flies as they look over the side. Now the little boat moves out further from the ships and is preparing to fire missiles from its AT4 missile and rocket launcher so they are not hit by the flying debris from the ships.

Mitchell takes careful aim at a pirate in the crow's nest and he falls to the deck almost hitting the captain. Capt. John Wallace is standing at the helm looking surprised he can see the chaos of the two ships in the water inlet set on fire and exploding this is not what he had planned for and he is frightened. He remembers what Christopher told him it is now coming true, if you screw with Navy Seals you can kiss your ass goodbye. Capt. Wallace can see the two ships that were in hiding now a ball of flame he realized a little too late that he was not properly prepared to fight the Navy Seals from the future. He is now in a panic mode never having faced an enemy quite like this before, using weapons that he has never experienced before. His crew can see their captain's panic and his fear is catching as his crew is more afraid than ever before. Mitchell lines up a pirate in his sniper sites with the night vision sight making him out clear as day standing right beside the captain and he pulls the trigger his head explodes his skull, blood and brains covering the captain. Capt. Wallace now screams out loud in panic not knowing how this man standing beside him one minute could have been killed like this with no noise what so ever. Mitchell fires again at a look out up high on the rigging he is dead on arrival hitting the deck only a few feet away from the captain. Mitchell thinks to himself, "Captain I have a bullet with your name on it you evil bastard." Mitchell can see Capt. Wallace trying to hide behind the sailing masts or any other barrier he can find and looking around. Mitchell screams at the top of his voice, "Up here you miserable rat bastard, I'm up here take a long last look your evil ways and miserable life is over this bullet is for Christopher." Mitchell pulls the trigger Capt. Wallace's head explodes like a watermelon hit by a sledge hammer and a real mess of his brains covers the deck. Next Mitchell aims at another captain on the farthest pirate ship away and fires his chest explodes his body parts hits his men standing close by. Then Mitchell takes careful aim at the third pirate ships captain and fires his head in no longer attached to his body and his men panic not knowing how this can possibly happen, what kind of weapons can the Devil men possibly have? Mitchell watches closely at who looks like he is taking charge and kills them instantly, creating total panic because no pirate can understand how their captains and the other pirates can be killed like this and by what for they see and hear nothing creating this is true horror.

Hunter quickly maneuvers the boat to the opposite side of the three pirate ships where they are not prepared to fire their cannons. The pirates have their guns ready to fire on the starboard side and the Navy Seals are on their port side surprise, surprise. The bright lights can see pirates scurrying like cockroaches not knowing which way to run or to move they have never seen such bright lights before this is surly the work of the devil the Devil men can control the sun. Jacob is moving the Mini gun the

Gatling gun back and forth killing anyone that moves. The loud speakers are now playing Little Richard's song Long Tall Sally a perfect rhythm for killing pirates. Bobby Harold fires a rocket at the first pirate ship the Red Dragon and it explodes in a ball of flame then he fires at amidships hitting the powder magazine and the ship now really explodes in a ball of hell fire. Pieces of the ships fly hundreds of feet into the midnight sky, no pirate ship can maneuver to fire its cannons they are helpless against the Navy Seals who are able to maneuver from side to side from bow to stern firing at will. The voices of the pirates can be heard cursing and screaming not knowing what to do they were not prepared for this kind of fight tonight, as their battle plans go up in smoke. Pirates are jumping into the sea only to be killed by Lt. James assault sub machine gun. The night has now turned to day with all the fires burning and explosions all around. The pirate ships that can try to mount an attack by firing off their cannons at anything that moves in the water. All the cannon balls do is make a splash in the sea. Jacob Blum is firing the Mini gun the Gatling gun at the sailing masts on the ships cutting them in half and the sound they make crashing to the decks in a horrendous sound, he's feeling pride of duty. The pirates never thought that killing one Devil man would bring such revenge, devastation and destruction so quickly and with such furry. Bobby Harold fires two missiles at the ship that just fired their cannons at them onto the center of the ship creating a massive explosion that tears the ship in half.

The second pirate ship is now in their sights and Bobby Harold fires his missiles at the water line creating gaping holes as the sea rushes in, on his third missile firing he hits the powder magazine creating another hell fire, fire storm. So far no pirate ship has fired one cannon ball that even got close enough to splash the Navy Seals with sea water because the Navy Seals have surprised them and approached them on the opposite side they were not prepared for. Hunter throttles up and maneuvers the Apex Pegasus boat so they can witness the last battle cries of the pirate's ships with their bows and sterns gone and masts cut in half. The pirate's ships are listing hard to port it will only take a few minutes longer before the three ships are below the sea and sailing with Davey Jones and his crews at the bottom of the ocean. The third ship is still floating but not for long the bright search lights catch the pirates on deck pointing their blunderbuss rifles at them, Jacob points and fires the Mini gun the Gatling gun at them BRRRRRRRRRRR, BRRRRRRRRRRRR, BRRRRRRRRRRR killing the pirates and creating pure chaos and panic where they stand and cutting the main mast in half it falls with a terrible crashing sound onto the deck. Another 50's song is playing by Jerry Lee Lewis, Great Balls of Fire a perfect song as the Navy Seals sing along. Bobby Harold fires three missile rockets into the third ship and it explodes in a great ball of fire and the sea is covered with red pirate blood. Lt. James and the other four Navy Seals are all yelling at the pirates still alive and holding onto anything that floats. "You started this fucken war we ended it your lesson is never start a war with Navy Seals we will shove our boot up your ass and twist it and yes we are the Devil men from hell. We will not kill any more of you evil dastardly pirates tonight; do enjoy your swim home that is if you know how to swim."

The three pirate ships setting at the horizon can see the explosions the fire balls going high in the night's sky and the odd bright lights from a little boat and they can hear the screams of the dying pirate's way across the water. This sends chills of absolute fear and panic into the pirate crews and all three captains. The three pirate captains Capt. Caesar Demantie his ship the Italian Stallion, Capt. Bellamy McVaine his ship the Anne Bonney and the temporary Captain, Capt. Juan Lopez McGill his ship the Black Pearl are the three ships that are sitting at the horizon ready to enter the fight tonight. Capt. Demantie watched as Capt. McVaine is throwing his arms up cursing and yelling at his crew to raise the sails and get the hell out of here, he wanted no part of the destruction and chaos taking place he can see the five pirate ships in a battle with the Devil men are on fire and destroyed. Capt. Demantie is thinking the same thoughts as Capt. McVaine to get the hell out of here now. The temporary captain Capt. Juan Lopez McGill is watching as the two ships turn to leave as fast as they can he knows that he is not a hero and follows giving his order to raise sails and turn the bow around getting the hell out of here. The three captains are hoping that the Devil men in their little boat will not be following them since they did not enter the battle or try to kill any Devil men. The three ships separate taking different routes to the Southern Caribbean.

There is mostly silence now across the blood soaked water the five ships are at the bottom of the sea the explosions have stopped; only the moans and groans of the pirate's still alive and some are crying out for mercy and hanging on to the debris of their ships can be heard. Lt. Darren James stands and surveys the battle zone shakes his head and says, "Let's go get Mitchell from Jamaican Point and make like a tree and leave this dead zone." As the Apex boat enters the cove Mitchell was waiting for them, he jumps in and Hunter puts the boat on fast mode and within the hour they are back at the docks of the governor's mansion. At least it didn't take all night its only 4:00 A. M., in the early morning the Navy Seals take showers to get the grime of battle from them and flush it down the drain and then sack time. Lt. James gets in bed he notices a large lump that turned out to be Lilliannah wearing her beautiful smile and nothing more, Darren thinks there is no rest for the wicked. The day is now Friday only one day remaining before the earthquake strikes it is late in the morning around 10:00 A.M. even with last night's battle most of the seals are up and cheery eyed, smiling, and walking around ready for a new day to begin. Perhaps because they know that the battle with the Brethren of the Black Spot pirates is over, done, finished, and no more bloodshed oh what a wonderful feeling it is to celebrate a new day. All the seals are up except Darren some are thinking what a sleepy head he is, others are envious because they know Lilliannah is in his bed. Governor Beeston is looking for Bobby Harold and spots him in the dining room. The governor takes a seat at the table and confirms with Bobby that he remembers volunteering to go into town today and he does. Bobby says, "Of course I remember I am looking forward to going into town today."

The governor speaks up, "I want to introduce you to the Commander of the Guard, David Getingzer the man I trust most to get things done he is my number one man in Jamaica. He is well liked and respected for being fair and speaking the truth and is courteous and respectful to every person he meets, when he talks people will listen to him. The two of you will travel to Port Royal by horse back and talk with as many people as you can to convince them of a terrible earthquake coming tomorrow. This I believe will save many precious lives I can only hope that many people will believe what you have to say. I also believe that the two of you are better than one telling the story and you can also protect each other from the unknown. Hunter looks around the room and declares, "Today is a good day for a swim in the Caribbean ocean to at last relax and enjoy our lives. Who wants to join me?" Only Jacob and Mitchell remain and think that is a great idea. Then Carol Kay and Cassandra over hear what Hunter said and they want to join them in their swim. Jacob speaks up, "Ok ladies get your bathing suits or ware nothing at all like we are going to do, swimming nude is so much more relaxing and fun to do being all natural." The five of them heard for the beach to go swimming and playing in the ocean in the nude feeling as natural as they can this is a wonderful, beautiful, perfect, relaxing, day. Jacob says to Carol Kay, "Bring your blanket with you to the beach," "Now why would I do that?" asks Carol Kay. "So we can lay on it and not get sand up our you know what." explains Jacob. "What a great idea that is, we never thought of that," says Carol Kay. Mitchell, Jacob, and Hunter are sitting and lying on the blankets on the white sandy beach with Carol Kay and Cassandra they are getting used to being in the nude and really liking the feeling as the cool ocean breezes flow over their bodies. Cassandra and Carol Kay are very curious about these strange men; about their world, what marvelous things they have, and all sorts of questions. Cassandra starts the questioning and says, "Carol Kay and I are very curious about your world and where you come from, would you please share some of your stories with us? Your boat is so wonderful you must have so many more wonderful things in your world." Jacob is the first to answer, "Yes we have many wonderful things, cities where hundreds of thousands of people live and work and the cities do not stink of raw sewage. Buildings so tall you cannot see the tops of them because the clouds cover the tops, cars that carry people not horses. We have gigantic long highways that cross our country from coast to coast where the cars can travel as fast as 100 miles per hour. We have busses that fit over 88 people on board and airplanes that fly through the sky carrying hundreds of people safe and relaxing." Mitchell joins in the conversation, "We have what is called electricity that lights up our cities and streets and homes and buildings like daylight, we also have telephones that people and talk with other people hundreds of miles away.

Then Hunter joins the conversation, "We also have a square box that is called a television we can see pictures of other people from around the world. We have so many things that would blow your mind for instance washing our clothes we have a washing machine we put our clothes in and the machine does all the work and cleaning. Then we put the wet clean clothes in another machine called a dryer and all the clothes come out dry no work at all. Oh yea Jacob told you about the airplane it can fly from Jamaica to England in only 8 hours carrying hundreds of people not the months it now takes on an uncomfortable ship. The three seals look at the two ladies whose mouths are wide open from astonishment with their eyes focused on them they have their listing ears on because the stories are so fantastic and mesmerizing. Cassandra says, "You know what you are saying to us is very hard for us to believe, these things you describe are impossible for us to comprehend, it just sounds like magic." Hunter says, "Ok when and if we are able to find our way back to our time if we can through the time portal of that dark blue and crimson fog would you two ladies like to join us in our time?" Carol Kay is shocked by the question and scared at the same time and says, "No way would I want to go I'm too afraid and not that adventurous at all, please do not ask me that question again." Cassandra is sitting wide eyed and has a very adventurous mind and says, "Damn right I want to go that sounds so wonderful. So do you really mean it or are you just joking with us? Hunter speaks up, "I am serious if you want to come with us you are welcome." "Then I am ready to go can we go today?" asks Cassandra. "No not today but soon after the earthquake is over and the tsunami is over and the ocean settles down then we will begin our search for our way back to our time," answers Hunter. Cassandra is beside herself with excitement she gets up and runs into the ocean waving for the others to follow her.

Bobby Harold and David Getingzer head for the stables to pick out two good and fast horses, the horses are chosen and saddled. Bobby provides David with one of the seals side arm pistols and instructs him how to use it, strapping them to their right legs. Bobby has also brought along a TDI Vector sub machine gun with plenty of ammunition in his saddle bags always be prepared that way you live longer and wearing his navy fighting fatigues. "Were off to town," says David to the governor. The governor responds, "I will pray that both of you come back safely I'll see you both later on this evening." They both begin the 15 mile ride down the trail to Port Royal. David turns to Bobby and says, "Thank you for showing me how to fire your magic pistol I have never fired such a weapon that fires and fires or ever thought gun like this could even exist." Bobby responds, "You're welcome we always travel with protection, glad to share our pistol with you. You never know when it will be needed especially in your crazy town with all those evil, uncivilized pirates around." David says, "Your weapons are really fantastic the future must be wonderful where you come from." Bobby answers, "About our weapons you haven't seen anything yet, I can only imagine what the weapons of the future will be like in 2306 that would blow my mind. Today is a good day and a good thing what we are doing warning people of the earthquake tomorrow, and saving as many live as we possibly can." They start their journey on a beautiful day the sky is blue puffy white clouds float in the sky, it is such a clear day it seems like you can see forever as they ride along a path close to the shore. The small white caps slap the beach; the day is warm and will be getting warmer. Bobby looks with caution at the sea hoping not to see any reminisce of last night's battle with the pirates coming ashore. Bobby Harold only wants to enjoy his ride in peace not to be reminded of the chaos of the last two nights and only thinking of his mission ahead. As they are riding into town they notice a lot of domestic animals walking and running in the opposite direction. They see horses that were not tied up properly they see dogs, cats and squirrels, birds and rabbits and so many outer animals hurrying away for town even a duck with her 8 ducklings are waddling away. Bobby realizes that this is the natural instincts of animals that feel and fear impending disaster.

Capt. Caesar Demantie and his ship the Italian Stallion sailed away from the battle with the Devil men the other night not wanting any part of that engagement. He was so frightened by what he saw that he ordered his ship to continue to sail south, way south until it found a safe harbor on the island of Aruba. There Capt. Demantie gave up command of his pirate ship took the bounty that he had earned as a pirate, left the ship and the pirate life behind vowing to never to return to that life again. Mr. Demantie now proceeded to open a tavern and men's club called the "Blue Goose Tavern" and settled into a completely different life in Aruba. Capt. Juan Lopez McGill and his ship the Black Pearl sailed his ship in the Southern Caribbean Ocean for a number of years but never returned to Port Royal, Jamaica. Capt. Bellamy McVaine ashamed of his running away from battle with the Devil men returned to Port Royal the next day to say to himself and his crew he was back and not afraid. Capt. McVaine is the only captain left of the ten captains who once were the Brethren of the Black Spot, his ship the Anne Bonny has dropped anchor in the harbor. He removed the red flag with the black spot in the center that used to fly at the top of his forward mast and threw it in the trash. Capt. McVaine told his crew if any man speaks of his fear and running from the battle with the Devil men he will personally cut their hands off, they never said a word. He is still angry at the demise of his friends, and fellow pirates and ashamed that he ran and did not fight.

Capt. McVaine is very angry at the demise of his friends and brothers in arms he misses their comradery, friendship and brotherhood. Deep down inside this behemoth of a man is mad at himself living with the thought perhaps if he would have attacked them he might have saves his pirate brothers. Capt. McVaine still feels he has a score to settle with the Devil men but how he has no idea blaming them for taking his courage away. Like so many men that have come before him and will come after him try to find their courage in the bottle, 180 proof rum that is. The only men who understand their captain are his crew, they saw what he saw and experienced the same fear and were all glad that they did not join in the battle and they are alive today. The pirate crew all took a pack never to speak of the last battle with the Devil men again, to no one never ever.

All they want to be is regular pirates of the Caribbean rousting merchant ships and stealing their bounty, and enjoying lap dances at the Catt & Fiddle Tavern eating and drinking.

Bobby Harold and David Getingzer continue their ride towards town Bobby speaks up, "Do you know how many people live in Port Royal?" David responds, "Yes a count is taken every year it is 6,500 people with approximately 2,000 dwellings today." "That is a lot of people for us to reach in such a short period of time but we will do our best." David says, "One of the first places I want to go is to my parent's home and warn them then my brothers home only a few blocks away. We can't just stand on the street corner yelling there is an earthquake coming get out of town the people would think we were crazy people, what would you suggest Bobby?" "Does this town have a mayor or someone in charge of the city?" responds Bobby. Davis says, "Yes they have a council of sorts the head of the council runs a jewelry store," answers David. "Good let's see him first and let him pass the word on if he will. How about a printer perhaps he could make some posters and place them around town warning of the earthquake," suggests Bobby. "Let's go and see them first then we will go to your parents and brother house next." Good thinking on your part Bobby I'm glad you came with me," answers David.

The first stop they make when they enter the town is the Golden Jewels, jewelry store they walk in and tell the owner why they have come and what they would like him to do. The owner of the store is thinking this is a bad joke perhaps they want to rob his store when he leaves, he tells them to just leave his store and go away. This reaction really upsets David and Bobby they now head for the printers shop to explain their mission. The printer tells them that some of his friends had attended the grand party at the governor's mansion the other night and were advised of the earthquake by the governor but no one believes this farfetched story. The printer suggests that they leave his shop and he is not interested in printing any posters about a crazy earthquake that will not happen. The two of them continue to try to tell about 12 more people to help them to leave before the earthquake comes but no one believes their story and most people laugh at what they are saying. "That really pisses me off," says David, "I never expected that kind of reaction so let's go to my parents and brothers house next." They ride up the street and cross a large section of town to David's parent's home. His parents listen to what they are being told and believe their son and prepare to leave to safety immediately. Next they ride a few blocks more to where David's brother lives, he listens and believes his brother and prepares to leave to higher ground.

"Now what in the hell do we do," asks Bobby, "Who do we tell, how do we convince people about the earthquake that will happen tomorrow morning so far no one believes us." David speaks up, "The governor is not going to be pleased with our efforts so far no one wants to believe us. It is getting close to supper time we didn't have any lunch and I could use a drink, I know of a good tavern that has good food and drink only a few blocks away." "Damn good idea, but perhaps we should return to the governor's place for food and drink." answers Bobby. "No, no don't be afraid of staying in Port Royal after dark, I'm with you the pirates know better than to confront me the Commander of the Royal Guard and anyone that is with me." says David Getingzer. "Trust me David I fear no man but at the same time I am a cautious man and I listen to my trained instincts and my inner voice they are sending me a warning to leave." Speaks Bobby, "Ok my inner voice be damned the sun is still up we'll have one drink and something to eat my stomach feels empty anyway and then begin our journey back while it is still light. I have seen and experienced enough things with the pirates in this town to last a life time, I just feel very uneasy." The two of them ride a few blocks on their magnificent chestnut horses with the most exquisite riding gear and saddles on the island of Jamaica; they tie up in front of the Pig & Whistle Tavern that is David's favorite place to stop. What they do not seem to notice is a small contingent of pirates gathered outside a tavern across the street, drunk from a day of drinking 180 proof rum and grog. They now have their courage up and common senses down with a desire hell bent on looking for trouble and a fight with someone.

A little true history about Port Royal, Jamaica 1692

Port Royal, Jamaica was known by many names in its hay day of its existence; Sodom and Gomorra of the Caribbean, the wickedest city in the world, the Devil's house. Port Royal had one drinking house for every ten residents; by 1692 the population was slightly more than 6,500 people including 2,500 black slaves. The town supported over fifty-five taverns and 250 buildings crammed onto 52 acres of land that jutted into the sea all built on sand with no rock structure underneath. Prostitutes were plentiful and most worked the taverns and brothels and some walked the streets no man was denied love no matter how ugly he looked as long as he had a doubloon in his pocket. Drink was cheap wine and rum were made on the island, the food was expensive most food was imported very little grown at this time. Plenty of sea food was available with a large variety and prepared to perfection. Some innkeepers would have as many as two or three establishments in the same building, one would be for upscale customers and they would be served the very best wines, whiskeys and brandies from as far away as France, England, and Ireland. Then there would be another room for the fisherman, seaman, and local workers that served beer and rum that was produced on the island. Then a third room was for the pirates and buccaneers that served debauchery at its best, the whores and prostitutes and stews and grog. The tallest building was four stories tall most were only two stories tall, and not a lot of room between the buildings the streets were narrow some were only two people could walk side by side and a lot were paved by cobble stone but most were just dirt streets. Many shops did extensive business, gunsmiths, clothing stores and Jewelry merchants and fine jewelry designers were common places of business. It seems that there was a fair share of doctors and dentists that practice their medicine in town along with other tradesmen from carpenters to furniture makers, cordwainers and fish net makers. Just about any business that you sought out is here ready to serve you and fulfill your needs.

The bartender quickly walked up to David giving him a friendly welcome and showing them a good table and to make sure they were well taken care of. The best wine for my friends the bartender called out to people behind the bar. A very pleasant waitress came to their table in a few moments to take their food order and recommended the fish of the day would be their best choice. The wine was red and warm with no name on the bottle, red wine was the only wine served. David did the ordering since he knew the place best and he went with the fish of the day. As they were sitting at the table two ladies came over to their table to see if they could be of service in any way if they had any personal needs that needed attending to. Bobby took one look at the ladies and almost gagged. David seemed to know them and was impressed with the ladies, they had long stringy hair it did not appear to be combed in days, the dresses were off the shoulder style but unwashed in perhaps a couple of weeks. They had too many teeth missing to make a nice complete smile. David asked, "Bobby which lady to you choose I choose the one in the red dress." Bobby was dumbfounded that David was impressed with these ladies, not wanting to hurt the ladies feelings. Bobby said, "I am sorry ladies but I am not feeling at all well today I will have to pass on any selection."

The pirates outside were walking around the horses admiring them and their saddles and hardware, touching them and patting their necks. Just then a huge man with a full beard stepped out from the tavern across the street called The Mad Hatter, he looks at the horses and yells, "Who be ye horses belongs to?" his name is Capt. McVaine along with 20 of his pirate crew. The men on the street stepped back and say, "Dem horses belong to David Getingzer the Commander of the Guard and his friend who dresses oddly." "I have to see for me self who dee is," says Capt. McVaine. Then he steps into the Pig & Whistle Tavern, and notices that the man with David Getingzer is a Devil man by his dress and his facial appearance. Because he remembered the kind of clothing Christopher had on it was the same. Capt. McVaine steps back to catch his breath and then steps outside of the Tavern and reacts as though he had just seen a ghost, his crew observed his reaction and was concerned. Capt. McVaine is thinking of a plan on the spur of the moment, should he just walk away, or capture this Devil man to bring back some of his lost honor? He is thinking this time it would be different they are not at sea and me and me men know dis town like de backs of me dirty hairy hands. We should capture him by rushing at him wit me 20 men hold him for ransom say only 100 pounds of gold dat be fair me not wanting to hurt him just get me honor back is what Capt. McVaine is thinking.

Bobby Harold being who he is a highly trained Navy Seal; his personal radar is on high he is detecting what may become a harmful situation. He is curious about the man who briefly walked into the tavern and left so quickly. So Bobby turns to David and asks, "Who was that huge man who just walked into this tavern looked at us then immediately turned and walked out again?" David answers, "Oh he is Capt. McVaine a captain of a pirate ship the Anne Bonney and a member of the Brethren of the Black Spot, do you know him?" All the hairs on the back of Bobby's neck stand on end and he gets goose bumbled flesh, he goes to the window and is observing Capt. McVaine franticly talking and gesturing to his men to get them to do something, Bobby is able to make out the words capture them and bring dem to me. He hurries back to the table and with a very stern no-nonsense look on his face and a tone in his voice that means business he says, "Come with me now, do not look back, and where is the back door?" David does not understand but obeys Bobby's command, out the back door they flee leaving David's lass disappointed. "Listen to me, David and do exactly what I tell you if you want to live. The pirates outside by our horses that are members of Brethren of the Black Spot whom my seal buddies and I have been in battle with and we destroyed a lot of their ships and killed hundreds of them. I know in my mind that they want to take revenge on me and perhaps whom I'm with. I overheard them say at the window to capture us and bring us to Capt. McVaine."

"We need to get to the horses in order to escape so when the pirates rush into the bar to capture us we had better be in position to get our horses get your pistol at the ready and fire on my command. Then 20 or more pirates rush into the bar but find the table that they were sitting at, empty. The command is given David and Bobby rush towards the horses firing their side arm pistols hitting several surprised pirates how many they killed some they couldn't stop to count. They jumped on the horses and headed out of town on Queen St., what they didn't count on was pirates waiting for them at the end of the block firing their pistols, killing their horses. Bobby remembers he has his semi-auto sub machine gun in his saddle bags he grabs it along with the ammo. Bobby and David now fire at the pirates standing in the middle of the street hitting them. They have to take time to reload their guns killing and wounding a number of them, they run for cover into a building nearby. "Oh fuck this is not the way this day was supposed to go and that I thought the fighting with the pirates was over," thinks Bobby. Bobby Harold looks at David and can see his left arm is hit and bleeding. Then he realizes that his left leg hurts quite badly and that he cannot stand on it, in the excitement of most encounters adrenalin masks any pain. He looks at his leg and realizes it is broken below the knee it most likely happened when his horse fell on him as he landed wrong. Bobby also feels terrible shooting pains in his right side he lifts his shirt to find a hole in his side, damn that lucky shot. Together they are able to stop the bleeding in David's arm and find some wood sticks to make a splint for Bobby's broken leg and stop the bleeding in Bobby's right side helping somewhat but the pain is excruciating. Bobby also realized that this is not David's fight but his and his Navy Seals fight with the pirates.

Bobby knows he cannot ride a horse in his condition David must ride back to the governor's mansion and get the Navy Seals involved to rescue him before the earthquake hits tomorrow morning the time is 7:30 P.M. there is time but not a lot of time. He turns to David and says, "I will be ok I have my weapons and I can manage my pain and believe me I know how to keep out of site. What I need you to do is get back to the governor's place and get my Navy Seal buddies aware of what the hell is going on and hope they will arrive soon. They hear the pirates talking and moving around on the street they are searching for them. They are trying to figure out where the two men are that they are searching for the pirates split into two groups. The pirates seem confused and disorientated in their search moving away and down the street searching other buildings. David speaks up, "I know this city and its people and how to move around I will find a horse that is tied up to a post take it and ride like the wind to get help, but I am concerned for your safety." "Thank you for your concern, but your concern will get me killed, you can't do anything for me here." explains Bobby, "So find a horse and bring my buddy's back you have a pistol, how is your on ammo?" David checks his pistol and says," Yes I could use some more ammo." Then he checks the window seeing no pirates in the street he gives a pat on Bobby's shoulder and says, "I know what I need to do I will not fail you, help is on its way stay safe." With that Bobby is heartened by David's attitude and believes that help will soon be on its way. David checks the window again and moves carefully into the street.

Capt. McVaine realizes that he has just stuck his arm up to his elbow in a hornets nest but cannot figure out how to pull it back without getting badly stung. He has involved himself with the task of trying to capture a Devil man in the city on a Friday night with the whole town watching. He knew he had a choice to walk away or pursue this man eating dinner in a tavern with a friend minding their own business. His pride stood in the way of making a rational decision and he thought this would be so easy. Now he has gone and done it six pirates lay dead in the street and another nine are wounded and need medical attention. The pirates from his own ship were there to watch another debacle of trying to capture a Devil man. No turning back now he is in the city and the sun is setting, darkness is coming to Port Royal just like it does every evening. Where in the hell can this Devil man be hiding, in what building, how far away can he possibly be, he does not know this city so capturing him should be easy. But the Commander of the Guard David Getingzer knows this city and he is with him. So his life is on the line along with the Devil man to capture and kill both of them. Capt. McVaine is starting to get back some of his macho attitude that he lost the other night. He is sitting at a long table with 15 of his men in a tavern called The Mad Hatter and they are listing to his every word and willing to follow his orders. He realizes how odd it feels to be the last captain standing of the Brethren of the Black Spot and holding court so to speak. He, Capt. Demantie and Capt. Juan Lopez McGill are the only three captains left and who in the hell knows where they are or if they will ever be seen again. Capt. McVaine slams his huge hand on the table and declares, "De man or men who brings to me da Devil man he be rewarded 80 gold doubloons, what ye be waiting for go find him." The pirates leave the tavern some are drunk with rum and grog searching they figure that they have to be close where their dead horses lay in the street he must be close by but they have no idea that the Devil man is wounded. Bobby is watching from a second story window a couple of blocks away from where their horses are laying.

David has already left the building searching for a horse to get the hell away and to bring help. Bobby's Navy Seal training is coming in handy staying awake in uncomfortable surroundings when you would like to sleep or pass out from pain, he has to stay sharp and be able to think and plan effectively. Even though the pain is so bad from his broken leg and bullet hole in his side his thinking has to stay sharp. Bobby can see eight pirates walking back heading for the building he's hiding in, time to move so he moves very carefully dragging his leg and body to the roof top and is able to hide under a large wooden box with a large sail covering it, he thinks the building must belong to a sail maker. David is on the move he is frustrated that he has not found a horse to ride he is not able to see a horse tied up to a hitching post and it's a Friday night. That would be ideal because the horse would already be saddled and ready to ride. Then he remembers the livery stable that is over two blocks and decides to head that way as quickly as he can. Not wanting to be noticed he walks in a hurry but decides not to run that would bring curious eyes watching him. As he turns a corner he almost bumps into four pirates they stop him to ask a question, "Have you seen a man dressed in long green black and blue pants with a shirt to match?" David answers, "Not likely haven't seen a man dressed like that, why are you looking for him?" Because there be 80 gold doubloons reward on him head by Capt. McVaine, ye call out of ye see him." says one of the pirates. It has been 25 minutes since David left Bobby alone he knows time is going by very fast he needs to get on a horse and ride as fast as he can. David keeps moving now only a block away from the livery stable, he arrives and is able to saddle a horse quickly and ready to ride out of the livery stable when he sees three pirates standing at the door blocking his way with their pistols drawn and pointing at David's head. "Ye are wit da man we seek in da Pig

& Whistle I see ye," shouts one of the pirates. David responds, "Are you sure perhaps you are wrong?" He is doing his best not to spook them into doing something rash like shoot him as his right hand slowly moves to the pistol strapped to his right leg. David is setting on the horse looking down on the three pirates and measures them as to which one is going to die first. The one man who confronted him seems like the leader of the pack; David pulls his pistol fires a bullet clean right between his eyes then he keeps on firing until all three pirates are dead lying in the straw on the stable floor, with 45 caliber bullet holes in their heads and bodies. David thinks to himself as he kicks his horse in gear to run as fast as he can, "Damn I like this gun perhaps they will let me keep it."

Dinner is almost over at the governor's mansion, and another fantastic meal was served to the Navy Seals. Mitchell turns to Cassandra and asks, "Are the meals always this wonderful at the governor's home?" Cassandra answers, "Yes they are we may not have fancy boats but we do have fancy meals." Everyone at the table smiles at her answer because it was friendly and good natured. The governor says, "I am beginning to worry about David and Bobby Harold they should have returned by sun set do you think anything could have happened to them?" Lt. James answers, "I believe they are ok perhaps David is showing the town off to Bobby after a day of getting the word out regarding the earthquake." "Perhaps your right I do worry needlessly a lot of times and everything turns out just fine," says the governor. Lilliannah asks Darren, "Would you like to take a walk with me in the garden?" Darren says, "Yes I would very much." Lilliannah smiles because she was playing with the question and believed what the answer would be. Off they go holding hands and looking at nothing else but each other. "I do believe we have two love birds on our hands," says the governor, "And I give them my blessing." The four Navy Seals sitting at the table remember the picture of Lilliannah and Darren in the museum hanging on the wall at the naval base and would really like to say something about the picture but think better of it so the seals just smile in agreement. Jacob leans over to Carol Kay and asks, "Would you like to join me for a walk along the sea shore tonight I am sure that no pirates will be there to ambush us." She responds with a big smile and answers, "I would really like to walk with you tonight it is such a beautiful night."

Cassandra looks at Hunter and smiles and asks, "Hunter would you like to walk with me along the sea shore?" Hunter without hesitation answers, "I would like that very much let's go." Now at the table sits Mitchell and the governor so the governor asks Mitchell if he would like to join him in his study and have a nightcap drink. Mitchell responds, "I can't think of a better way to end a perfect day" Hunter and Cassandra are walking along the sea shore feeling the small waves wash across their bare feet as their toes dig into the warm wet sand. Hunter says, "Cassandra I was very serious when I said you were welcome to join us in our search to find a way back to our time, are you really anxious to come with us or were you just kidding?" "I really meant it I would love to go with you guys, it sounds so exciting and your time sounds like such a wonderful place." answers Cassandra. "I do have adventure in my soul I am always looking to try new and different things and this would be the greatest adventure of my life." "We have to find the portal again out on the ocean or we will never return to go to our time that is if it even exists. "Ok then it's on to a new adventure and new horizons," says Hunter. "Tell me one more thing that would see in your world," asks Cassandra. Hunter responds, "Let's see we have very large ships that are larger than 100 of your ships put together that cruse the Caribbean on happy friendly cruises with families to see the wonderful sights of the Caribbean and its islands. That is called a vacation hundreds and hundreds of people are on board eating great food, enjoying themselves and going into different towns on different islands all for the fun of it." "Now with everything you have told me this is the hardest thing for me to believe it just sounds too fantastic," says Cassandra." Hunter says, "I will make you this promise when and if we get back to my time and I have to believe we will I will take you on a Caribbean cruise on one of the gigantic ships and we will stop in Kingston, Jamaica." "I love your stories and really love what you just promised me, I will keep you to your promise." smiles Cassandra. And she gives Hunter's hand a loving squeeze and a loving kiss as they walk along the sea shore.

Mitchell asks the governor, "Could you please tell me more about your time and your island I find it so fascinating." "It would be my pleasure," answers the governor, "I know that you men have engaged in battle with the pirates the Brethren of the Black Spot since you arrived and it all started with you men saving my daughter and her two friends. There are a lot of good people who live here as plantation owners, merchants and honest citizens just wanting to make a good and productive life for themselves and their wives and children. The pirates are a part of our wealth as a city and I know they steal for a living and are not good men but are evil men. No one has a way or the amount of personal and resources to bring law and justice to Port Royal at this time, come to think of it perhaps the earthquake will change everything for the good. You see I am English, I was appointed to my position by the government of England we are at war with the Spanish and the French there are two kinds of men who sail the seas. One is called buccaneers they are paid by my government to attack Spanish and French ships, bring in the bounty we keep some the buccaneers keep some and the majority is sent to England. The second kinds of men are called pirates they work for no country or no man but themselves and they have no allegiance to any country. When they attack a ship which could Dutch, French, Spanish or even English they keep all the bounty be it gold, silver, jewels or the rigging from a ship, they spend a lot of their loot in Port Royal the capital of the pirates of the Caribbean. I know that, that creates the debauchery but that is what we are known for and that is our present day existence. I have a good life and have made a good life for my daughter, we really love Jamaica. I believe that civilization will soon come to us in Port Royal, by that I mean no more pirates and no more buccaneers will be needed to bring about our prosperity. Just honest trade in sugar, rum, coffee, cattle and legitimate business trade and with imports and exports will be our salvation. Believe it or not we have just about every religious denomination represented on this island, and the people are free to practice their religion without any interference not like England imposes that is a good thing."

"The weather is heaven sent mostly mild throughout the year, never really cold with reasonable welcoming rain and the sun oh God the wonderful sun it is fantastic warm sunshine. When I grew up in England in all my years' warm and hot sunshine was very rare and mostly cold dreary days all year long, I will never go back to that weather I will live out my life right here in Jamaica. Oh and the food even though it is expensive, I have never tasted such flavors and spices and the heat of the food is wonderful. The food is prepared by people that have lived and eaten throughout the world and are food adventurous, it seems like every week there is something new to eat and enjoy. The bland food of England is in my past my country does not have any idea how to prepare food it is tasteless with very little spices mostly stews and beef pies. But now one last thing our drinks, they are getting better every year, with new methods for distilling and new and adventurous ingredients keep on being developed along with better methods of making ice. As you can see I am happy with my life, are you happy with your life?" Mitchell ponders the question without answering.

Lt. Darren James and Lilliannah walk alone in the garden; Lt. James thinks this is the Garden of Eden, such a wonderful and beautiful place as he is holding hands with an angel and he has never been happier in his life then right now. Darren says, "Lilliannah I love you with all my heart and soul, you make me happy by just walking beside me, holding hands and the way you look at me I know that I am your man with your serious blue eyes I never want to leave." Lilliannah responds by gently squeezing Darren's hand with that love look in her eyes and speaks, "I love you I have never believe a love like ours could exist, you are my life and I would be lost without you I never want to let you go." Darren says, "When my men go searching for that elusive colored fog that brought us here in the first place I will not go along I want to stay with you for the rest of my life. Our life has been preordained I saw it in a picture on a wall in a museum over a week ago in our time I questioned how it could possibly be but now I understand. I will gladly explain at a later date but not tonight what I just said."

"But for tonight my big question is will you marry me?" Lilliannah is beside herself with joy, she was hoping that question would be asked of her. Lilliannah throws her arms around Darren's neck and gives him the most passionate kiss he has ever had. She responds, "Yes, a thousand times yes you have made me the happiest woman in the world I will marry you." Off in another part of the island Hunter and Cassandra are walking along enjoying each other and the night holding hands. Both of them are contemplating a future together but not ready to verbalize it right now. Jacob and Carol Kay are also enjoying each other's company looking forward to a night of love making when they return to the mansion. As they walk they feel rain drops falling on their heads a little summer rain tonight. "We better get back to the house before the rain really becomes heavy," says Carol Kay.

Bobby Harold feels the light rain drops that are beginning to fall and he knows with his present condition he had better get out of the rain. This light rain doesn't pose a problem but if it becomes a down pour he would be in serious trouble with his broken leg and bullet in his side. He begins to move ever so carefully from his hiding place the box on the roof even a little noise could possibly be heard. A pirate on the second floor hears something and climbs the stairs to find out just what he is hearing. The pirate opens the door to the roof carefully and sees the man they are searching for trying to get out from under the box with the sail on top. The pirate screams at the top of his voice, "I see da man we is searching for on da roof." Bobby is trying to clear his mind and decide his best approach should he stand and fight killing as many pirates as he can or just surrender. Bobby decides to stand and fight he gets behind the large box for as much cover as it will provide moving best he can. He reloads his pistol and his TDI Vector 45 caliber submachine gun getting ready to fire at a rate of 1500 rounds per minute and waits for the battle to begin. The pirate that found Bobby is directing the pirates that came running to keep an eye on the Devil man but do not fire until Capt. McVaine arrives. Another pirate runs a fast as his big lard ass can carry him to the Catt & Fiddle Tavern to tell Capt. McVaine that the Devil man has been found. The pirate runs into the tavern out of breath, takes a moment to recover then walks over to Capt. McVaine and says in a rather nervous voice, "We found da Devil man ye be searching for, follow me I will show ye the building he's on da roof." Capt. McVaine stands up reluctantly thinking why did I start this search in da first place? I be having a really good time wit da wenches. But out the door he goes to finely face a Devil man and kill him for all the chaos and destruction they have cause him and his mates.

Capt. McVaine is back at his favorite tavern the Catt & Fiddle with about one quarter of his crew the other quarter is out searching for Bobby hoping to get the reward. He is having more rum then he should considering the rum is 180 proof even though he is a very large man 6'6" tall weighing in at 360 pounds he is staggering more then he should and beginning to slump in his chair. He loves the wenches of the night and the pleasure they bring him it is party time in his scrambled mind and does not stay focused on the mission at hand to find the Devil man. There is a very good reason why Capt. McVaine was not chosen to be the leader of the Brethren of the Black Spot he is not very bright and is easily distracted by rum and wenches. Capt. McVaine arrives at the building where Bobby is hold up but does not fully realize the fight that Bobby Harold is able to still give. In his impaired thinking process by consuming too much 180 proof rum he orders five of the pirates that are standing at the door on the roof to rush and take the Devil man alive. They do as ordered because they are more frightened of Capt. McVaine then they are of the Devil man. The pirates rush forward screaming and have their cutlasses raised this tactic would normally scare the hell out of any merchant seaman, but they have no idea whom they are fighting to their demise. Bobby raises his TDI Vector submachine gun and fires off a few bursts ZZZZZZZZZZZZZZZ, ZZZZZZZZZZZZZ, ZZZZZZZZZZZZ immediately killing three pirates and wounding the other two who now are without an arm or a leg. Now what do they do to take this devil man alive, and what in the hell kind of gun does he have anyway that fires so may bullets at one time that you can put a fist through the holes in their bodies.

The rain is now beginning to fall with a vengeance, Capt. McVaine really does not want to be here but rather be with his wenches and a tankard of rum. But he realizes he has a real puzzle on his hands if he walks away now without capturing the Devil man he will appear weak and afraid and if that happens he most likely will lose his command. The pirates start looking around the building for something anything that will help them out and give them an advantage. They find a large iron plate large enough for four pirates to hide behind figuring they can hold it up and rush him and the iron should protect them. Capt. McVaine like the idea and orders four men to rush him and grab the Devil man along with ten other pirate's right behind. Mission accomplished the Devil man is taken alive, he is wet and his broken leg hurts like hell along with his side where there is a bullet hole and Bobby Harold almost passes out from the excruciating pain. The pirates take him to another building on the docks, a warehouse that Capt. McVaine owns that faces the water. Bobby is partially dragged to the warehouse and thrown up against a center post on the cobble stone floor, and they bind him to the post. Capt. McVaine can see he has a broken leg smiles and kicks it as hard as he can Bobby passes out from the excruciating pain. "Tomorrow we have da funk fun wit ye, Arrrrr I'll be back," screams Capt. McVaine as he stands over Bobby tied to a post just like the bully he is. Capt. McVaine runs from danger if he believes he may lose in battle or be harmed. He shouts at Bobby even while he is unconscious, "Ye an ye mates have destroyed me life and killed me best friends they be all dead because of ye, I am going back to the Catt & Fiddle Tavern to celebrate ye capture but I return in a few hours to finish ye life.

End of chapter 5

CHAPTER 6

David Getingzer is riding as fast as he can back to the governor's mansion best he can with a bullet in his left arm it is to his advantage that he is an excellent rider. He suffers blood loss and feels the pain but because he is such an excellent rider he can stay on the trail and is able to control the horse with one hand. David arrives at the mansion but no one is awake all the candle flames are out so he begins to scream as loud as he can and a house servant hears his cries for help just as he passes out at 2:00 A.M. in the early morning hours. The servant wakes up others for help, the governor's aid is able to summon the governor from his sleep. The governor comes down the stairs quickly and tells his house servants to wake up his house guests and to come quickly. Carol Kay is already helping with David's wounds and the seals come bounding down the stairs in a hurry. Now the entire house hold is up everyone is trying to help David and understand what happened. David regains consensus and begins to tell his horrific story, "Bobby and I were having supper in the Pig & Whistle Tavern minding our own business after we tried to tell others about the earthquake. Then a huge pirate by the name Capt. McVaine of the Brethren of the Black Spot with a full black and gray beard came into the tavern and spotted Bobby and he then went back out into the street. Bobby got a strange feeling as soon as I told him who the large man was, he got a strange feeling like something bad was about to happen. Then he went to the window and over heard them talking and saying to capture us and bring us to him. Bobby told me to follow him and to get the hell out the back door if I wanted to live. When the pirates rushed into the Pig & Whistle to capture us we got on our horses killing some of the pirates and started to ride away."

"We had just begun to ride away when we were ambushed and our horses were killed and I got a bullet in my arm and Bobby was shot in his side and he broke his leg when his horse fell on it he is in serious condition. The pirates are searching for him right now and if they find him the pirates will kill him they seek revenge. Bobby instructed me to leave and seek help with his buddies to come as soon as possible. I saddled a horse in the livery stable and three pirates were blocking my way I pulled the gun Bobby showed me how to use and killed the three pirates. Now I am here to get help to save Bobby." The four Navy Seals are all pissed and mad as hell they thought that the battles with the pirates were over and now this, they have pulled us back into battle again. Lt. James says, "Saddle up men we have got to save Bobby before the earthquake happens in the morning." The governor orders that four of his best horses be saddled and ready to ride as soon as possible. The four Navy Seals hurry and get dressed in their battle fatigues along with their Dragon Skin bullet proof vest. They head for the boat where their devastating weapons are kept to kill more pirates. Each man puts in his saddle bags a; TDI Vector 54 caliber sub machine gun, and they take two Atchisson Assault Shotguns, two Chey Tec sniper rifles 50 caliber and each man takes a Barrett M468 6.8 sub machine gun with plenty of ammunition for each weapon along with their side arm pistols. Today is early Saturday morning at 3:00 A.M. Lt. James yells out, "Son of a bitch the fucken earthquake will happen today at 11:45 A.M. Port Royal is the last place I wanted to be. Not only do we need to find and rescue Bobby but we must get our asses out of town or we will all be dead men." Lilliannah speaks up, "Why are you riding horses into town what about taking your fast boat?" Because the ocean waves are starting to kick up it is too rough out on the ocean and it would take us twice as long to reach town my love," answers Darren, "I can feel the weather changing, at least the rain has stopped but the wind is blowing from the northwest at around 20 knots right now it feels like the island knows and is preparing for the earthquake to happen. You all here in the mansion better prepare as well take all things on the shelves and put them on the floor and stay away for the windows get out on the lawn, it won't last long but when the ground shakes and feels like it is coming alive it is a scary thing."

"All I ever do it seems is wave goodbye to you and your mates as you go off to battle with the pirates. I pray that this is the very last time that you and your mates have to battle those damn pirates. Return with Bobby and return unharmed come back to me safe my love," says Lilliannah. Mitchell has a song playing over and over in his head for the last hour and is also singing along with it, "Don't take your guns to town son, and leave your guns at home." Mitchell shakes his head trying desperately to get that song out of his head. The Navy Seals move quickly getting everything ready and getting prepared for battle one hour has passed since David arrived now it is 4:00 A.M. and it will take approximately one hour to get to town. Darren places his arms around Lilliannah giving her a tender kiss trying his best to assure her that everything will be ok. Hunter is reminded of what he is doing like four cowboys in a John Wayne movie are riding into town to save a friend. Carol Kay, Cassandra are crying and worrying about their men even the governor has a tear falling on his cheek. The four Navy Seals mount up sitting tall in the saddle and all yell out in a commanding voice, "Lets ride." The sun will begin to rise soon before they enter the town, time is very important and not on their side they know they will be cutting it close.

As the Navy Seals ride towards town they can hear rustling of animals moving away as fast as they can away from town not thinking much about it at the moment they continue their ride on the trail. Lt. James says, "We need a plan when we get to town and need to move fast and find Bobby Harold before that damn earthquake hits and get as far away from town as possible or we are all doomed, who has an idea speak up." Hunter speaks up, "Why don't we go to that first bar you guys went into and talk with the bartender, you said he was helpful perhaps he knows something." "That's a good place to start, great idea Hunter," says Lt. James, "We will start there the people in this town seem to be frightened and do not understand us I don't think they will offer us much help so stay together, there is strength in us staying together. The sun has now risen and what the seals see can now is what that rustling sound of animals was all about. It's an eerie sight; cats' dogs' horses that can get away and wild animals of the forest moving away from the town going to high ground. Even birds are flying away they look to their right and see an assume sight a mountain lion walking alongside of a number of dogs their only intention is to get away from town. Mitchell says, "This confirms what I have been saying about the earthquake, animals from the beginning of time have a natural internal since of earth's tragedies to come." Jacob sees the movement of the animals and comments, "Son of a Bitch those animals freak me out that is a real eye opener. I will stay focused on our mission and to get the hell far away from Port Royal." Lt. James is worried but stays focused on what they have to do. He thinks back and is thankful for his seal training as hard as it was when he was going through it such strenuous training drills you question why. But not today, today you appreciate and understand what it means to be a well-trained Navy Seal. Lt. James lifts his head to say thank you to all the navy instructors who have trained and formed him and his buddies into the men they are, thank you.

Capt. McVaine is still in the warehouse and he hasn't left yet as he begins to leave he notices that the Devil Man is coming out of his unconscious and walks back to him smiling just then a pirate picks up the TDI Vector submachine gun never having seen one before and he doesn't know how deadly it can be or how to operate it. He is smiling and holding it and pointing it all around the room thinking how smart he is. Then he happens to put his finger on the trigger and pulls it and the gun fires, zzzzz, zzzzzzzzzzzzz, xxxxxzzzzzzzzzzzzz and he sprays the room with deadly bullets, killing three pirates standing by the door and putting holes in the bodies of a few more pirates wounding them. Capt. McVaine is so damn mad at the stupidly of what just happened he takes out his cutlass and with a clean swipe cuts the right hand off of the pirate holding the gun. And he yells, "Ye dumb ass ye almost kilt me, ye lucky I only cut ye hand off, I will deal wit ye when me return, throw ye Devil Man gun in da harbor now." Bobby Harold has been watching the entire chaos taking place and a smile comes over his beleaguered face, he is thinking those dumb ass, pirate bastards just got what they deserved. Capt. McVaine and a few of his most trusted mates go off to the Catt & Fiddle Tavern to enjoy a morning meal and more rum, leaving a number of pirates to guard the prisoner 12 to be exact. The pirates make a grand entrance into the Catt & Fiddle Tavern as though they have won a great battle. Finding his favorite large table, Capt. McVaine places his large body in a chair and loudly demands service, "Rum bring us rum and not da ladies rum but da man's 180 proof rum now. Bring us food for we is hungry from capturing da Devil man he be in my warehouse by da docks Arrrrr." He announces his accomplishment for all to hear proud of his dirty deed. The bartender Jeremy Bartholomeus at the Catt & Fiddle Tavern has been preoccupied looking for his dog and cat all morning. They usually sit at the end of the bar and greet all the people that come in, looking forward to getting their pat or head scratched and bits of food that a customer might share with them. Since before sun up they were nowhere to be found, Jeremy loves his two pets they mean more than anything to him they never leave the bar or Jeremy's side except when nature calls. He is concerned and asks everyone if they have seen his two pets they are well known all over town without any luck the cat's name is Meow, Meow his dog's name is Peg Leg. Meow, Meow is an all-white rather fat cat and Peg Leg is a large bull dog who seems to love everyone although his left leg is missing from a pirates stray bullet.

Capt. McVaine in the last day or so has become more obnoxious, drinking heavily and just being a bigger ass then he usually is. After the announcement that he captured a Devil Man and he is being held captive in his warehouse by the docks this is bad news. Jeremy knows from the last experience when the Devil Men rescued the three ladies all hell broke loose in his tavern. He knows that this is not going to turn out well for Capt. McVaine, and where in the hell are the other pirates of the Brethren of the Black Spot they have not been seen for a few days. In fact Jeremy Bartholomeus got along quite well the three men who are now referred to as the Devil Men and really like them. That is because they rescued the governor's daughter and her two friends and that was a good thing to do stupid but oh so brave. Bobby is tied to a post in the warehouse, he is moving in and out of consciousness do to the pain of his injuries and being kicked on his broken leg didn't help his condition. The 12 pirate guards watching over Bobby are talking about what they are involved with; what if his mates come looking for him what chaos will take place. They are talking over whom do they fear more Capt. McVaine or the Devil Men; they decide that Capt. McVaine is more fearful and decide to stay guarding the Devil Man rather than run away. A pirate that is standing outside the tavern sticks his head inside and yells, "There are four very strange odd looking men on horseback way up da street coming this way all dressed in da same clothing of our captured Devil Man. Capt. McVaine knows exactly who is coming down the street and quickly leaves the tavern and heads directly for his warehouse.

Lt. Darren James is trying to remember the bar they were in maybe it was on another street, ah yes it was close to the docks that I do remember, how about you Jacob do you remember?" Jacob says, "Stop for a moment I will go into this bar and see if it looks familiar the name of this bar is 'The Boars Head' no, that's not the one let's keep looking closer to the docks." Darren yells out, "By God I think I remember that sign up ahead with a cat on the sign playing the fiddle that bar is called 'Cat & Fiddle Tavern that's it I'm sure of it. The four seals arrive and tie up their horses very secure because they don't want them running away with the rest of the animals as they walk into the bar. Jeremy Bartholomeus the part owner and head bar tender welcomes the Navy Seals with a friendly hello he also recognizes them as the ones who were in his tavern about a week ago and got into the fight with the pirates. He thinks to himself this time the trouble will be at the docks at a warehouse not here. The merchants, seaman, and pirates have filled this tavern even at this early hour of the day some came last night and never left.

All the men are having their fun with the wenches so one seems to notice the odd looking Navy Seals with their odd looking clothes walk into the tavern. The tavern is crowed with wenches everywhere, sitting on pirate's laps, dancing on top of the tables, performing lap dances, swinging from a wood pole in various forms of dress and undress, singing and caring on like there is no tomorrow. Jacob says, "Hell this place reminds me of the Cheetah Club in Las Vegas I didn't know that lap dances was an ancient art form, I thought it was developed in the 70's." "Your right, son of a bitch this does remind me of the Cheetah Club in Vegas," says Mitchell, "Except the women there are all gorgeous and smelled fantastic, one important thing is they have all their own teeth and don't chew and spit tobacco. This fucken town has a stench about it that I will remember for the rest of my life. It needs a good cleaning hell these people have no idea what a sewer pipe is they just use the streets perhaps the earthquake today will wash away most of the stench."

Lt. James looks around and says, "This is the bar we walked into the first night, you bartender you look familiar to me." Jeremy speaks up, "I remember you from the other night about a week ago, please I don't want any trouble in me tavern today." "Now why would you say something like that to me? Were only peaceful hairy legged country boys just trying to get along?" The other three seals smile with what Darren just said. Jeremy says, "What would you men like to drink it's on da house, for saving da governor's daughter and her two friends from Capt. John Wallace that's me way of saying thank you. Come to think of it I haven't seen Capt. Wallace for the past few days perhaps he's out attacking merchant ships with his mates the Brethren of the Black Spot." Lt. James speaks up, "No drinks for us we are here for a serious mission to find one of our men who was captured last night do you have any idea where he might be? Jeremy looks into Lt. James eyes and knows he had better tell him what he knows and to tell the truth the whole truth and nothing but the truth and says, "Capt. McVaine a member of the Brethren of the Black Spot just announced in me tavern this morning that your man he captured and he be in his warehouse on da docks everyone knows where it is." "I want to thank you for your honesty, I will reward you with this information. An earthquake will happen at 11:45 this morning and your entire town will sink into the sea and thousands of your people will die so get the hell as far away as you can. As we were riding in we saw hundreds of animals running away because they know what is about to happen," says Lt. James. Jeremy thinks about his two pets and now realizes where they may be. What happens next is hard to believe 50% of the tavern patrons believe what they just heard and flee as fast as they can, the other 50% do not believe and stay to party hardy.

Jacob makes an announcement, "Who will show us were Capt. McVaine warehouse is?" A prostitute who hated Capt. McVaine for his brutal, cheap and disrespectful ways agreed to show the Navy Seals the location of the warehouse on the docks it is only three blocks away. The Navy Seals ride their horses as close as they dare and tied them up and proceed to make their plans to rescue Bobby Harold. The buildings are all two stories made of wooden timbers, bricks and mud and adobe hay walls, some have glass windows. Mitchell speaks out, "I can see a lot of openings for windows that have wooden shutters and some just have drapes covering the openings. I still have a hard time believing we are back in time and all the buildings we see will be under water in a few hours." Jacob speaks out, "We are going to be fighting for our lives to save Bobby in the next minute or two, by my watch we have less than three hours to get the hell out of this God forsaken town. Lt. James says, "Keep your eyes open for anything thing that moves and your weapons at the ready stay out of sight for now. These bastard pirates will be putting up a fight that you can be assured of, what we want most is to get Bobby back safe and sound." The weather all around is giving hints of what is to come, the sky is getting darker in the early morning, the wind is cold still blowing from the North East at about 30 knots now not the warm wind like usual. The sun is giving off an ominous glow; there is a terrible feeling in the air. The sea is churning like never before, waves are now 5' high some that are higher are crashing onto the docks the sea just looks angry as hell with a very dark uninviting dark blue color. The hundred or more pirate ships anchored in the harbor are seen shifting in a violent way from port to starboard tethered by their anchors as though the ships what to sail away from what is coming.

Lt. James lays out the attack, "This will be our plan of attack, Jacob and Mitchell will be on point stay close to the buildings signal if you see any movement at all be careful. Hunter you stay with me you have the sniper rifle if you see a pirate's head poke out of the building fire your rifle or if they are standing at the door or looking out a window opening. The building where Bobby is being held is a two story building the third one on the left, with the large door facing the street; I count six windows also facing the street. With your suppressor on very little noise will be heard the very surprise of their head exploding will scare the hell out of any one who is watching. Hunter take your position behind those large wooden boxes and crates that will give you a perfect position of control from the outside of the building." Jacob and Mitchell move along the side of the buildings. Hunter throws a flash bang grenade into the street to get the pirates to stick their heads out to look around. Then Hunter fires his sniper rifle at the curious pirates able to hit any head sticking out, all the heads are hit and explode like a pumpkin being hit with a sledge hammer, with all of its insides, seeds, and the pieces of shell go flying about. The pirates inside the building that are watching scream out in terror, because they heard no noise and watched as their mate's heads explode all around them how can this possibly happen. Capt. McVaine is looking as well and is terrified at what he sees; no noise and heads explode how can this happen in the blink of an eye. The Navy Seals move quickly to the large door they know that they must be in position to see and save Bobby. The large door opens and the pirates fire their blunderbuss pistols and rifles at Jacob and Mitchell as they rush through the door hitting them in their chests and nothing happens to them because of their bullet proof vests. Now the two Navy Seals return fire with their Barrett M468 automatic machine guns with its deadly fire power hitting many of the surprised pirates. Lt. James and Hunter are close behind firing their weapons spraying the warehouse with deadly fire killing pirates where they stand.

They see Capt. McVaine standing over Bobby sitting on the floor tied to a post. Capt. McVaine screams out in his loud and scary voice because he is more frightened then he has ever been in his life, "Get ye out of here or I will kill ye Devil man Arrrrrr." Hunter is in the rear of the building he takes a sitting position and sets his sights on Capt. McVaine large head a perfect target he makes the perfect target. Capt. McVaine thinks that his threat to kill the Devil man would make the other Devil men leave the building. (NOT) Hunter pulls the trigger and Capt. McVaine's head is no longer sitting on his shoulders it is a mess of brains, bone and blood spread across the floor of his building. The rest of the pirates those who are still alive only three of them to be exact throw down their weapons and surrender pleading for mercy. Jacob kicks their weapons across the floor out of reach and tells them to get on the floor with their hands behind their backs and they do. Mitchell bends down and cuts the ropes holding Bobby to the post careful not to hurt him. Bobby Harold looks up and says with a big smile, "What took you guys so long?" Lt. James says, "Get Bobby to our horses and let's make like a rock and roll we have only an hour and a half before the earthquake hits. Lt. James instructs the seals to tie him to his back on his horse in case he falls into unconsciousness on the ride back to the governor's home. As the seals ride along the cobble stone and dirt streets they are sadden by what they see. People just walking around not aware of what is about to take place and some of them were warned and did not believe. The Navy Seals need to get off this long strip of land before it collapses into the sea. They need to get on solid and higher ground as far away from the peninsula that serves as the land bridge that Port Royal is built on, as it turns out the land is only sand. They have less than one hour to get to safety, or as safe as they can be, the entire island of Jamaica will feel the impact of the earthquake. They still see more animals leaving on their own they did not have to be told so what species is smarter animal or human? A few people can be seen leaving they are the ones that did believe what they heard or were told. The sight of some humans leaving pleased the Navy Seals they are thinking that their warning did save a few humans from this horrible event. Mitchel is watching his watch as they continue to ride, time is now only five minutes away from the time the earthquake is to happen. The Navy Seals stop turn around and look back they are on solid ground high on a hill giving them a perfect view of Port Royal especially with their high powered binoculars.

As they wait and watch the time is now 11:45 A.M. the time that Mitchell warned everyone the quake would happen. Now they can hear a low rumble and the trembling begin high on the hill. "Oh shit," proclaims

Mitchell, "The earthquake has now begun." The ground is not just shaking like other earthquakes, but the ground is rolling like waves in the ocean, the land where Port Royal stands is disappearing as water replaces land. The sand that Port Royal was built on is slipping underneath the sea. The ships in the harbor are beginning to bob in the ocean like toy boats in a bath tub like a child hits the water with his hand. Since they are anchored they cannot ride the waves out as the ships struggle and pull against their anchor chains and some now begin to roll over and sink. The buildings are collapsing the stone and brick buildings go first because they are the heaviest now wooden structures are leaning over the sounds of the buildings sinking give out a horrible groan. Some of the voices from the people screaming and yelling for help can be heard as people are buried up to their waists and necks in sand. Liquefaction is taking place what once was land is now quick sand pulling people and everything else down under, as the ocean reclaims what once was. The ground is splitting and opening up creating large pools of water. The land cannot support any weight at all, not people, not buildings. The sounds that can be heard are horrific and very disturbing these sights and sounds will live forever in the minds of the Navy Seals as they watch from the safety of a hill top. Buildings that once stood four stories tall less than nine minutes ago cannot be seen as screams fill the air and buildings tumble and disappear. Thousands of people are drowning and dying and there is nothing that can be done to save any of them.

The cemetery located just outside of town on the Palisadoes opens up and most of it slips into the sea, causing wooden caskets by the thousands to begin to float in the ocean were the town once stood. Skeletons and decomposed rotten bodies rub up against the people buried in the sand not able to run or move out of the way. In just a short period of time the stench of death is over whelming. Mitchel shouts out, "Look at that 5 mile stretch of land connecting Port Royal with the main land it is gone and what is left of Port Royal now is now a small island sinking into the sea. Oh God look the ocean is moving away from the inlet harbor and leaving a lot of shoreline exposed that means a tsunami is about to occur a title wave. Oh shit here it comes the water must be over 16 feet high maybe higher it is going to crash where the city once was. I can still see people struggling waist deep in the sand now they are under water drowned this is so horrible to watch but at the same time mesmerizing the horror of it all. Over three quarters of the town is gone underneath the ocean what is left will soon disappear as well. Look at the hundred or more of the ships that were once anchored by Port Royal most are sitting on some land, smashed together, sinking or are now sunk what a terrible chaotic mess."

Bobby Harold has been gently set beside a tree so he could watch the chaos taking place in Port Royal and speaks up, "I owe my life to you great guys and thank God for you and our training. I was never going to give up I am sure Christopher never gave up. I was positive that you would show up and rescue me, but you have to admit it, it was a close call we all could have been caught up in that earthquake. My leg is broken below the knee I have this damn bullet in my side, but all in all I am feeling pretty damn good about my life and our narrow escape. The town of Port Royal the jewel of Jamaica and the Caribbean is no longer a shining city by the sea. I don't see how this town will ever be able to rebuild or recover from this devastation today. I really feel bad for this town its future and the fact that it could all disappear in a matter of minutes and so many thousands of people perished. God works in mysterious ways and perhaps the evil, sinning and the debauchery were getting too much for even God to handle and he just took care of business." Jacob speaks up, "I wonder if the governor's house is still standing and everyone there is all right, the earth quake must have affected the whole island it was one hell of a good sized quake. It is a good thing for us that Mitchell studied the history of this part of the world, we all thank you Mitchell or we would not have known or been prepared and probably could have been in the town when it hit." Lt. James says, "Yes we are all grateful for your knowledge and your warning, great work we are truly indebted to you." Mitchell says, "Forget about it, we are one for all and all for one that is what was hammered into us at our seal training and I am grateful for our tough training it prepared us for this adventure and what an adventure it was." All the seals give Mitchell a pat on the back and smiles all around, everyone is just glad they are all safe. Darren speaks to Bobby, "Are you ok to continue the ride back?" Bobby answers, "You bet your sweet ass I am I'm sure that they can make a better splint for my leg and possibly take this damn pirate bullet out of my side. I am looking forward to some good food I haven't eaten in a day or two." Lt. Darren James says, "Let's get back, help Bobby up and tie him real secure to me, let's ride."

The governor is standing outside of the mansion as Mitchell recommended as well as everyone else. Governor Beeston says, to everyone, "Mitchell was right on with what he warned us about the earthquake the time and the day. My house didn't receive much damage only a crack here and there and some pictures fell off the wall over all we are good to go. "Daddy, I am scared and worried for our friends," laments Lilliannah, "I can only stand here and pray that they are ok I really want them to return now, when do you think they will return?" The governor ponders the question and says, "If they survived the quake and are now riding here they should arrive by 2:00 P.M. give them a half hour or so. I know you're afraid for them all especially Darren, but I believe in my heart they are ok and safely on their way my daughter." Cassandra speaks up, "We owe a lot to those strange men, to start with our lives and they will always be in our hearts." Carol Kay says, "Don't forget when we first saw them they also scared the hell out of us we didn't know what they were or if they were even human." "You have that right," adds Cassandra, "Now look at us we're so worried about them in a strange way these men have changed all of our lives and just in the nick of time."

Governor Beeston speaks up, "Now my concern is with the town of Port Royal and the island of Jamaica how much of it was damaged and how many citizens may have died or are injured crying out for help. Tomorrow somehow, someway I need to inspect the town and to organize help to somehow help the citizens that is my greatest concern right now. Right now I will send twenty five of the guards to the city to assist in any way possible. What will become of Jamaica and the city of Port Royal, all I can give is my belief and hope that this earthquake will not stop us from being great and taking our rightful place as a leading nation in the Caribbean again. Lilliannah says, "Let's go to the house and help clean up the mess and straighten it out at least that will take our minds off of our worry." Cassandra and Carol Kay agree and proceed into the house to help with the cleanup and wait for the Navy Seals to return. The time is now 3:00 P.M. and no men have returned one hour later than they were expected and they now all start to show their signs of worry. Just then they hear men on horseback on the property, they all rush out of the house and can see it's the men they were waiting for. Happiness fills the household as everyone rushes out to greet them. Bobby is helped down from the horse carefully and Lilliannah gives Darren a great big welcome home kiss that he was looking forward to. Carol Kay gives Jacob a fantastic welcome home kiss and Cassandra gives Hunter a wonderful welcome home kiss. Then everyone is giving hugs all around it is a happy time as the governor gives handshakes all around. David Getingzer walks forward happy to see that Bobby is safe and welcomes all the seals back. Lt. James says, "Bobby needs medicine and medical care for his wounds and pain he has a broken leg and a bullet in his side." Carol Kay steps forward and says, "I have some medical training when I worked in the hospital. I believe we do have some things that will help with his pain, get him into his bed where I can better attend to him. Carol Kay is able to examine his wound and finds that the bullet passed clean through his side that is a good sign she is able to properly dress his side and provide a much better splint for his leg making Bobby more comfortable then he has been in days. Carol Kay provides a potion that puts Bobby into a peaceful needed sleep.

Dinner is announced and what a fine dinner it will be fresh fish from the sea fixed the Jamaican way with fantastic tasty spices fresh vegetables from the garden and plenty of the best wine to celebrate the Navy Seals return. Governor Beeston says, "After dinner I would like you men to give me a full report on what you saw regarding the earthquake today, I am very concerned about the people and how help can be arranged." "Yes sir we will be able to provide you with some gruesome details but after dinner this unfortunate event should not be discussed at the dinner table," says Hunter. Smiles and small talk fill the room trying to be in a happy mood but the events of the day make it impossible to not let your mind wonder back to 11:45 A.M. Dinner is over and into the study the men go, ladies you are welcome to hear the details if you like and they follow as well. Mitchell starts by saying, "Governor I will be very frank and honest with you and you deserve that from us. Port Royal as far as we could see three quarters of the town is under the sea. The majority of the population is gone, drowned. The only way to describe it is. Hell came calling the ships anchored in the harbor most are destroyed that is well over 100 ships. Some of the ships are sitting on land and a lot sunk just destroyed from the title wave that came crashing on shore that also devastated the city along with the quake. The 5 mile long land causeway that connected the town with the main land is gone what you have is what little remains of the town now is an island no way to get to what remains of the city except by boat, and they are mostly destroyed. In the coming months what people have survived the earthquake will be subjected to disease and starvation they need to be brought to the main land as soon as possible. One last thing as soon as Bobby Harold can travel perhaps in a few days we will be going out to sea to see if we can find our way back home." You could feel the sadness in the room with Mitchell's last comment.

"We thank you all for your wonderful hospitality, but our lives and our reality are in our world our time I do believe you understand our need to get back home if at all possible," explains Jacob, "We have had life changing experiences, wonderful experiences with you all and horrific experiences at the hands of the pirates and watching the earthquake today wash away a whole city." Hunter adds his thoughts, "I personally would never change what we experienced here in your time, the good, the bad and the ugly. And especially meeting you fine, wonderful people has made a big change in my life, I thank you for this experience." Lt. James has been silent tonight and has not added anything to the conversation he seemed satisfied to just smile and nod in agreement with what the other Navy Seals said. Jacob speaks again, "Another concern we have is the health of Bobby Harold, and Carol Kay you have provided great medical help we thank you for that but our doctors in our time should take a look see to make sure he is ok." "That is another reason we need to find our way back home if at all possible but maybe we will never be able to leave we don't know," chimes in Mitchell.

"This evening get together will have to end," explains the governor, "I thank you all for you telling me what happened to Port Royal today, and your thoughts and your concerns the news was devastating. I never thought it would be as bad as you described, tomorrow I will get as many of the people I trust together that are still alive to help the survivors." Lt. James stands and holds out his hand to Lilliannah, she stands and they walk out into the garden together. Lilliannah says, "Darren you didn't say one word tonight in the study why was that?" Darren finely speaks, "I know I have had a lot of thoughts going through my head tonight and thinking of our adventure in your time. My decision to stay is weighing heavily on my mind and not to return with my buddies as they seek a possible way home. We have talked about it before and now it is fast becoming a reality, a reality that I must face to live out my life with you in your time. I haven't told my seal buddies of my decision yet but I want to share my decision with them alone I hope you understand." "Yes I understand you are so thoughtful that is just one reason I love you so much," laments Lilliannah, "It's getting late lets go to bed my love and face tomorrow with our good thoughts and smiles." This day has finely ended with so much chaos and stress taking place tomorrow should be a much better day. Today is Sunday June 8th 1692 the sun is rising to warm the day, the wind has died down to a gentle breeze and it is a typical tropical day in Jamaica. The Navy Seals, the ladies, and the governor are all up it is 9:00 A.M. ready for another wonderful breakfast of island fruit, scrambled eggs and tasty spices and sausage, homemade biscuits and plenty of hot coffee.

Bobby Harold is just waking up from a much needed restful sleep; he looks around the room and sees David Getingzer sitting in a chair with a smile on his face. "Good Morning my good friend," says David, "I was very concerned for your good health and safety, I prayed that you would be rescued and brought home safely by your mates before the earthquake happened and God answered my prayers. Bobby looks at David and says, "David you are a good friend and I thank you for all your help and concern. Now if you will help me to get down stairs I can smell that great breakfast and I am so damn hungry." Bobby and David make their entrance into the dining room and receive a great big applause. Seeing Bobby and David means that they are on the mend and feeling better joining the group is a good thing. Lt. James makes an announcement, "I would like to see my seal buddies in the garden in about one hour that includes you Bobby. I have something I believe is important to share with you." An hour passes and the seals are gathered in the garden, sitting on benches and large rocks anxiously waiting for Darren to make his announcement.

Darren makes his announcement, "Men you are the greatest Navy Seals I have ever served with, I am proud and honored to have served with you. I love my country you all know that, America is a great country my love of America will always be on my mind and in my heart. The decision that I have made will have a radical change in my life, I am not going back with you I am staying here in this time." No Navy Seal seemed surprised by that announcement because it now all makes perfect sense. The picture on the wall they all saw at the Jamaican military base in their time now is explained how Darren and Lilliannah were depicted honoring Darren James as a great governor in 1706 of Jamaica. The seals just didn't think that they would be here to see it happen and be a part of it all. The seals all stand and shake Darren's hand patting him on his back and giving him their full support for love and success. Hunter speaks up, "This is what I believe our time frame should be today if we are to go searching for that time fog portal. When we came through it the first time it was about 4:00 P.M. there is no guarantee that it will be in the same place and time or if ever. We could be searching until the end of time and never see it again or perhaps it is there waiting for us to go through the time portal again. The time right now is 11:00 A.M. we should be underway by 2:00 P.M. three hours from now if we are to find it today.

Lilliannah can see that the group meeting is over and hurries over to join Lt. James and the other seals, they welcome her with their smiles and hugs and give her and Darren their blessings for a wonderful and happy life together. Hunter sees Cassandra standing off to the side and invites her to join everyone. Hunter places his arm around her shoulder looks her in her beautiful eyes smiles and says, "Are you ready to come with us as we search for our way back to our world and our time? If so you better get packing." Cassandra rushes off screaming and yelling for joy, "I am going to go on a new life's adventure a new life is waiting for me." The lunch bells ring inviting everyone to a great lunch maybe their last lunch together no one really knows for sure. The governor walks into the room after he has met with his most trusted people all morning about the Port Royal catastrophe and how to being help, aid and hope to those remaining the citizens who are still alive. This fantastic and grand lunch prepared by the staff believing that this may be their last lunch together. They have out done themselves producing a grand feast for everyone to remember; a whole baby pig was put in the ground at 6:00 A.M. roasted to perfection and served with fresh vegetables and local fruits along with fantastic red wine. Everyone is enjoying what could be their last lunch together, even the governor is enjoying himself and this unexpected grand lunch. The governor is remembering what the Navy Seals have done; first rescuing his daughter and her two best friends, and bringing about devastation to the Brethren of the Black Spot that evil pirates association. And the warning of the earthquake that saved many lives.

Lt. James stands up and says, "I want to say a few well-chosen words and to make a toast to those at this table. I never in a million years thought that I would be here to meet such wonderful people that would change my life forever. I am going to stay here till the end of time and make a new life for myself and my future wife Lilliannah. A lady I love more than life itself and I feel in return her love and passion for me is beyond anything I have ever known." The people at the table give a big cheer and clapping of hands in support of their happiness. "My toast is, no one knows what the future holds or how the past can change your life." "Here, here." is the next cheer heard at the table. The great afternoon lunch is quickly coming to an end and the remaining Navy Seals and Cassandra will be on their way in less than an hour in search for that fog time portal. The goodbyes are now getting serious with more tears flowing than anyone ever expected.

The Apex Pegasus boat has been cleaned, the gas tank topped off with more 180 proof rum and made ready also an additional 25 gallons of 180 proof rum is stored in a compartment for today's journey. The seals all know there is no guarantee that they will find what they are seeking today or on any other day but they must try. The sun is shining brightly in the sky the sea is calm hardly a white cap wave in sight and the sky is a bright blue the weather today is 180 degrees from what it was yesterday. Hunter calls out, "Everyone on board who's coming on board." The seals help Bobby take a seat and make sure his broken leg is protected and he is strapped in. Cassandra steps on board with the biggest smile she has ever had happy and seeking a new life's adventure. Jacob gives Carol Kay a great big goodbye kiss and steps aboard. Mitchell jumps on board happy to be on his way hopefully back to his time. A large flower wreath is placed on the sea in remembrance of Christopher Kirk. Hunter turns the key and the water jet engines come to life the two lines holding the Apex boat to the dock are disconnected and slowly ever so slowly the Apex Pegasus boat begins to pull away from the dock. The governor, David and Carol Kay are waving goodbye, Lt. Darren James and Lilliannah are also standing on the dock waving goodbye but with tears streaming down their cheeks. The Navy Seals turn around for the last time wave their goodbyes then turn back around to hopefully begin their journey back to their own time. The sea is smooth so the ride will not be bumpy smooth sailing is what they want. Hunter pushes the throttle forward getting up speed to what is comfortable and fast at 20 knots. The people on the boat can see dolphins jumping in the water just ahead like they are showing them the way.

Mitchell is checking the gages figuring out the direction they should go, Cassandra is sitting back enjoying the ride of her life time. "I believe we should go 90 degrees to the west towards the entrance to what was Port Royal," says Mitchell. "You're the navigator turning 90 degrees west." shouts Hunter. Jacob is keeping a sharp look out with the binoculars, scanning from port to starboard and directly over the bow.

"Nothing as yet no fog bank on the water how close are we to the spot when we first incounted the dark blue and crimson fog bank?" asks Jacob. "We should be in the vicinity in the next half hour," answers Mitchell. Then thirty minutes passes, then another thirty minutes passes still no fog bank they are all getting anxious with no fog bank in sight. The time is later then they want in one hour the sun will set and with it their hopes of finding their way back home today. Jacob is beside himself starting to use fowl langrage to express his frustration, Mitchell is upset because he believes everyone is depending on him to find their way home. Then at the last moment of time Jacob shouts, "I believe I have spotted the fog bank we're searching for, I hope it is not just a regular fog bank, Hunter take a look see in the binoculars tell me what you see." Hunter takes a look and shouts out, "I think your right Jacob everyone hold on tight to whatever I'm going to go full speed ahead." Hunter pushes the throttle forward to obtain maximum speed everyone can see a fog bank now about a mile ahead of them, but it is now a race of time before the sun sets and the mysterious fog bank dissipates. Hunter now declares, "With my naked eye I can see a fog bank with a dark blue center with a crimson color all around. That's it hang on tight, damn it hang on we will be in the fog bank in a minute or two. The entire group of men and a lady are excited as they enter the center of the dark blue center with a crimson color all around and emerge five minutes later from the fog feeling no different than before. They all wonder is that all there is. Then another five minutes later Hunter shouts, "My GPS gages are back on all my electronic gages that I depend on connected to the satalights they are working I believe we are back in our own time.

Jacob is still looking through his binoculars and can see an inflatable boat just like theirs about 600 yards to starboard and shouts out what he sees. Mitchell picks up the radio still set on the 312 radio channel. To his amazement and everyone else's the seal team answers and the loudest shout out of joy can be heard. The two Apex Pegasus boats get in close to each other it is early morning now around 4:00 A.M. they tie up to one another. Lt. John Schneider is happy as hell to see everyone but is puzzled as hell where they were. Lt. Schneider shouts out, "Where in the hell have you guys been you missed all the action with the Muslim Jihadists Terrorists we killed every last one of those bastards and recued the hostages. Now we are on our way back to the mother ship and you guys show up. Wait a minute there are two less Navy Seals and a new addition a beautiful lady what in the hell happened?" Hunter speaks up, "What happened to us will be very hard for you to believe that will take a few hours of explaining over a few bottles of cold beers. Yes two of our men are no longer with us Christopher Kirk and Lt. Darren James they are left behind in another time. Our experience will outperform your experience any day of the week. This is not the time or the place to discuss our experience, we will be glad to tell you our story in a bar over a few cold beers in a few days perhaps when we are back at the base in Jamaica." Hunter makes this challenge, "I bet our Apex can beat your Apex back to the mother ship." As the two Apex Pegasus boats go racing across the dark sea to the Mother ship.

The End

Be sure to read the next three books written by Dennis Davis The title of the three books are *They Live Among Us* and *Drugs are forever Evil,* and *Revenge equals Justice*—the three science fiction books that will take you on another great adventure beyond anything you could possibly imagine. There have never been any stories written before about human interaction and extraterrestrials like this ever.